PRAISE FOR JONATHAN BLUM'S *The Usual Uncertainties*

I love everything about this book. These are wise and richly imagined stories, at turns hilarious and heartbreaking. Blum is undeniably a master of the short story form, a writer of profound compassion and virtuosic talent, and these stories mark the arrival of a major new voice in American short fiction.
—Andrew Porter, author of *The Theory of Light and Matter*

In these wonderfully various stories, gentle and bizarre and tragic and very funny, there are characters the likes of which have rarely been given life in fiction: the young son of a pulmonary oncologist learns excitedly to read x-rays, and that excitement is very different than what his father feels. A widow makes a business of bringing a quality of life to elders, and a thirteen-year-old Roger, on the occasion of his Bar Mitzvah, has a T-shirt stamped: *I'd Rather Be Davening*. Herm is a one-man ad hoc adoption agency finding unwanted newborns and delivering them into well-appointed futures. Jonathan Blum descends from a great tradition of Jewish storytellers, Richler, Malamud, Michaels, and he brings the tradition into the twenty-first century, and he brings the tradition west, too, to Los Angeles. Oh, and south to Florida, and right up to the Shabbat table where Adam sits with his Thai girlfriend in "A Certain Light on Los Angeles." There is a certain light here in these stories and it is very much worth your time. **—Michelle Latiolais, author of** *Widow*

PRAISE FOR JONATHAN BLUM'S *Last Word*

A humorous and relatable depiction of a troubled family... Blum's novella is an engaging rapid-read that touches the heart as much as it strikes a chord. Blum is a rising star in the Jewish literary world." —*The Atlanta Jewish Times*

A masterful finesse of unreliable narration...Blum writes with tremendous economy and compression. *Last Word*, at eighty-six pages, punches far above its weight, as does every one of its paragraphs and sentences...*Last Word* is gripping. It's also incredibly funny...a precis on misunderstanding." —**Stephen Lovely,** *The Iowa Review*

Last Word makes the reader really think about who is innocent and how one event leads to another. Despite this book's brevity, Blum is able to create a multi-dimensional family and community that come to life on the page. This book focuses on an emotionally charged and complex situation highly relevant to twenty-first century digital concerns, teenage bullying, and the parenting skills needed to help teens navigate this confusing time." —**Jamie Wendt,** *Jewish Book Council*

Blum is highly skilled in showing the reader the complexity of contemporary Jewish life...I see in his work the melancholy and astuteness of Bellow and the humor of Roth. —**Jason Christian,** *World Literature Today*

THE USUAL

UNCERTAINTIES *stories*

RESCUE PRESS
CHICAGO, CLEVELAND, IOWA CITY

THE USUAL UNCERTAINTIES
Copyright © 2019 Jonathan Blum
All rights reserved
Printed in the United States of America
FIRST EDITION
ISBN 978-0-9994186-5-9

Design by Sevy Perez
Adobe Caslon Pro
rescuepress.co

ALSO BY JONATHAN BLUM

Last Word

THE USUAL UNCERTAINTIES

UNCERTAINTIES *stories*

Jonathan Blum

CONTENTS

THE WHITE SPOT

When I was nine, my parents went through a bitter custody battle over me. In the end, the judge decided that I should live with my mother Mondays through Saturdays and go for visits with my father every Saturday night and Sunday. Back then, my father was on call at the hospital seven days a week, and he had no one to look after me during the hours he had to work, so he started bringing me to the hospital with him on Sundays and keeping me in the break room on the same floor where his patients were located.

The break room was only about the size of two closets. It had a coarse plaid sofa, a low-hanging spherical leather chair, a coffee maker and mugs, a sink, some cabinets, a telephone, and a laminated poster above the telephone that was called Screening Guidelines for Invasive Carcinomas, which was put out by the American Academy of Pathology. That first day in the hospital, which was my first time in a hospital since birth, I tried to sit up straight on the plaid sofa and read one of the sports biographies I carried with me everywhere, but I couldn't concentrate at all. My mind kept wandering, wondering what my father was doing—where exactly he was and who he was with.

My father never talked about his work, not during his residency, not now, but I knew a few things about what he did. This was because, starting a couple years earlier, I had skimmed through the back sections of two of his medical books and seen pictures of sick pulmonary patients. I had seen many pairs of lungs that were removed from their bodies after death and photographed. One such pair, which had belonged to a person with emphysema, had an oozing gray coating over the usual healthy red color. Another pair of lungs had holes, caused by black carbon deposits that were the result of smoking. I had also seen a smoker with a gangrenous, partly lopped-off foot, a smoker with a gaping hole at the base of his throat, and a smoker with no tongue in his mouth.

In my own shy, optimistic way, I took pride in the fact that my father treated lungs. Lungs were vital—and underappreciated. I thought of them as the unsung heroes of the human body. Unlike the much-celebrated heart and brain, no one ever talked about the lungs and yet we couldn't last four minutes without them. They took in and released breaths every three seconds or so, usually without our ever noticing. They moved oxygen to the bloodstream and removed carbon dioxide. They kept us going, even when we were sleeping.

After I had been daydreaming for more than an hour, my father, who was a big man—six-feet-two, a hundred-and-ninety pounds, with curly black hair in a white lab coat and brown Wallabees—came back into the break room, sat himself down in the low-hanging chair, and crossed his legs, his feet close to my feet. The air conditioner wasn't working right that day, and there were beads of sweat on my father's forehead and odoriferous spots under his arms. His breaths were quick and confident. He had just seen all his patients, and he had to write up some notes. As he went through page after page of triplicate paper with a blue ballpoint, checking boxes, scratching words, signing his name quickly at the bottom of each page, I half-hid my eyes behind one of my sports biographies and pretended to read.

I was very curious what my father was writing on those pages—one white, one yellow, one pink—but I didn't dare ask. I had decided it was best not to talk to him at the hospital unless he talked to me first.

Finally he asked, "How's Roberto Clemente?"

"He died trying to help earthquake victims in Nicaragua," I said.

"Yeah, I remember that," my father said. "You ready to get out of here?"

My father got called into the hospital almost every Sunday. Sometimes these calls were for what he called real emergencies and sometimes they were false alarms. His beeper would usually go off while we were at his apartment playing chess or else squaring off at our favorite game, Encyclopedia, in which we picked a single volume of the encyclopedia, opened it up at random, and quizzed each other about the facts inside. After my father's beeper went off, he would usually say, "All right, kid. Let's go."

Some weeks my father just saw one patient; other weeks he saw many. Sometimes he went down to ICU; other times he did rounds only on the pulmonary wing. Just hearing him refer to the people he saw as *my patients* excited me; it meant that he was the one in charge of their care. I didn't dare ask him what he did when he saw his patients, although there was nothing I would have liked to know more. I just stayed in the break room, reading, while he was gone.

One Sunday morning, my father got called in earlier than usual. We stopped in the hospital cafeteria on the way. At the register, a ponytailed woman with a flappy chin smiled when she recognized my father, then asked him who was this fine young gentleman he had brought with him today. The woman was surrounded by a pot of chili and oyster crackers, a jar of Little Debbies, some loose cold cuts and cheese slices, and a box of mayonnaise packets. After telling the woman my name, my father bought a couple cinnamon buns, which the woman heated up in a microwave that was spattered with drops of soup. My father ordered a coffee.

As we rode up the elevator, I counted floors.

When we arrived at the break room, my father tousled my hair and said, "You're a good kid, coming in here every week and not complaining. You want to learn how to read a chest X-ray today?"

I couldn't believe my good luck.

Almost two hours later, after he had seen all his patients, my father came back to the break room, carrying his clipboard.

"Let's do it," he said.

He and I walked down the hall toward the pulmonary wing. He saluted nurses. I ran my fingers along the wall. We passed paintings of muhly grass and Tampa vervain. Soon we arrived at a narrow opening in the wall. Inside was a small alcove with a wall-mounted X-ray viewer. Screwed into the wall next to the viewer was a plastic box in which dozens of loose X-rays were haphazardly stuffed. Behind that wall was a closed door.

My father disappeared through that door, then came back a minute later with a small pile of X-rays in shabby paper envelopes.

"Okay," he said. "First you need to know how to read a normal piece of film."

He put an X-ray up on the screen and flicked on the viewing light. At the center of the image was a pair of long black regions, not quite symmetrical, one with a sharper, more curved bottom than the other.

"The lungs," I said.

"That's right," he said.

At first the two lungs in the X-ray made me think of lakes or pools, then of wings or windows, and then of the tombstones you see in cartoons.

"Can you guess why they're black?" my father said.

I shook my head. My shyness amounted to a terrible fear of saying the wrong thing.

"Cause they're mostly air," he said. "But you don't want them too black. That could mean air is getting trapped."

After my father had pointed out the features of a healthy lung, including the soft webbing of bronchi, he directed my attention to the white areas that framed the lungs: the ribs, clavicle, vertebrae, trachea, shoulder bones, arm tissue, diaphragm, and heart.

He then slid over the normal chest X-ray and said, "Now we're going to look at some pathology."

He posted an X-ray on the viewer, next to the normal one.

"What's different from the normal X-ray?" my father said.

This was an easy one.

"One of the lungs is white," I said.

"That's right," my father said. "The left lower lobe is white. In this patient's case, the small air sacs in the lungs, known as alveoli, have gotten clogged with dense liquid. The patient has pneumonia."

"Could the patient die?" I said.

"Not necessarily," my father said. "We'd have to know some other things. Like the status of the infection. And the age of the patient. But probably not," he said.

My father put up another X-ray.

"What's wrong here?" he asked.

This one was harder. I shook my head.

"Look at the lungs," my father said. "Healthy lungs are elastic. When we breathe, they expand and contract. But with certain diseases the lungs lose their elasticity. They hyperinflate. Look how narrow the heart is. You see the flat, low-set diaphragm? These lungs are too big and too dark. Dark, I told you, means air is getting trapped. The blood's not getting enough oxygen. This person has emphysema."

"Could the person die?" I asked.

"Yes, they could," my father said.

"When?" I asked.

"Anywhere from eight months to a year, maybe two years. Depends what treatment, if any, works."

I thought about this answer, wishing I understood death as well as my father did, as well as my grandparents did.

"Here's something that'll make you pause and wonder," he said. "By the time emphysema patients get to me, they generally have one foot in the grave. They're lifetime smokers. Their lung function is impaired or badly impaired. And yet these same people, who know that the only *possible* way to stop their disease is to stop smoking, go right on smoking. They sometimes sneak cigarettes in their hospital beds when no one's around. You can smell it halfway down the hall. What do you think of that?"

My father got out another X-ray.

"One more?" he said.

"Okay," I said.

He put the diseased X-ray up next to the normal one. The two looked virtually the same.

"Look closely," he said.

I couldn't see any difference.

"Here, below the clavicle," he pointed. "This opacity. This white spot."

I saw what he was pointing at. But because the spot was dense and white, like the bones and tissue nearby, it didn't look that different from the white in the normal X-ray.

"I see it," I said.

"That's cancer," my father said.

I didn't dare ask if the person could die from it. Of course he could. Instead, I wondered what my father saw when he looked around him every day. How much more did he see than an ordinary person did?

"Is there any way to get rid of it?" I asked.

"For most people," he said, "by the time it's detected, they're already a goner."

"How fast do they die?" I asked.

"Ninety percent of the patients I see with lung cancer die within a year of diagnosis. Often it's just three or four months. But I never tell them that. Unless they ask."

"Why not?"

"Don't you think people deserve the chance not to lose hope?"

I thought about this. I then asked my father to show me another X-ray that might or might not have a white spot. Then another. And then another. I wanted to be able to identify the spots as quickly and accurately as he could.

Finally, I got the hang of it. I identified three cancerous spots in a row.

"Now imagine having to break news like that to a patient," my father said.

The words startled me, because up until that moment, finding the white spot had been something exciting, like discovering buried treasure.

"All right," my father said. "Enough for one day. Let's get out of this place."

Within a few weeks of reading X-rays, I could tell the difference between healthy lungs and chronic bronchitis, tuberculosis, pneumonia, emphysema, and cancer. I saw collapsed lungs and severe asthma. I saw a rare lung disease with a long name that mainly afflicted younger people.

One Sunday, on the ride over to the hospital, my father told me that he was sick of looking after patients seven days a week. He needed a break. But he didn't have anyone he could call who could cover his patients on Sundays.

"I'll cover your patients," I told him.

He laughed.

"You know, that gives me an idea," he said. "How would you like to come around with me today and visit patients? You could just poke your head in the room and say hi. It would probably cheer them up. A nice kid like you."

"Any day," I said.

So the plan was hatched. I would walk the halls of the pulmonary wing with my father; he would tell me when to come into a room and when to leave.

"You're going to see some people who're in bad shape," he said. "Can you handle it?"

"Of course," I said.

"Actually, I think I'll start you with one patient today and we'll go from there."

When we arrived at the hospital, my father went down to ICU. He had a guy there who was barely holding on.

While I was in the break room waiting, I wondered what it was like for my father to lose his patients all the time, even when he did the exact right thing you were supposed to do to treat them.

When he returned, he pinched my shoulder and said, "All right, let's go."

We walked down the hall toward the pulmonary wing, my short legs unable to keep pace with his longer ones.

"This lady has emphysema," he said under his breath.

He wouldn't show me her X-rays; that would be an invasion of privacy.

"But you have a good idea, from experience, what her film would look like."

The lady's door was almost completely closed. Facing us was a work of art by a four- or five-year-old, some trees and flowers made out of paper plates, markers, Popsicle sticks, crayons, glue, and pieces of colored yarn.

"All right, here we go," my father said.

He knocked on the door. A woman's hoarse voice croaked, "Yes?"

"Halloooo, Mrs. Grinnell," my father said, his voice ringing out. He pushed open the door and put on a smile.

He stopped and then I stopped at the foot of the bed. An old woman with gray hair that had turned a dingy yellow was propped up in bed. She looked pale and worn out, as if the muscles in her face could no longer follow instructions for what to do. Stuck deep inside her nostrils were a pair of small, flexible tubes, which attached to a green tank on the floor that had some kind of valve on top of it. The old woman was wearing a blue hospital gown and watching a game show on TV, in which the audience was aahing because the contestant had made a mistake.

"How's your shortness of breath today, Mrs. Grinnell?" my father said over the game show. The woman was sucking in air every few seconds. "Is the oxygen helping?"

My father went over and took the remote control from the bedside and muted the game show.

"I believe so, doctor," she rasped, then sucked in air.

"You believe so? Yesterday you characterized your problem with shortness of breath as being a 2, 1 being the worst. Is it still a 2? We're trying to prolong life here. Are we making headways?"

The woman gathered her thoughts.

"Who's the boy?" she rasped.

"He's mine," my father said. "Can't you tell?"

In fact, my father and I didn't look a great deal alike. There were lots of ways I was probably never going to equal him; physical strength and size were just a couple.

"You want to show this lady what kind of head you've got on your shoulders?" my father asked me. "It's crammed with knowledge," he confided to the woman.

I cracked my knuckles to show readiness.

"All right," my father said. "What's . . . um . . . 24 times 48?"

"1,152," I said, without missing a beat.

"31 times 13?"

"403."

"What's the capital of Iceland?"

"Reykjavík."

"Who was the twenty-first president?"

"Chester Alan Arthur. Republican from New York."

"What year was Tampa founded?"

"Indians started living here twenty-five hundred years ago. But after the Spanish arrived in the 1600s, most of them died of diseases. Today's Tampa started forming in 1824, after the United States purchased Florida from the Spanish."

"All right, now you ask him one," my father said to the woman. "Try and stump him. See if you can."

"I may be up to a 2.5," the woman croaked, and gulped air.

"That," my father said, "makes me happy. That," he said, "is what I like to hear."

My father told the woman that he was going to keep her on oxygen twenty-four hours a day for the next couple days and see what happened. He was also going to start her on a medication that would help open her breathing passages and promote air flow.

The woman coughed deeply; her lungs sounded as if they had holes in them through which a wet substance was trying to escape.

"Just lay off the tobacco," he told her. "Or else."

An old man in a plaid shirt and a silver crewcut, clearly the patient's husband, entered the room and slowly made his way over to the far side of his wife's bed. He seemed as though he was trying not to look worried.

"I'll check on you tomorrow," my father said to the woman and her husband.

"Bye," I waved.

The following Sunday, my father let me visit a few patients. Mrs. Grinnell had been released, but there were plenty of others to see. A few doors down from Mrs. Grinnell's old room, we went to see another patient with emphysema. On the way, my father whispered, "This guy's finished. Three months max. He's not responding to anything."

Upon being quizzed by my father, I told the man the four nucleobases that DNA nucleotides are made up of—cytosine, guanine, adenine, and thymine. I told him the average life expectancy of an American in 1780 (thirty-six), 1880 (forty), and 1980 (seventy-three). I named a major league baseball player who turned a childhood disability into an advantage—Mordecai "Three Finger" Brown.

After that, we saw two other patients with emphysema, neither doing well. I told them both a joke my father loved whose punch line was, "Yeah, the food is terrible. And such small portions." Once the joke was finished, I took a small bow.

Then we saw a guy with chronic bronchitis who, my father said, might just walk out of this hospital in pretty decent shape, though if he doesn't lay off the cigarettes, he's sliding down the same chute as the rest of them.

"Ready to get out of here?" he finally asked.

The following week, my father said he was going to test my maturity. He was going to bring me in to see a patient who was dying of lung cancer. Tumors everywhere. She was on a ventilator, which eased her pain, but by next week there wasn't going to be anything left of her to ventilate.

We stopped at a soda machine on the way. My father dropped in some coins, which rattled in the machine's innards. He punched the machine twice and two cans of Mountain Dew came flying down. We both took long drinks.

"This is a lady you're not going to be able to cheer up," my father said. "I've been seeing her for months. Nothing amuses her."

We went inside. The patient, who was propped up in bed, had a thin netting of white hair, anger lines across her forehead, and the most liquid eyes I had ever seen. They were blue and welling up and staring at me, piercing me. She was wearing an oxygen mask over her nose and mouth that was connected by a tube to a red, peeling canister beside the head of the bed. Another tube led from a ventilator on wheels down into a hole in her neck. The ventilator kept making a whishing sound.

"Good afternoon, Mrs. Szabo," my father said. "Jó napot."

I was shocked. My father never spoke Hungarian, his parents' language. On the two or three occasions per year when we left Florida to visit my grandparents in Wilmington, Delaware, my father did everything he could to block out his Hungarianness and Jewishness.

"Look who I brought," my father said, examining the ventilator settings and jotting down notes on his clipboard. "My son, Jay."

Mrs. Szabo stared at me with stern brows and liquid blue eyes. She looked as if I had somehow just personally offended her or was about to.

I looked at my father. I didn't want to say the wrong thing.

"Mrs. Szabo's family is from the city of Pécs, in Hungary, isn't that right, Mrs. Szabo? In the beautiful Carpathian Basin. Not far from my mother's home village."

Mrs. Szabo's chest rose a little when she inhaled and fell soon after. I could see the outlines of her toes underneath the bedding.

"Mrs. Szabo came to the United States as a young girl. On the eve of the First World War. Her family was poor and uneducated. They were looking for opportunity. Her father found work as a coal miner. In Western Pennsylvania. Hard life, but, income-wise, he did better than he would have done in Hungary. Raised four kids. Spoke Hungarian in the home."

My father's voice sounded tinged with malice; I had never heard him speak that way.

"His dream was to make enough money in America to be able to go back to Pécs and buy a plot of land and plant orchards. He wanted to have a family business that shipped out fruit to the rest of Europe. Sour cherries in the summer, apples in the winter.

"Mrs. Szabo's told me all about her family," my father said. "Their ups and downs. Their hardships and disappointments. But she's never asked about mine. Even though I have a Hungarian-Jewish surname. Maybe she doesn't want to hear about mine. What do you think, kid?"

Mrs. Szabo's liquid blue eyes stared out across the oxygen mask. They looked like they were permanently geared up for a fight.

"Hungarians don't like to hear our stories, do they, Mrs. Szabo? The way we Jews go on and on about our miseries, you'd think we were the only ones who ever suffered.

"Well, I want you to know how *my* parents came to the United States."

The ventilator went on whishing.

"This is where you come in," my father said to me, crossing his arms.

"When we go see my parents," my father said to the woman, "the kid just sits there at the table for hours and listens. Soaks it all in. Me, I can't sit still for half a minute. I go for jogs. I listen to rock and roll on headphones.

"What year was my mother born?" my father asked me.

"1926," I said.

"And tell Mrs. Szabo about my mother's life when she was a young girl."

"Like what happened on the way home from school?" I said.

"Yes, like that," he said.

"On the way home from school," I said, "two girls in her class would kick her and make her nose bleed and say, 'Rotten Jew. You will all die.'"

"And what did my mother do?"

"To get them to stop," I said, "she did their homework for them. And gave them money every week. It was a time of Depression in Hungary."

"And what else do you know about that time?"

"Her two favorite people were her older brothers, Lajos and Sanyi. Lajos taught himself how to make leather so that he could make her a pocketbook for her birthday. The next year he made gloves."

"Mmm," my father said. "And what happened after that?"

"Hitler's armies entered Hungary."

"When?"

"March 19, 1944."

"And when did the Jews have to start wearing the yellow star of humiliation?"

"April 5, 1944."

"And when were the Jews in my mother's village forced into the ghetto?"

I lowered my eyes, which I now realized were filling up with tears. I couldn't remember the date. I would have rather said no date than the wrong date.

"Tell Mrs. Szabo about the ghetto," my father said.

"All two hundred Jews from the village were forced to live there."

"Two hundred out of how many people total in the village?"

"Seven thousand."

"You see how much he listens?" my father said to Mrs. Szabo. Her liquid blue eyes seemed to be burning with rage.

"They all had to sleep in the temple," I said. "Or else jam themselves into three small houses around the temple. Everybody said, 'Something bad is going to happen.'"

"And what happened?" my father asked.

"First, Lajos and Sanyi were taken away to forced labor camps. With some of their friends."

"Right, right," my father said. "And after that?"

"All two hundred Jews from the village, including my grandmother and her parents, were shipped off to Auschwitz. It was a three-day ride with no food or water."

"Oh, Mrs. Szabo doesn't want to hear about Auschwitz. We

Jews, obsessed with talking about Auschwitz."

My father, standing beside the ventilator, bowed his head gloomily, placed his hands behind his back, and squirmed.

In fact, at Auschwitz, my grandmother's parents were sent right to the gas chambers. On arriving, my grandmother's mother said to Mengele, in German, "We are mother and daughter and we would like to stay together." He separated them. If my grandmother had insisted on staying with her mother, she would have been sent to the gas chambers too.

"This kid could tell you stories—100 percent true—of what went on there," my father said. "But weren't there some good Germans at Auschwitz? I once heard my mother say she'd have never made it out if not for the German who put an extra piece of bread in her pocket or the ones who took care of her in the clinic when she got diphtheria. At any moment, they could have just gassed her."

Mrs. Szabo's eyes were boiling over with rage.

"What happened next to my mother?" my father said.

"By miracle, she got sent to Lenzing. With three hundred other girls."

"What was Lenzing?"

"A subcamp of Mauthausen. In Austria. She did factory work. The girls all became skeletons."

My father's beeper went off. He silenced it. A nurse popped her head in the door. My father raised a finger and she disappeared.

"I hope we're not taxing your patience, Mrs. Szabo," my father said. The old woman's liquid blue eyes were burning inside the masked pouch of her face. "We Jews. Can't stop broadcasting our troubles to the world."

"So what happened after that?" my father asked me.

"The Americans liberated Lenzing on May 5, 1945."

"And where did my mother go?"

"Back to Hungary," I said. "By train."

"And here we get to the part of my mother's story that you're really not going to enjoy, Mrs. Szabo. Mrs. Szabo is a true Hungarian," my father said to me. "She goes back to Pécs once every three years. As often as she can afford. Speaks fluent Hungarian. If there is such a thing as an American with a Hungarian world view, Mrs. Szabo has it."

The old lady's eyes narrowed. Her chest rose and fell more slowly, as if she were starting to fatigue. For some reason, I found myself picturing what her chest X-ray must look like, white spots everywhere. And if she was at death's door, why weren't any of her loved ones here?

"What happened on the train ride back to my mother's village?"

"She met a boy. The boy who became my grandfather. He had been doing forced labor in Germany, repairing railroad tracks. He went back with her to her village."

"And what happened when they arrived?"

"There were no Jews there," I said.

"And what did she do?"

"She went and knocked on the doors of some people she had known. And they all said to her, 'No Jews live here.'"

"How long had she been gone?" my father said.

"A little over a year."

"And what happened next?"

"She went to the temple. And the temple was now being used as a warehouse. And she went to the homes of some family and Jewish friends, and all the homes were occupied by other people. And she went to the Jewish cemetery, and the cemetery had been cleared and replaced by a lumberyard.

"Finally, she went to see the man who was the publisher of the village newspaper. She said, 'All I want is to find my brothers.'

"'We have no Jews here,' the man said.

"'Jews have lived in this village for over five hundred years,' my grandmother said. 'May I take out an ad in your newspaper in order to find my family?'

"The man agreed. But nobody answered the ad."

"Continue."

"Two days later a cousin arrived. She told my grandmother that both her brothers were dead. Lajos had been shot by a firing squad after he injured his foot on a long march in Austria. Sanyi perished in a camp in Yugoslavia.

"My grandmother broke down in tears and said to my future grandfather, 'I cannot stay in this country another day.'

"They began making plans to come to America. My future grandfather had five sisters in Wilmington, Delaware."

Once again I realized that I was about to cry. What if I had made some factual mistakes in the telling of my grandmother's story that would invalidate everything I had said? The idea upset me terribly. My grandmother had warned me more than once that non-Jews often don't believe our stories, so don't make errors.

"How many members of our family went to the camps?" my father asked me.

"Forty-two."

"And how many came back?"

"Three."

"Gratulálunk!" my father said to Mrs. Szabo. "You see? That wasn't such a hard story to have to listen to. Now we can both go back to forgetting all about it."

Mrs. Szabo's eyes were closed, wet at the edges. My father went over and put his hand on her shoulder.

The following week, as my father and I were driving to the hospital, he told me that Mrs. Szabo had died.

"That old Jew-hating buzzard," he said. "We showed her what was what."

Up until that moment I had never given much thought to how anyone could hate a group of people so much that they would want to get rid of them all. When my grandparents told their stories, that was never posed as a question. It was just a given. People hated Jews.

Now that I had kept my composure while visiting a patient at death's door, my father brought me in to see his sickest cases.

I usually kept quiet and put on a cautious smile. While my father examined and interviewed the patients, he would go on quizzing and quizzing me.

A few weeks later, my father found someone to cover his patients on Sundays. In exchange, he would cover for the other doctor on Saturdays.

While my father told me this, he looked at me as if I would be automatically relieved that I wouldn't have to come into the hospital with him any longer. Now we could do fun things together on Sundays. Watch football. Go fishing. Barbecue. Get out of town. We wouldn't have to be afraid that anything we did would be interrupted by a call from the hospital.

But I wasn't ready to stop going to the hospital. I was learning things there that I could not learn anywhere else.

On my last day at the hospital, I told my father I didn't want to stay in the break room at all. I only wanted to be with him. So he let me trail him everywhere. He even let me wait for him outside the double doors he used to enter ICU.

By now, I had known four people, including Mrs. Szabo, who had died while in the hospital. Naturally, in every case, the room was reassigned to another emphysema or cancer patient who was in similar need of being cheered up.

Toward the end of the day, we approached Mrs. Szabo's old room. When I glimpsed inside, I saw a barrel-chested man with tufts of silver chest hair who was staring up at the ceiling. He gave a deep, wet cough. Then another. He cleared his throat, brought up mucus, spit the mucus into a tissue, and took a deep, gasping breath. My father bent over and whispered to me that this guy was not going to be able to stop smoking for all the tea in China.

"I give him six months."

THE KIND OF LUXURIES WE FELT WE DESERVED

My stepbrother Donny's twelfth birthday was all boys and Melanie, my stepsister. I deejayed, but it was no use. Donny and his friends just grouped up in a half circle behind the turntable and kept requesting the same three Van Halen songs. From our spot near the sink, Melanie and I watched the boys bump shoulders while one of them tried jumping into a half split in front of the refrigerator. After a while, Melanie got sick of the Van Halen and told Donny that his friends had no chance of ever getting girlfriends if this was the coolest they knew how to be. Finally, the boys got bored and began poking around the house for some action. A few of them ended up in the garage fooling around with my free weights and looking through Donny's new *Car and Driver*, and the rest took off behind the pool and started smoking a joint in the backyard.

Melanie wanted to dance now on the Chattahoochee stone floor of the screened back patio. She was looking tight and nasty, and she knew I'd want to see her shake that body. In the bathroom earlier I had stood aside while she whipped her hair around getting ready for the party. She'd asked me to smell the rose citrus perfume on her collarbone for whether I thought Bobby, her old boyfriend, would like it. I put my nose in her moussed hair on the way down. She knew I was in the bathroom to see what she had on. A black nylon shirt, a big yellow beach towel. We had bedrooms across the hall from each other.

When I wouldn't play the song she wanted, Melanie went to her room and called a guy. I could hear his truck gurgle up to the house a half hour later. She clapped her heels down the hallway tiles and called one of Donny's friends a starved little pervert on the way out. The boys who had been smoking came back inside and wanted to get into the liquor, but I wasn't about to let them do that.

"Stop giggling like it's your first time," I said, "and maybe I'll let you watch some cable."

Our parents came home before the good movies started. Liz had a sheet cake from Publix for Donny with a Matchbox car and the number 12 in blue plastic on the icing. For a present she had gotten him a pair of ten-pound dumbbells, the kind I had told him to ask her for. Donny's friends wanted to take their paper plates back outside and listen to more Van Halen on the patio. My dad asked where Melanie was.

"I have no idea," I said.

"What do you mean, no idea?" Liz said.

"She didn't tell me."

"So she just left?"

"I'm telling you, lady," my dad said. "Your daughter is out of control."

"Listen, friend. I'll worry about my daughter. You just keep worrying about you and your son."

"Everybody's been partying just fine without her," I said.

"That's right," said the scrawny pervert kid who had been hooting at Melanie.

"Let's enjoy some birthday cake," Liz suggested to Donny and all his friends, "and then Larry and I are going to have to drive you little guys home."

Melanie got back about 1:30 and cuh-clacked cuh-clacked down to her room. I could tell no one in the house was asleep when she threw her purse down on her bed. She went into the bathroom to take off her makeup, and Liz followed her. They were in there for a while. Melanie said, "Goodnight, mom" real loud, and they went back to their rooms. I could hear Liz creak into bed on the other side of my wall. My dad wasn't snoring yet. The fan was on but not the air conditioner. I had just a sheet over me. I was hot.

Melanie waited about ten minutes before she came in my room. The way she would do it, she really didn't give a shit. Melanie in pink heels, heavy stepping on the carpet, the collarbone I liked so much, baby bread-roll neck, acid-wash jeans with fringes along the seams, the blond bangs still curled with mousse and sprayed down to her eyebrows, fat, rolling, sexy, and I couldn't wait until she would kneel down in front of my pullout sleeper and put her elbows on my legs.

"You suck," she said.

"What are you talking about?"

"I'm just kidding."

"What did you do tonight?" I said.

"How much do you want to know?" she said.

She bit her lip and touched my chest. I flexed.

"Was it Bobby?"

"Bobby's an asshole."

"So where'd you go then?"

"Chris's boat."

"Chris the contractor?"

"He is so cool."

"I thought he lived in the Keys."

"I told my mom I went to the game. You better not say anything."

"Your mom's a bitch," I whispered.

"Oh yeah, and your dad."

We stopped talking and listened across the wall. Nothing but snoring and the cricking of bugs outside the window screen. It was dark in the room. I could not see Melanie's ears behind her hair. The hair was everywhere, over her shoulders and down to the top of her breasts, with smoke, perfume, beer coming toward me, and the harbor I could imagine down off Old Cutler Road.

We didn't start talking again. Something felt different. Melanie's fingers moved down the sheet to what was between my legs. She held it there. I swallowed my breath. She was looking at me, the stupid look, when her eyes got crossed and she looked like a retard. She had me. I was thinking of a twenty-six-foot boat and her sitting at the bow.

I kept holding still. She had the tip of her tongue between her lips. Then Melanie did something no girl did before. She brought that sheet down and she tied it around my ankles. I looked up over my head and saw a lamp.

Melanie said to me, "I can't help myself anymore."

"No problem," I said.

I wondered what she was thinking of mine, if it was ugly to her or if she thought Chris the contractor's was nicer, more mature. Afterward, she was biting her lip again, and her hair smelled a little like me now, too.

"I think I love you," she said.

"You can do that any time you want," I said.

The next day was Saturday, and when I walked in the kitchen for cereal, Liz was in her purple quilted robe and fuzzy slippers, picking at leftover birthday cake and browsing catalogs and junk mail. She was a board, no body, just long and bony like all the women my dad ever went out with. Donny sitting next to her with his new ten-pound iron dumbbells at his feet. I could hear my dad coming in through the garage from a run.

"Were there boys smoking marijuana cigarettes in this house last night?" Liz said to me.

"No," I said.

Donny sat sideways in his chair, facing the pool.

"Did you see any of the boys here last night smoking marijuana cigarettes?"

Donny curled a dumbbell with his right arm. I could tell she had already questioned him.

"I didn't see any boy doing anything."

"This is my house, Mr. Vince. And you're an influence on these children. What in the hell were you doing last night while we were gone? Dealing drugs at a birthday party?"

"What's your problem, Liz? You already know what I was doing last night. I was playing records, like Donny asked me to."

"And that's all you claim you know about the drugs?"

"I said I don't know what you're talking about."

"Well, I think you're a liar."

"Well, I think you're a schnauzer."

My dad walked in the kitchen in his little blue running shorts. His quads had some definition. Donny was still looking out at the pool. He knew if he turned around and looked at me, I might come over there and beat his face.

"Larry."

"That's me."

"Donny's friend Todd's mother called this morning. Todd told her some of the boys last night went out to the backyard and smoked marijuana cigarettes. While we were gone and your son was in charge."

My dad was breathing heavily. His running shoes had mud on the soles. Sweat was trickling into his headband and down the hair on his arms to his wristbands.

"You know about that, Donny?" he asked, holding up the side entrance to the kitchen with his hands.

"Donny wasn't involved. This wasn't all the boys, just some of them."

"Who started it?" my dad asked Donny.

"She's trying to tell me I gave them pot," I said.

"Who was in charge?" Liz said to my dad. "And watch your shoes please on the kitchen floor."

My dad jumped up and started curling himself on the lintel at the kitchen entrance. He did one pull-up, then two. He kept his legs straight. One of Liz's framed pictures, with oranges and grapefruits and a border of white blossoms, shook on the wall behind the table.

"If that breaks."

"You're hysterical," my dad said. "You know that?"

"Get out of my kitchen," Liz said. Then she hollered it. "Just get out of my sight, and take him with you. I don't want one more day of this."

My dad and I showered and went to the movies. After that we went looking for apartments. We stuck to the area near Dixie above 136th, near where we lived. Every manager wanted to rent to my dad. He had a decent job, and he brought cash. But my dad couldn't settle on an apartment. Not even the one that had a sauna, a jacuzzi, a pool, a basketball court, a shuffleboard court, a game room, a security guard, and about twenty fine single women in bikinis lying out and sipping drinks from fluorescent plastic cups. He just kept saying to me, "One divorce is one thing, two divorces—it's humiliating."

The next week Liz stopped talking to me completely. Two words at a time, most. "*My* refrigerator!" "*My* house!" I could see that she and my dad were going to start losing it on each other soon, but I didn't give a shit. I was working light construction during the week, and I was getting big. My upper body was smoking. Weekends I would bench rounds of 180 in the garage and polish it off with some lats. I kept wishing Liz would lay a finger on me the wrong way, so I could pick her up with one fist and crack her over my knee. Instead, she kept spazzing about little things. She would come out to the garage in the middle of my workout and stretch over me for a broom like my body was the biggest inconvenience to her. Or she would come up behind me in the pantry wagging a finger, and I'd flex my shoulders and pecs and just growl in her face—*ruff ruff, grrrr*. Melanie asked me to be nicer to her mom. I said, "For you, Melanie," and I brought my hips up closer to her chest and slid a leg across her cushiony body.

Melanie liked to come in my room when our parents were making up. She would kneel in the dark in front of my pullout sleeper making sexy breath noises in my ear while her fingernails skated across the rips in my abs. We couldn't hear the words our parents were saying on the other side of the wall, but we knew from their voices what they meant. If the TV was on, that was a peace sign. It meant the grownups had gotten in a better mood, and they'd be fucking the creaks out of the bedframe soon. Them starting in was like the sound of rails splitting to me. Their voices hush, Liz's legs spreading, cootchy-coo, and you could feel the jolting of the headboard. Melanie and I would stop what we were doing, sit up in the shadows of each other's bodies, me hating her mom, her hating my dad, and crack up to ourselves about the way grownups were until she was sucking on her lower lip and I was holding whatever parts of her were closest to my hands.

Melanie started spending less time at home. She was getting more involved with Chris the contractor, who was twenty-seven and had a mustache. Her mom didn't know about this guy. She was skipping school and going sailing with him. She kept telling me how mature he was. She would tell me this like I should be jealous. When she got D's in geometry and U.S. history, Liz asked her if she needed a tutor. Melanie told Liz her teachers hated her. Liz believed that that was the problem. At dinner my dad told Melanie her problem was laziness. He asked her if she planned to graduate. Then Liz cleared her throat and made my dad look at me.

"Living at home, almost nineteen years old, flunks his first exam at community college and decides he's just going to drop out. I think before you criticize someone else's child, you ought to take a good look in the mirror at the one that belongs to you. Speaking of laziness, not to mention a future."

"I'm saving for a car," I said. I wanted to call Liz a bitch. A nasty bitch with a slut daughter. "And a better set of speakers."

Liz wouldn't talk to me. She wouldn't look at me.

"You're not buying a car until we talk about it," my dad said. He was trying anything he could think of to bond with Liz.

"I'm getting a Testarossa when I'm twenty-one," Donny said.

"And you're taking me to the beach," Melanie said.

"If I feel like it."

One night, Donny knocked on my door when Melanie was inside with her fingers on my balls. He said he had to use the dictionary for a school paper. The lights were off, and I was wearing just a pair of sweatshorts. Melanie had on a plump white undershirt and dancing tights. I was so warm and stiff, I dragged the sheet up over myself like there was a chance Donny would be looking there.

"I don't care" is what he said.

I turned on the lamp. Donny was a porky little brown-haired dude in an Italian-striped racing shirt and colored underwear.

"You don't care, what?" his sister said back.

"Anything."

"Donny, are you just going to stand there half-naked or are you going to get whatever you came in here for and leave?" she said.

"I don't have to listen to your ass," Donny said.

I checked out Melanie's rolls in the light by the bookcase. I wondered what her and Donny's father looked like. Who'd mated with Liz and produced those two.

"Just wait till you need me," Melanie said.

"For what?" Donny said.

"Wait till you're trying to get a girlfriend. I could say whatever I want to them about you. Just remember that."

Donny made a pathetic muscle and showed it to me.

"When I do my curls, I keep my back straight," he said.

"You're getting there," I said. "Now you got to gradually increase your sets. And remember your breathing. But don't overdo it. You're just a kid."

"Why don't you go work some of that baby fat off right now, Donny? I don't think anyone invited you in Vince's room," Melanie said.

Donny looked to me.

"You heard her," I said.

Melanie sat back against the wall on my sleeper. My dad shouted out to us to get in our own beds. Melanie made a face. There were sea-grape leaves and hibiscus bushes outside shaking from the long, whistling gusts of wind.

That Saturday we were supposed to all have brunch as a family at eleven o'clock. It was already storming when I woke up, the big raindrops popping against the shutters and bushes. We waited at the table for Melanie, who I knew would be hungover. At about three in the morning she had shown up in my room wasted, in heavy mascara and a pink net blouse, blubbering "Chris is an asshole" onto my leg. She smelled like puke and rose citrus. I didn't want to see her cry. I lifted her into her own bed.

At eleven, Liz was walking through the kitchen in her quilted robe like she had something to say and she wasn't saying it. I was sitting at the table across from Donny. My dad was flipping French toast in a paper-thin jogging suit and singing "Rain, Rain, Go Away." He put out the napkins and the silverware. None of us could hear Melanie moving in the back of the house.

"I'm going to count to ten, and I promise I will not lose my patience," my dad said.

I turned around, and Liz took a hard look at me.

"Do you know what time she got in last night?"

"What are you asking me for? Didn't you sleep in this house last night?"

"Don't answer her like that, Vince," my dad said.

"I don't know when," I said to my dad. "You guys must have heard her. Or maybe Donny knows. Donny knows all."

Donny had wandered out onto the patio floor, which had puddles all around the edges of the pool. He was barefoot with his head down, punting up little splashes of water with his toes. He was moving away from us. The sliding glass door to the patio was open, and it was moist in the kitchen and loud from the rain.

"Do you know or don't you?" my dad said.

"I don't know," I said.

Liz walked to the back of the house. My dad put the oval serving plate of French toast in the middle of the table next to the syrup, the jam, and the margarine. Everyone had a cut grapefruit on a plate.

"Now!" my dad called to Donny.

Then he lowered his voice and leaned down to me.

"I'm asking you not to push Liz."

We ate brunch without Melanie. Liz kept giving me looks in the silences. My dad finally asked about Melanie's status. Liz said she wasn't going to make it to the table, and my dad said that was obvious. He took Melanie's grapefruit and put it on his own plate. Then he realized he was about to start another fight, and he asked Liz if Melanie was feeling okay. Liz said she thought Melanie had a fever. My dad put his fist in his teeth and looked at his wife with puffy eyes.

After brunch Liz was going to take Donny to Cutler Ridge mall, but Donny couldn't find his money. He whimpered about how he'd put a twenty right next to his bed yesterday. Liz said they'd find it later, she wanted to get out of the house now. My dad said, after they'd left, "Let's just take a drive."

We ran out to the driveway with our hoods over our heads. He turned the ignition, but he didn't shift into gear.

"Do you think we should just move out?" he said to me. He was staring at the flat-tile roof of the house.

"I didn't marry her," I said.

Above my dad's head I could see the patterns of rainwater beating down on the T-top. His gold chain was outside the zipper of his jacket, and he had deep lines across his forehead that looked like ripples of muscle to me.

"I won't get anything," my dad said. "I'll get half of nothing. It'll all be hers."

"It was all hers to begin with," I said.

"That's not what marriage is supposed to be," he said. "It's supposed to be half and half."

"It was never equal. Her last husband was loaded."

"But we've bought a lot of things together," my dad said with a crack in his voice.

"Well, we'll take them," I said.

"If we do leave," he said, "you have to treat Liz with dignity."

I looked at my father. I didn't know what he was talking about. I knew Liz had some kind of control over him, and once he told me he was in love with her. I felt sorry for him. I wondered what it was like to be forced to still care about someone like Liz six years later. I clicked the garage door closed and looked in one more time at my bench and free weights. I could picture Melanie lying on her back with stuffed animals and messed hair all around her, winding the curly phone cord across her bed, talking on the phone with some other guy.

The next day when my dad got back from a long run, he told me the plan for how we were going to move out. He sounded scared, but like he was going to do it. Tomorrow he would make a deposit on a two-bedroom apartment in that complex I liked with the sauna and all the females. Since Liz worked three days as a hygienist, 8:30 to 4:30, my dad and I would both take a day off work one of those days, rent a van, and move out as much stuff as we could while she was gone. We could probably make it with all our stuff in three trips.

My dad set the date for a week from Wednesday. It was in the middle of the work week, in the middle of the month, so Liz would never suspect.

"The way we're doing this is the best way," he said to me more than once, confidentially, that week. "Because I want to be fair, and at the same time I know that if I sat down with her and tried to reason out a separation, there'd be fireworks. You've seen how unreasonable she's been getting the past few months."

Now my dad was telling me every reason he had ever

thought of why it was a good idea to move out of Liz's house. What a temper she had, how bossy she could be, how moody. He busted on Melanie. She was proof that Liz was a bad deal. Melanie was an overweight, out-of-control delinquent, and Donny a spoiled child. If Liz had ever really cared about their marriage, she'd have put him before them once in a while.

Alone in my room, I practiced how many clothes I could carry in my arms at one time. Then how many magazines, lamps, and porcelain figurines of Liz's. The move on Wednesday was making me feel like I was leading a two-man adventure quest. I would stand on the thin foam mattress of my pullout sleeper and strike Mr. Universe poses. "Can our hero safely liberate the palace treasure before the dragon witch returns and starts breathing down spears of fire?" I asked out loud.

I consoled Melanie about Chris. She told me her problems, and I listened to them. If she wanted to give me a blow job afterward, I let her. I would rest my head back on my hands and let her get to work. I was out of there. I didn't give a shit.

The morning of the move, all of us wound up in the kitchen at the same time. Liz was wearing her all-whites, and she had her wiry hair up in barrettes the way she always wore it to the office. Melanie had on a large football jersey from our high school with a lineman's number on it. Tight-ass jeans and plenty of lip gloss. She was pouring two glasses of Five Alive by the sink for herself and Donny. My dad was next to the refrigerator, chugging coffee.

"I'm leaving," Liz said. "Be good."

"Love you, Mom," Melanie said. "We will."

"All right, Larry," Liz said.

"I'll see you," my dad said, like he was about to cry.

Liz kissed Donny on the forehead. Donny had pretty much stopped talking to me, too, lately. He picked up his things and walked to the bus stop.

In a few minutes Melanie went out the front door to wait for her ride. I went down the pathway after her. Her jeans were tight and looking good.

"Is No. 61 Hector Villanueva?" I said when our feet were on the edge of the street. I used to play some JV cornerback.

Melanie was looking up the block to see if anyone was turning our way.

"Uh-huh," she said.

"I know that guy."

"Yeah, he said he knew you."

"That guy can squat," I said. "Especially for a Cuban."

Melanie wasn't saying anything about him.

"How much is he squatting now?" I asked her.

"I only just started hanging out with him," she said. "I can just tell you he's built."

A car came up our street, but it wasn't Melanie's. Already the sky was blue like the middle of the day, with a sun you couldn't put your eyes near, and all the big white clouds whizzing by over other people's houses.

"Are you into him?" I said.

I checked out Melanie from the side. She shrugged, and she pushed out her lips.

"Doesn't he have a black Trans Am?" I said.

"Stick."

"I bet it's nice inside."

"Leather interiors."

"When were you guys hanging out?"

"Why are you asking me all this shit?"

"I don't know. I'm just trying to remember what the guy's like."

"He's hot," Melanie said. "He's fuckin' hot is all I can say."

Melanie had her fingers combing through the back of her hair and her curvy ass sticking out in my direction. She was wearing Wayfarers and looking upward slightly. I was standing there taking her in and not just her body. Her face. What it really looked like in the daylight, the shape of it around the sunglasses. The way her mouth would smile and perk up when she saw Villanueva in the parking lot before school.

"That guy's on 'roids, isn't he?"

"Excuse me?" she said.

"I knew it."

I wanted Melanie to look at me, at my arms, the color of my tan, and the definition.

Then I said to her, "You're going to be late." I said it twice.

"Could you write me a note, please? Daddy?"

"Funny," I said. "Nice mood today."

"I'm just kidding."

"That's cool," I said.

A bunch of girls pulled up in a white Rabbit on the other side of the street, and Melanie got in on the far door with her books against Villanueva's jersey. I walked back into the house past the banyan tree with its long mossy branches set up along the gutters of the roof.

My dad started getting panicky in the garage, but I calmed him down. We got the van with the luggage rack on top.

"All right," he said in the driveway with the garage door

open. "I just want you to get our stuff. I don't want you even touching anything that belongs to Melanie or Donny. You understand me? We're going to do this completely fair and square. You carry, I'll load. Then I'll go do a check inside and make sure we got everything."

My dad kept stopping and catching his breath.

"What about stuff that's both of yours?" I said. "Like the bedroom TV. And what about the gas grill? That stuff?"

"Anything we bought while we were married, we'll deal with that at the end. Just get all the stuff that's only ours first. That's going to take at least two trips by itself."

I had on my brace for lifting. The first thing I grabbed was my dad's exercise bike. Then all the other things of his that took two hands. Most of what was in my dad's bedroom belonged to Liz anyway—the bed, the artwork, the chest of drawers. I emptied his half of their walk-in closet and laughed at how lopsided it looked. I got almost all of what he said was his out of the house before I even looked in my room. I just kept gathering the biggest clumps of anything I could see and stretching my arms around them.

We took the first load over to the new apartment complex around 11:30. Our unit was on the second floor. We unloaded the van and stacked everything in a mixed-up pile right inside the front door. A shoe falling in a blender, a jump rope around a jockstrap. I was bolting up and down the stairs about three times as fast as my dad, leaping from a few steps up and landing on the run.

"You got to pick up the pace," I said. "Don't get beat by the heat."

We were both sweating like animals when we got back to

the house. No shirts. My dad was bouncing on the tips of his shoes on the hot driveway, waiting while I cleared more stuff out of the house. He kept looking around the crazy trunk of the banyan tree to see if anyone was coming. He told me to go faster, just get the important stuff. He was starting to get worried that Liz would come home before we were finished, think we were stripping the house, and lose her mind.

The more worried my dad got, the rowdier it made me. I was starting to want to do everything he had instructed me not to. Just take random shit from everywhere and throw it in towels and load it up. I had the air conditioner down to a nice moving temperature. A rolled bandanna around my forehead, cutoff blue jeans, the leather brace, and steel-toed work boots. I felt wild.

In front of Donny's room, I plotted what kind of damage I could do and how quickly. What could I take that would piss Liz off the most? I jumped up and slapped the hallway ceiling, straight vertical, ten times in a row. The idea that I was never going to have to look at Liz's face again was making me feel like anything was possible for me. I did twenty clap push-ups and ten more on fists.

With my chest out as far as it could go I flung open the door to my room. I didn't own very much. What I had in there didn't even fill up the van. My dad said don't forget the rest of his kitchen stuff, and living room stuff, and patio. While I was back inside, I started doing some rearranging. I tucked Liz's diaphragm under Donny's pillow. Then I dropped one of her silver rings in the toilet tank in the master bathroom. After that I turned over all the photographs of her and my dad together.

A few more trips, and I wasn't satisfied. So I began taking. I wanted Liz to know that she hadn't gotten away with the last six years. I took all the quarters out of her change tray in the pantry, dumped them in a pillowcase with some other things she would notice were missing, like her two-liter plastic bottles of Diet Coke, and carried the whole package out to my dad in a paper grocery bag. I took Donny's ten-pound dumbbells wrapped in one of my sheets. I wanted more, so I went for Donny's baby teeth that Liz kept in a little lined box in her bathroom. I put the clasp box in my front pocket until I could decide if I really wanted to take it.

By 3:30, the second load was at the new apartment, and my shoulders were getting pooped. Now my dad had to make the big decisions. What to do about the three major items that he and Liz had acquired as a couple: the Sony color television in the bedroom, which had remote and a better picture by far than the living room TV; the gas grill, which he had gotten the deal on from knowing the floor manager at Service Merchandise; and the Chinese screen that Liz had picked out at an art fair on Key Biscayne, and that my grandparents had bought for them as an anniversary gift.

My dad wanted to discuss these three items with me. He said, "Disregard all the money I've spent over the years on repairs and improvements to the house."

I said no question, the gas grill was ours. My dad did all the grilling, replaced the canister. Liz would not miss the grill. My dad agreed.

The other two items were a different story. Liz was attached to that television, and she had a possessiveness about the painted bamboo screen, too. We were going to have to pick one or the other.

I uncabled the TV and hoisted it with my elbows. My dad

wanted to make a final sweep of the house while I packed up my weights and gear from the garage. Then we would roll out the gas grill together as the last thing, close up the house, and stop for subs on the way over to the new apartment.

In the doorway leading out to the garage, with the sweaty TV almost slipping in my fingers, I practically knocked into Melanie and Donny. Melanie had a fat new hickey. Her breasts were shapes of hills coming up out of the 6 and 1 of Villanueva's shirt.

"You really think you're taking my mom's TV?" she said.

I was looking at her neck. I could feel the weariness in my arms.

"I know you didn't take anything out of my room," she said.

"I'm just doing what my dad told me to," I said.

The garage smelled like a swamp. I tried to let the two of them by, but they didn't want to move.

I kept waiting for Melanie to do something extreme. Grab the TV, beg me not to leave. Maybe wrestle me down and have Donny pile on.

"What, did you and brainiac just skip work and try and get whatever you could out of the house when my mom wasn't looking?"

My dad came around the front of the garage. He was gesturing something to me in confused hand signals. Melanie shot a repulsed look at him, and she and Donny took off past me for the back of the house.

A second after Melanie passed by I felt a cool little rush of breeze from her. I held the scent of it in my nose. I let it wash across my face.

"I think we probably ought to get going pretty quick," my

dad said. His gold chain was swinging against his chest of hair. His work slacks looked tight around the middle.

"No shit," I said, walking the TV to the van.

I started hating the van. I started hating everything that was going on the whole day. The bags in the back, everything I'd switched around. I threw my brace into the van and shut the doors.

"What time is it?" my dad said. "I got to make sure I get everything I need out."

"I'm not leaving without every single one of my weights."

"First you're helping me get the grill."

"I'm telling you, Donny is not going to get those weights."

"I'm telling you, she's not going to walk away from this with two out of three."

I followed my dad to the back patio, and we started rolling the gas grill across the Chattahoochee floor. The sound of the squeaking and rolling made me want to kick something hard. Donny opened a door from the bathroom and shut it right away. I could picture the expression on his pudgy white face when he realized his little curl bars were gone. His box of baby teeth kept rubbing against my thigh. I was walking backward. He saw my eyes.

My dad and I were pulling the grill across the grass to the driveway when Liz showed up. My dad's arms clenched. His mouth was a straight line.

He walked slowly toward the van, and I stayed put on the grass. Then I walked behind the van on the other side of it from my dad and her. I didn't know the plan. I stayed at the back of the driveway behind the van, almost on our next-door neighbors' lawn.

"You are shit," Liz said to my dad from in front of the garage. "You are so full of shit I can't believe it."

They were less than three yards away from each other, and Liz was standing, guarding the inside of the garage. My weights were behind her. She had taken out her barrettes, and she looked like she had a black-and-gray terrier lying across her head.

"Where are my children?" she said.

"They're in there," my dad said.

"So what are you going to do now? Pack up the grill, call it a day? Huh? That's not your grill, partner. *Not* yours."

Liz waited. My dad didn't talk.

"God help you if you took one thing out of this house that didn't belong to you."

Liz waited again for my dad to say something.

"You just stay right where you are," she said.

"This is my home as well as your home," my dad said. "And I'm going to go in there and get the rest of what's mine."

"Don't threaten me, Lawrence. Bad idea."

Liz went inside. Her white hygienist outfit made everything feel more serious. My dad stepped back toward me, and I came up close to him.

"I'm not taking any chances with her," he whispered. "I want you to go call the police. I mean it. I'm not taking any chances. I'm going to try and settle this with her the peaceful way, but I want them here just in case. There's still important things I need to get out of the bedroom—and we're taking that grill."

The way the sky was, and the sun, it felt like it had been the middle of the day all day.

I took my dad's car up to Old Cutler Road and called the police from a gas station. I said there was a domestic situation. The whole time the lady on the other end was talking to me, I was thinking of Melanie's bedroom. Me with my knees on her comforter and Melanie doing her nails over the carpet, telling me things in private.

I drove back to the house about ten miles an hour. I kept punching the buttons, looking for anything decent that wasn't love songs or talking. I parked a ways up from the driveway and walked very slowly across the front lawn toward the garage.

I didn't have to see anything to know Liz was on the warpath. My dad had apparently done something to piss her off royally. And not just my dad. Vince is a lying thief, Vince is a bully, Vince thinks he can bluh bluh bluh bluh bluh bluh bluh. Talking about marijuana and a twenty-dollar bill and bullshit from five years ago that I didn't even know what she was talking about. I got up closer until I could see her. She was standing with her knees in position like an ogre hermit in dentist's office clothes ready to defend her cave. She said if either one of us touched another thing that belonged to her, she was going to go into that kitchen, get her sashimi knife, and cut him up.

Now I had my boot against the back fender of the van. All five of us again. The dumb faces of Melanie and Donny on the steps at the back of the garage. Our parents between us. My dad wanting to whisper something in my ear, but I wouldn't lean in to hear it.

"Well, I guess she told us," I said pretty loud. I was ready to go toe to toe with Liz. Once and for all. I was ready to pick her up by the hair, swing her around the garage a couple times over my head, and whack her up against my bench set.

Melanie pfffed like she was so disgusted about something,

she couldn't take it. I gave her a look. I let her know she wasn't all privileged and special now that she was letting some 'roid-freak lineman suck on her neck.

My dad said to Liz he had only wanted to divide things up the fairest way. She didn't need to overreact like this. "The marriage has run its course," he said. "We can both agree on that."

He said to Liz, "I just want to get some papers from the bedroom. I'm not even going to discuss the grill right now, okay? We'll let the lawyers do that."

"Just get out!" she said. "Leave. And don't you dare stand there and tell me I'm overreacting. Goddamned coward. You and coward junior slinking around my house all day with a moving van while I'm at work. How in the hell do I know what the two of you took or didn't take?"

Liz was turning pink and red. I was just standing back, checking out my triceps, letting my dad do all the work. The teeth were mine.

Liz waved Melanie and Donny back inside the house. Donny looked at me the way I raised him to look at me, like he better respect me or keep his fucking head down. Melanie I wondered. What she might start saying to people about me when I wasn't around.

I could see the green-and-white sheriff's car pull up in the front yard under the banyan tree while Liz was still screaming her lungs out about dignity-her-ass. One big old flappy-cheeked Dade County sheriff behind the wheel with a writing pad and a shotgun right there next to him.

Liz saw the car on the lawn and started patting herself all over, nervous. She put a barrette between her lips, then pinned back one side of her hair. I waited for her to pin back the other side, but she didn't, and by the time the sheriff was walking up to us, she looked even battier than she did before.

My dad didn't bother to put on a shirt. I didn't either.

"Folks," the cop said, pacing toward my dad. He was about my dad's age, nicely shaven, with a big beige patrolman's hat on, and uniform pants tucked into knee-high black boots. "Came to check on a disturbance. This the proper residence?"

"Yes it is, sir," my dad said.

Three of Donny's friends came by on motocross bikes, saw us in back, checked out the sheriff's rifle and his V8 Caprice, and walked their bikes into the house through the front door. It was the first time all day I noticed anyone on the block even around.

I had my eyes on the cop, his mirrored sunglasses hanging off his shirt pocket. He was nodding and sweeping his eyes around. Taking notes.

"I don't see any disturbance," the cop said.

"Actually, sir, my wife has stated that I am forbidden to enter my own house."

"You let your wife talk to you like that?" the cop said.

"Not usually," my dad said. "No. But she's been getting a little rough around the edges today. You know."

"This your residence?"

"It is my residence. My son and I live here, and we want to be able to go into the house peacefully and get the rest of what belongs to us."

We all looked at Liz. She had a face like she was choking on ideas.

"Officer, I can't believe what's going on here."

The sheriff stood there and gave Liz the once-over. Chewing on his ink pen, jotting down notes.

"Officer, that man and his son went into my house while I was at work today and put things in that van that do not belong to them. The definition is stealing. Stealing is what that is. That grill belongs on my patio, and that television they took belongs to me too. And my son is missing things. Valuable things. You can put that in your report. And there's going to be other things except I haven't even looked around yet to see what else. You know, if the chicken-liver wanted to move out so much, nobody was stopping him. Do you see me stopping him from moving out now? I'd prefer it if he left."

"Lady, let's get this straight. I am not the judge, and nothing's getting divided up now."

The cop paused and made sure we were all listening. His radio was steady, the static over the dispatcher's other calls.

"Festivities are over. End of round one. Going to be nothing else going, nothing else coming. I'm working on sixteen hours straight, and I've seen all the trouble I'm going to see for today."

My dad was starting to get mopey now—drooping his eyes, hanging his face, holding himself like you'd think someone was forcing him to be there and stand up on his own two feet.

"And there's been plenty of it," the sheriff said. "First thing this morning took a dashboard out of a baby's sternum. Going to be half the right side of that kid's face. Bloodbath. Perfectly avoidable too. Vehicle trying to pass on a two-lane across a double-yellow. So spent all morning with the kid in emergency, then spent the rest of the day helping out on a kook with a hostage, and my work isn't done yet. Got to stop at Eckerd's after this, pick out some vapor rub for the mother-in-law, or no one's letting me in the front door when I get home. See, it's trouble and a mess out there, but so easily avoided. You gentlemen have another place to sleep tonight?"

"Yes, sir," my dad said.

"Suggest you lay it down for today."

I'd never taken my eyes off the sheriff. His bulletproof upper body, the knife strapped to his belt. He had a legitimate chest, too, I was judging from his upper arms.

"Excuse me," I said. "I have one request."

I looked the sheriff in the eyes. I wanted him to know I was different from my dad and Liz.

"What if there's one thing of mine, right in the garage, that I could just load up in about five minutes? It's all it would take. Anybody can watch me."

"Son, how's your hearing?"

My dad muttered that we were on our way. He said we would get the court to give us the rest of what was ours.

Liz was still standing in front of the garage, waiting for us all to take off. I looked in behind her at my 180-pound bar on the bench stand. I could picture her throwing the iron wells one by one against the floor of the garage after I was gone, or just clearing out everything that was mine in there and promising to buy Donny a whole new set of weights someday.

The sheriff nodded to us and got on his radio. Then we drove toward the new apartment complex in a kind of procession. First the sheriff, then me, then my dad in the rental van. When we got to Dixie, the sheriff turned left. I honked goodbye and waved out the T-top. The sheriff flashed his yellow roof lights, and I honked some more and blasted the speakers.

The rest of the week I called in sick. I kept going for swims and taking showers. I used Liz's quarters on video games. I set up my stereo, but that was it.

My dad kept bellyaching how much worse this was. He ate frozen enchiladas by himself on the carpet. He asked if I thought things were really over with Liz. I put on some trunks and went down to find the sauna.

I had never actually been in a sauna before. It was just a wood slat stall with a wood slat bench. I shut the door behind me and stripped naked in the room. I found the heat dial on the wall and turned it up to the max. I was thinking about that baby that lost half its face.

I tightened my abs and let them go. I pretended I lost half my face. With my fingers like a cutting knife, I cut myself down the line of my nose and all the way down the middle of my skin. I kept one eye shut the whole time I was cutting. Then I cut the base of my belly in half. Then halfways diagonal across my chest. I cut an X where my sternum made the center. I made squiggle cuts all over my flesh.

Afterward I took a jacuzzi and let the water swirl around in the net of my trunks. It was Saturday afternoon, and there were bodies galore. The whole scene outside the community building was blowing me away. The landscaping of the walking paths, the vanilla smell of lotion, the row of green coconut palms in the turf around the pool. The place was loaded. I approved. I could hear Jimmy Buffett playing on somebody's tape deck. I saw guys at the hibachi getting high. There were girls with loose bikini strings getting rid of their tan lines, rubbing their shoulders down with cocoa butter and tropical oils.

I had my left arm at ease along the edge of the tub. I was sweating good and clean. Across from me a couple of stewardesses were dipping their toes in the steaming water and talking about their hectic flying schedules. Now they were laughing about the bubbles and climbing in. They had one-piecers on but some action underneath.

As soon as they were sitting down, one of them reached into her shoulder bag and pulled out a cold bottle of pink champagne. "We've got to celebrate, Julie," that one said.

Behind me, in the rush of the water's jets, I could feel Melanie's excited hams around my ass, the pulse from her body streaming under my legs. I felt the grip of thighs, the press of breasts to my back.

The stewardesses raised a toast. They clicked their cups and smiled at each other like they were about to sail off on a cruise somewhere.

Now I could feel Melanie sitting up beside me, and I tried to think of some way that all of us in the hot tub could get acquainted. We live in the Palm Springs apartments too, I began rehearsing in my head. Personally I work construction, and Melanie here's still in school. We used to have a house together not far from here, but it didn't have the kind of luxuries we felt we deserved.

On the other side of the tub Julie was pinching herself about her new promotion and tipping some champagne on the other one's hair. "Par-*ty*," they said together.

I still couldn't get over the landscaping job. I stretched an arm a little farther around Melanie's shoulder and asked her if she could believe all this was ours. I was pretty sure she was starting to feel more at home in the jacuzzi. Just the way she was biting her lip and not saying anything, moving in closer like nobody was watching.

ROGER'S SQUARE DANCE BAR MITZVAH

Roger, of course, would have been 13. So Imonie would have been 11, I would have been 10, and Lianne would have been 6. Lianne in those days looked after the pretty little Vehemente girl from down the street, the Venezuelan nightclub owners' daughter, so really there were five of us usually around somewhere. We lived in a split-level townhome at the western edge of Miami. To our right were the synagogue and the dialysis center and the other split-level townhome developments; to the left, the pole bean/wax bean/snap bean/black-eyed pea farms, Krome Avenue, and then the swamps.

Roger didn't want a party—all he wanted from his Bar Mitzvah, it seemed to me, was permission from Jewish law to wrap tefillin every morning when he stood and shuckled, praying toward Jerusalem by our bedroom window an hour before school. But Mother had decided on a square dance. Hay was cheap, and every girl would have a boy to dance with. She had gotten a tip on a caller in Vero named Buddy Miley, who *knew how to get a room going*. A square dance, Mother's friends agreed, was just the thing. Once Buddy Miley was booked, Imonie began walking out to the bean fields around sundown and promenading up the mud rows. Palming fast circles against her breasts, she gazed north at the sky, sniffing it like a lightning rod. Back in the front doorway, she would hold out an imaginary side of skirt and, blushing, say to the full-length mirror, "Honor your partner." Then, "Sashay right. Star through." What no one would say—including Alessandra Vehemente, lovely, long-haired Alessandra who was always running downstairs in front of Lianne rasping scandalous stories about the larger world, Alessandra Vehemente who at four-and-a-half had lived in Caracas, Puerto Azul, New York, who had taught Lianne and I to dance *pachangas* and *guarachas*, *boleros* and *son montunos* and was the first person besides Lianne I was sure I could spend every day of the rest of my life with—what no one in the house would say was that Daddy, who was very assimilated, loved a square dance. Daddy could move bluegrass and beautifully he did. This square dance must be for Daddy—wherever he was, whenever he'd come home. Daddy agile, Daddy slide, Daddy small and lean like a barefisted fighter.

Where was Daddy? This time we hadn't gotten postcards; these six months we hadn't received collect calls, or trinkets from Indian reservations; no bad word yet from the credit card companies or the authorities in Tarpon Springs or Bayonet Point, towns along the Gulf Coast he wandered to selling home and office security, deep-sea fishing trips; no contact—and this time Mother wasn't going to fetch him home. She would not, she said, this time, swing wide the gate of love for him. That had been the first fret: What, then, to invite Daddy's people to? Saturday morning service and kiddush? Kiddush and party?

Kabbalat Shabbat and service? Daddy's people will want food, we shouted. Let them pay for the meat, Mother answered. If we don't invite Daddy to the dance, Daddy may show up and knock strangers around. Let Daddy pay for the hay. Let Daddy pay for the bourbon. I'm not afraid of your Daddy, Mother said.

None of us believed this, but I think we liked hearing her say it, whatever it meant.

None of us, I think, knew really what to believe in those days, except for Roger, who believed so strongly, it seemed he was always making up somehow for the rest of us. Roger had begun to converse openly now only with the rabbi and with a handful of other boys he met at youth group conferences and inter-synagogue weekend retreats—as if everyone else around was too simple, or savage, or just didn't exist. He walked through the months leading up to his Bar Mitzvah with such self-possession—such plump, new, wire-rimmed, hunch-shouldered, head-covered self-possession—that kids at the bus stop loudly called him Mister Superior, Tight-Ass, Kikazoid Jewboy, and enough other names that I wondered why he didn't just adjust back to the person he had been six months ago who didn't get his face bashed in. Mother might have wondered this too. She hated to see Roger leave the house now, even for a Sabbath overnighter, even knowing beyond doubt he'd be sleeping nowhere but the floor of a synagogue youth hall in Pompano Beach, in a crowded, monitored row of Jewish preteens. Imonie could walk into the swamps, I could stay out all weekend playing basketball, Lianne and Alessandra could catch rides to Mr. and Mrs. Vehemente's club on Key Biscayne and run about till four a.m., jingling in jewelry, clinging to the bouncer, engraving his name in their arms—Mother might not notice. But Roger mystified Mother; he was like her leader.

Once, I was pretty sure, things had been more believable. Daddy had looked after Mother, Mother had looked after Roger, Roger after Imonie, Imonie after me, and I had looked after baby Lianne, guarding her and bathing her in the sink and walking her around the townhome development naked at my hip. Alessandra Vehemente hadn't been born yet in Caracas, and her parents Mr. and Mrs. Vehemente didn't know yet that they would stop manufacturing handbags, leave their two teenage daughters in Queens, move to Florida, and renovate a nightclub. We knew who went where. Afternoons when Mother ran activities at the Peaceful Winter Assisted Living Plantation, Roger started dinner. Days when Daddy growled at classifieds on the living room floor, Imonie hugged him upways from behind. Roger picked guitar and Daddy played fiddle. Lianne clapped knees. Even when no one was around, even when you had to bike half an hour to the basketball court, even when your friends had never met your family and never would, and you were always waiting to be 12, everything had been easier to know what you were supposed to do, even when you didn't know why.

Lianne had seen Daddy last. The dark face had been rising in him; she was always the first to notice. She would tell Alessandra, Alessandra would tell me, and I would say I don't believe you, either of you, and I would be wrong. That morning, Daddy had chosen Lianne and had taken her to Aunt Jackie's for a visit and had kept her overnight and had not driven her to school the next morning, like he had told Mother he would. It was the kind of thing he did just before he disappeared. Take someone and leave her in a ditch by a low-lying canal and let her find her way back.

That last morning he chose Lianne, Daddy had been staying on our Aunt Jackie's floor. He and Mother were *trying out an arrangement*. They had had a disagreement over signing credit cards and Mother had slipped in the kitchen and her tailbone had changed places, and she had had to shriek, "What do you want from me, Gary? What do you want from your woman?" Jackie's floor was not a place Daddy liked to go. Jackie lived near Jackson Memorial, in an SRO by the incinerator. She kept red lights on her dark ferns. She sat all day on a couch with a levered footrest and brushed her hair and watched programs about shopping. Daddy said a person shouldn't see Jackie too much—she rubbed off on you. She was his older sister by one year. She used to live in the state home in Pembroke Pines and now she was on assistance. I was always glad when Daddy didn't choose me to go for visits to Aunt Jackie's; I was glad when he did, too. He didn't keep much there: just his essentials—his speedbag and his Palm Beach sales suits and his nicked snakeskin toiletry bag that you could feel right away *had seen the road*. With what he carried, you knew he could take off north any time, and I remembered wanting to steal anything belonging to him just so he wouldn't be able to go.

That last morning, we could all see him through the glass, through Mother's sunny garden of hanging violets. He knocked once at the front door and let himself in. The four of us had lined up on our couch in birth order, the way he liked us to wait. Alessandra was in Lianne's lap, and he made her get out.

Daddy clapped once for us to stand forward, twice for us to turn around. He didn't inspect us this day. He didn't snap out his steel pointer and make us jump over it—jump back, jump forth; he didn't take any measurements. He waved the red tip of the pointer high, cutting shapes in the air, and said, "Someone needs to draw you children a diagram of reality." He wasn't making much sense after that. Roger hadn't gone full-blown religious yet. Imonie's chest heaved and heaved; she might have been saying "Daddy is too sexy a man for me" or that might have been later. Lianne looked straight at her feet—like the little girl who covers her eyes and thinks, Now no one can see me. Mother stayed in the kitchen, tailbone out of whack, quartering chicken, wringing hands, and we didn't blame her. The dark face had risen in Daddy.

We sat back down in birth order, and Daddy said, "So I assume I have made myself perfectly clear here." Imonie's eyes watered and she thrust up her hand and said, "Yes! Yes! Yes!" until Daddy pressed the red tip of his pointer to the center of her waffle-batter chest, heaving thick, in leotard top, and silenced her.

Roger stretched his socks to the knee. We closed our eyes the way we did, like in "Duck, Duck, Goose," and each hummed different songs to ourselves. I could smell Mother come out of the kitchen with chicken on her hands. Three times Daddy paced in front of us with the pointer, then he tapped Lianne on the head. Lianne said, "Oh." Mother said, "Oh, no." Roger tore the elastic on one sock. Imonie broke into sobs: "You never! You always!" Those were the things she said.

With Daddy gone, I began wanting to see another state. I wondered if the trees were different. And what, really, was a mountain? *Alabama and Georgia are our two neighbors to the north*, Mr. Panadero taught us in geography. Tennessee was a state I thought I might like to see. I might also like to see Venezuela, Jamaica, the Dominican Republic, but not Cuba, Mr. Panadero's birthland, which was 220 miles from our bedroom, the same as Clearwater, where Daddy had once sent Roger and me an autographed Polaroid of himself standing next to a Philadelphia Phillie at spring training. That was the time he brought home Mother a giant stuffed dog that he won at a carnival, and they started kissing with the dog pressed to their chests and we didn't see them for two days. Cuba was not like that. Cuba, Mr. Panadero told us, was like a mother who is being held hostage by a fanatic. She is the dear object of your heart whom you may never see again. The few times Mr. P spoke of Cuba, of its mountains and shorelines, its rivers and fields, when his face turned sweaty and blood-red, until at last he covered his mouth and said, "But I shouldn't talk this way to jou," I was sure Daddy was out seeing great and important things, things he locked away. However far he went, I wanted to go farther, higher. At the basketball court I tried muscat. If I could just see the Great Smoky Mountains of Tennessee, which Mr. P had showed us slides of in class, where he had visited with his wife—with the word *altitude* he used so dreamily—I knew I'd have seen the beginning of what a person needed to see to be able to feel, when he looked west toward the bean fields and out to the swamps, that he had seen somewhere.

The week before the Bar Mitzvah, a black ceiling of clouds rolled in from the south every day after school and dropped half-hour-long torrents of lightning rain on the wooden vegetable stands and on the townhomes and on the flat-roofed dialysis center, then disappeared. When we moved we slogged, and when we dried it all off, we still trailed an acrid puff, as if we could not step out of a hamper. As soon as the sky was brilliant and high again and the colors stretched wide in every direction, Imonie would track in from the bean fields, panting for a listener, and say she had just heard from Daddy, Daddy was on his way to see her and Mother, her and Mother and no one else—to which Lianne would answer, "*Eschizo*, stop being *eschizo*," an expression I took it she had picked up from Alessandra. Back and forth the sisters would argue about who needed a head transplant operation more, until Mother called them both downstairs to train to be hosts Saturday night—to look available, to say yes for one dance, *even to a man who might not be their favorite.*

"Ladies, circulate" was an expression Mother favored. "Don't be slow."

That was the week Roger began referring to himself in third person as The Lonely Man of Faith, a phrase he spoke also in Latin and Hebrew. He seemed entirely oblivious to the preparations being made in the rest of the house for his cross-over into adulthood. Usually he was shut in our room studying; either that, or sewing himself a heavy undershirt with symbolically tied fringes, a *tallit katan*, that he declared he was going to wear every weekday for the rest of his life, no matter what the humidity or the heat. When he tried it on, his chest looked packed with protection, like the police. He hardly made eye contact with anyone except Mother—you would ask him what he said when he moved his lips first thing in the morning and last thing before sleep, what was the significance of the steps and shuckles and toe lifts he performed, praying at our bedroom window, and he would answer sharply that he was seizing the subjective flow of experience and converting it into enduring and tangible magnitudes. The rabbi gave him ideas. Every Saturday morning Roger walked to synagogue alone, setting out along the shoulder of the long road east in an awkward-fitting blazer; then went over to the rabbi's house, so far as we knew, for lunch and studied. The rabbi lent him books that I wasn't allowed to touch. This rabbi was something else. His whole little body was always bobbing about something. His nimble hands looked like they were continuously spreading a tablecloth or stretching dough. In the shed behind his house he souped up old Spitfires and Camaros for the goyim who drag raced Krome Avenue, then used the proceeds from the mechanical work to help the needy. He danced and sang on local telethons, though he had no voice or feet. He could sermonize, though. You'd find yourself swaying in agreement with him even when you hardly understood a word he was saying.

All the while, the meat began to mount. It was quite a scene. Mother was now expecting fifty-two family members, including thirteen of Daddy's people, whom she'd invited to the whole thing after all. When the out-of-towners arrived, she could stack them along the walls for sleep, but they'd still need to put something in their mouths. So she charged bags of bulk parts and chewing bones from the kosher butcher Roger made her patronize and jammed them into our freezer. The counters flooded with defrosting parts. We knew she was spending past our means—I'd found a crumpled envelope of NSF slips in her stocking drawer—but who could gainsay? All snacks were now meat. "How does a little sweet and sour sound?" she'd nudge. "How about a little roast?" You'd open the door for a Popsicle and catch a discount block of rump on your toe.

One night, shortly before the guests poured in, Imonie in undershirt, smelling sharply of fertilizer, stood up on a chair and announced that Daddy was going to walk through our front door any minute in glory and the sun was going to blaze so fiery and white, it would burn a skylight through the roof of the den. All would be forgiven, all would be repaired. A raven had told her this today in the sugar snap pea field just before he died. *Unify, and be one family in love* had been its last words. Mother was a terribly flexible woman, which we all knew and in most cases took easy advantage of, but you could see that she didn't approve of this manner of mixing words, which sounded, to me at least, a lot like the way the freckly blond children sounded when with mournful faces they handed Lianne and me folded rainbow-covered leaflets at recess, inviting us to Message of Hope meetings at the First Glades Baptist church. Mother glowered at Imonie and, straightening her back, rubbing her tailbone, repeated what she had been saying for six months, in one form or another—that Daddy was not welcome in this house, that the on and off, back and forth, up and down, yes and no of our past was ended, and if need be, she would ask Jared to enforce the matter.

This last part no one had heard. Jared was a name not lightly spoken in our house. Back when Mother was big with Lianne, Daddy had barricaded all the doors of our house one day, saying he *needed an accounting* of everything that belonged to him. None of us went to school, no one did anything but account. On the next day, when still no one had left or entered our house, Mother's water broke, and Daddy wouldn't drive her to the hospital until the accounting was made. "Mine, mine, mine, ours," he assessed, while Roger tallied switches on a tall sheet of wood. When Uncle Jared, Mother's younger brother, showed up that afternoon with a creel of pondfish and saw Mother splayed on the couch in a writhing tent of maternity sweats, he broke in the front window, flicked out a boning knife, and drew a crescent in Daddy's gut, then rushed him and Mother to the hospital.

If Mother called in Jared to defend against Daddy, who would Daddy bring to offend against Jared? I glanced at Lianne. Most matchups between our two sides were even. Uncle Moises, Uncle Ray. Cousin Lance, Uncle Billy. Granddaddy, Grampoppa. Jared, Daddy. Mother had more veterans, Daddy had more lunatics. It could go to third cousins—and women. The hayride our granddaddy had organized through the streets of the townhome development could turn into a Florida free-for-all. The parquet floor of the square dance: a fifty-two-card body pickup.

Just then, Alessandra began howling upstairs. Mother sprinted toward the sound of pain. Imonie, it turned out, had left the dead raven on the floor of her and Lianne's closet. She had cut off its feet to make square dance earrings, forgotten where she'd put the earrings—and the raven—and now mice had shown up and were eating the damp, shiny raven carcass.

"Violation," Imonie screamed, pointing at Alessandra.

"She's not right," Lianne accused, as Mother beheld the clamoring mass of gray tails and fur. "I'm moving to Barcelona with the Vehementes."

"You are not moving to Barcelona," Mother answered. "And what have you to say for yourself?" she asked Imonie.

"*Be kind to each other*," my older sister sniffed, again quoting the raven. "*Stop eating of the flesh of other beings. Simplify.*"

"What raven would say that?" Mother asked.

"*Unify, and be one family in*—'"

"I shall not be rebuked by my daughters," Mother said sternly. Then, pointing to the nibbling mania on the closet floor, she said, "Mice eat meat. We all eat meat. Are you saying you're better than mice?"

Imonie broke into sobs. None of us took criticism well.

"Thanks to you," Lianne said to Imonie, "we'll have to get a cat."

"How I hate cats," Alessandra exclaimed.

Imonie swatted a pile of Lianne's fake club jewels off their dresser.

"If I find your earrings anywhere touching my stuff," Lianne snarled, "I'll cut your neck with the claws in your sleep."

"Everyone favors you," Imonie screamed. "They always have."

"I'm moving to Barcelona," Lianne cried to Mother.

"You are going to the Bar Mitzvah," Mother said. "And not another word. Run and get me a plastic bag and gloves," she told Imonie. "We'll clean this mess and put it out of our minds. And Chaim, find your sisters a cat. I'm concerned now that we've been disturbing Roger's studies."

Saturday morning the winds gusted so hard, the rain was swept back up toward the blackened sky before it could fall. You didn't know which way to put your umbrella or your face. Down was up, left was right. Palm fronds snapped and whizzed by you like saws. You'd catch needling eyedrops of rain that nearly keeled you over in tears. Cars fishtailed down the lane, seeming to hold their breaths and pray for passage. It was like the days at the basketball court that seemed like nights when as soon as you lofted a free throw, the ball carried back to the other basket. Roger insisted on walking the miles to synagogue, and we followed him in a headlit, wiper-beating, five-mile-an-hour convoy of autos and trucks. Every time a big rig hit a skid of puddle in the passing lane, Mother white-knuckled the wheel and Lianne and Alessandra and I made exploding next-of-kin noises in the backseat. The way the wind and rain battered Roger in the headlights, he appeared like a lone heroic figure marching for an important and overlooked cause.

We were late to the service—which was probably for the best, since soon enough we saw how few friends we really had and how absurd the ones we had thought we were. It was something I had always suspected, but it took a Bar Mitzvah to prove. The sanctuary was half-empty, sprinkled mainly with Mother's small chorus of friends, a few happily married pillars of the congregation, and about ten van-lifted-in residents of the Peaceful Winter Assisted Living Plantation, who grunted and lobbed their heads with the rabbi's biblical exegeses while we host children walked around the periphery of the synagogue, dipping in classrooms, fingering art displays, with about sixteen relatives each stacked on our heads. Keep the people busy and don't cause a commotion while Roger chants his benedictions, Mother had instructed us in perfume and white doily, applying lipstick, in the car.

By midmorning, Lianne and Alessandra and I had begun escorting the bored and restless relatives around the shopping plaza next door—past the ten-foot golden safe in the West Dade Capital Bank building, to visit the sunglasses emporium, the pharmacist, the car spoiler shop and the iron-on T-shirt stand where last month Roger had had the phrase I'd Rather

Be Davening stamped on a blue V-neck. Thunder crashed. Our noses filled with the damp, fertile weight of the air. Swamp birds circled and croaked above.

The morning's biggest surprise came with the emergence of Maxine during Roger's Torah reading. Maxine was a shambling girl from Fort Lauderdale whom Roger had apparently met at an older youth group's two-day dramatic reenactment of Nineteenth-Century Jewish Immigration through Charleston, South Carolina. She wore blue old lady's clothes and appeared completely and toweringly in love with Roger, which Alessandra and Lianne giggled about over dress flounces and cigarette puffs near the janitor's office while I took sips from Uncle Billy's bourbon flask. Maxine tried to sit devout and ladylike in the third row, yet however she sat, wherever she set her purse, whichever way she moved her mouth while she prayed, her lips and cheeks shot forth voluptuously, almost obscenely, from her face. Something made me know then why Roger might have loved her, but I will never be able to tell you what it is. Till then, I had never pictured him even talking with emotion to a girl. He noticed her and tried not to; his heart seemed to go out to her while he chanted, even more than it did to Mother or the rabbi or even God. He kept reconfiguring himself and then configuring himself again toward her. A giant with a denim skirt in her carry bag—she looked ready for a square dance.

The whole congregation, including the janitor and grounds-keeper, not to mention the rabbi's wife and every pillar of the congregation and offspring of pillar who'd heard how much meat we had garrisoned at home, followed us back for a luncheon. While we drove west, a hot white hole burned through the clouds, and by the time we got to our lane, the neighbors were standing in their driveways without clothes, like any other Saturday, looking up at their own townhomes. Mother and I walked in the door first. There stood Daddy in an undershirt and khakis at the dining room table, placing a slice of salami in his mouth.

"You didn't have to do all this for me," he said, looking terrifically pleased. Taut, charming Daddy.

He walked straight to Mother, who was a head taller than he, shook her arms and planted a long tough one on her lips.

Wheelchairs, oxygen tanks, fishing poles, tallis bags, deodorant sticks, gold chains, knife sheaths, loosening brassiere straps, rolled-up cuffs, little fountain pen boxes wrapped with Stars of David and a comet-tailed number 13, all were passing through the front door along with a herd of warm legs and chests. Imonie in her raven's-foot "Bar Mitzvah luck earrings," bulging in pink tights, walking arm in elbow with Aunt Jackie up the sunning violet path, charged suddenly through bodies and leaped onto Daddy from behind, feet in the air. "I knew you'd come," she gasped, as Daddy swatted at his back like at a stand of seagrass insects. I shook his other hand. "Good to see you, son," he told me with a warm, even smile and kissed my cheek. "It's been too long, I know."

The fifty-two Garbers and Shenkers filled the house. Seeing Daddy, men, women and children on both sides made horseshoes around him, reacting to his every gesture and tale with whopping grins. Good Daddy, big-hearted Daddy, Daddy *who could sell the poorest cracker in Dixie a two-hundred-thread-count sheet set at twice retail, couldn't he, Mabel? Stack of bibles.* In-laws seemed proud of him, and inexplicably composed. Maybe they suspected he had made a lot of money at something. Even Jared was tossing tangerine slices in the air for Daddy to catch in his mouth. Cousin Lance clapped knees. Would next come the fiddle? An old lady I didn't know, who looked eerily like me, confided to me in a Maitland drawl that she was experiencing "just a whale of *nachas* on this wonderful *simcha*"—and when she adjusted my lips to a smile, I told her I felt the same way, though by then I didn't know what in hell's name she was talking about or what nearly anyone around me was doing or why. If my friends from the basketball court could see their holm j. holmes now, what kind of freaky whiteboy would they think he was? Maxine arrived, like Kong. The rabbi and Roger followed, perspiring. When Roger saw Daddy-Man in the middle of everything, he tugged at Mother as if she had failed him irrevocably, and she kissed and kept kissing the side of his bushy head and telling him *he* was the big mensch, *he* was. At the head of the room, the rabbi jumped up and down, waving for order, then made a stupefying kiddush toast, celebrating life, work, family, the Sabbath, the State of Florida, endings, beginnings, Hashem, and country music. People sang the shehechiyanu and began eating so ravenously, I thought someone might barbecue the cat. With her small chorus of friends, Mother served; the center of her eyes glowed, the lids trembled and cracked. Lianne and Alessandra vanished, to make believe somewhere in another language. The crowds, like ocean waves, who massed around Daddy—drinking, punching arms, eating stuffed cabbage competitively—began, I could see, to dispirit Imonie too, whose prophetic visions of Daddy never did come true, or else came too true. Leaning against the poker cabinet, holding herself tight round the middle, she seemed to wish for something like a third side of the rainbow, that someone would sweep her up and carry her that way.

After the luncheon, relatives napped shirtless in our bedrooms in stacks of about ten. With the last of the cake polished off, the rabbi and his wife, Roger and Maxine, and Roger's three friends from youth group (all named Jeremy) pulled out annotated copies of the Torah and began haggling over marginalia in the den. Each time Daddy walked past, Roger would lower his eyes and pull up his navy Dacron dress socks farther above the knee until at last he tore one to the ankle, prompting two of the Jeremies to cry out, *Sabbath breaker!* "Transgression involves intentionality," Roger shouted back, tweezing the torn sock with two fingers and hopping about the den as if he had exposed himself in front of Maxine—at which point the third Jeremy began rapid-firing Talmud passages accusing Roger of crimes against the fourth commandment and of bearing false witness against himself, which sent the rebbetzin into unaccountable laughing spasms and launched the rabbi into a wandering tale from *Sayings of the Fathers*, which everyone in the room insisted proved his position. Meanwhile, in the backyard, a team of Shenkers was vying against a team of Garbers to see who could poke a fishhook all the way through his pointer tip and keep it there longest without wincing. Bizarrely, each team kept pronouncing the other the winner. Who were we? I snuck a rum shooter in the pantry and watched Mother's divided eyes as she plastic-wrapped and unplastic-wrapped casserole trays—washed, dried, sighed, chirping little melodies to herself over the mesmerizing name Buddy Miley. There was a lot of man in the house that day. Mother made trips back and forth to the townhome rec center, anxiously checking on the hay and the hooch and a thousand other points of detail.

Finally, one trip, she asked me to accompany her, to carry a tall box of loose eggs for the toss. I had a real buzz going. The sky now was as blue as could be, the air filled with dripbags of water we skipped through on hot little stones.

"Careful with those eggs," she said. "They're the only ones we've got."

"Mother, are you going to be Daddy's partner again tonight like you said you would never," I asked, "and bow to him like you said you would never and dance 'Honey Do'?"

"Heavens, little Chaim," she answered. "When did you start thinking about older people's business like that? It's not something you learned from me," she said.

"Can a person love two people equal," I asked further, "or do they always love one person most?"

"Of course a person can love two people," she said. "Equally," she emphasized.

"What two people?" I asked.

"My brother and my father I love equally," she declared. "Your brother and your father—you love them equally. Your two sisters you do."

I squinted.

"So if Daddy sleeps at home with us like you said he would never, does that make us one family unified in love under one roof again?" I asked. "Is this a joyous occasion? And what does *no* mean? And *never*? And *always*? What do you want?"

Mother didn't have answers right away. She peeked at the eggs I held in stacks of thirty-six and tried to make it seem as though my whole line of questioning was so out of order, it did not merit a response.

"Sometimes it doesn't matter what people want," she said at last, and I could tell I had made her heart wearier, which saddened me, though at least I felt I knew her, though what was the good in it? "If all of us did whatever we wanted whenever we wanted," she said, "what kind of world would that be? What kind of children would we raise."

"But what *do* you want?" I asked. "I've always wanted to know."

"I want the caller to get here on time. I want the family to dive into the potato salad. I want Roger to know somebody thought enough of him to make him a party. Why, let's you and I go shine up his and your daddy's boots right now," she ahemmed. "That's something I want."

"But right-now-this-instant," I demanded, as if I were making an important point, the way Roger and Daddy knew how, when they put their foot down like men. "What do you want right now?" I said.

"I want my children and my husband to love me," she said.

We waited for Buddy Miley. Squares and squares of us waited. We waited on the rented parquet dance floor. We waited in murmuring pairs. We waited in pressed plaid shirts. We waited with alfalfa sprigs in our teeth. We waited pinching each other's asses. We waited calling each other lady and gent. Mother a shaking mess, Daddy a strutting rooster, we waited. Roger a no-show, Imonie hurling herself at uncles, we waited. We waited with hooch and bourbon. We waited with hooking puncture bandages on our fingers. Alessandra Vehemente, equal of no one, whom I had, for once in my life, managed momentarily to partner, waited, yawning, declaring this to be the most fatiguing social event she had ever attended; and Lianne, her corner, my sister, assented, strategizing that if either girl got swung at the waist by someone who made her ill, they would slip out together, call a cab to Key Biscayne and make Sergio, manager of Nightclub Valentino's, pay the fare. We waited a good hour.

When the first fight broke out—between one of the Jeremies and Uncle Ray—I think everyone was a little relieved. There had been nothing to look at till then, except each other; a fight meant you could pay attention to the fight. Of course, it wasn't much of a fight. It was a skirmish that threatened to break into a fight but probably wouldn't unless somebody got shamed more deeply. My belly felt like a tank of liquor—the day was catching up to me—and while the skirmish escalated, with Jeremy crying out *Open your eyes, would you, son of Israel? Assimilation is genocide!* and with Ray touch-shoving him at the chest, warning, *If you do not get out of my face and out of my nieces' faces, I will knock the lights out of you, boy,* I showed off to Alessandra how much older my belching sounded.

Mother kept talking to herself—hopefully, rapidly, calmingly, combing and crossing and recrossing the floor. "If Gary got his fiddle and Cousin Blini borrowed the Shostaks' banjo, we could still do this. We must. We could. Where is my Roger? Where is Buddy Miley?" Celebrations of Daddy's advent went on.

Just then, a young square-jawed man in a ten-gallon hat with a 45 rpm record player in one hand parted the main room. He plugged in the record player to a large speaker Mother had hauled in on wheels, hooked up a small microphone for himself, then faced us with a broad smile.

"The fact that you are standing in denim and petticoats in

paired groups of eight, awaiting my arrival with excitement and anxiety," the young man said, with the strangest calling accent I had ever heard, "lets me know you are ready for a good-time square dance filled with quality song selections and innovative choreographic ideas."

The room tilted with bemused heads and mulling fists. Imonie, dangling raven's claws, stepped forward and curtsied at the man, who bowed back gallantly toward her, toward all of us, like he had been sent here solely for our solidarity.

"I think the time came to introduce myself," he continued into the mike. "Evidently I am not the great Buddy Miley and punctuality does not belong to one of my best points. I am Jiri Slini, also known by my calling nickname, Sliniak, originally of Karolina SDC Bratislava, later Vienna Swingers Club, also Munich Promenaders, and at long last chief apprentice caller to the great Buddy Miley of Vero Beach, Florida. This evening I bring to you a special message from the great Buddy Miley, who regrets to me he could not be with you in person: Hoes down, Bar Mitzvah boy up!"

Hoots, hollers, and hallelujahs followed, with the Bar Mitzvah boy nowhere to be seen. Jiri Slini dropped the needle on the first fiddle record and began calling instructions and formations over it. Daddy, roused like a cobra, and rippling, swept his side of the family into merry form. Mother and her side looked more doubtful. My aunt Frieda, my granny's cousin's aunt or else my cousin's granny's aunt, who had lost four brothers in four different concentration camps during WWII, tiny aunt Frieda who wore square sunglasses at all hours, resident of a dingy Miami Beach retirement hotel, who was presently wearing her body weight in fringed rhinestone jean jacket and skirt, did not look at all amused by this Sliniak. Likewise, my impish elder cousin Melmude, who fluttered from square to square dropping ice shavings down the back of people's pants, hooting "Come on Pancho, circle the rancho!" along with an assortment of Slavic patter he was picking up from the caller.

I didn't have a good feeling. I kept one eye on Mother (promenading with her father, serving in apron), one eye on Daddy (partnering and repartnering), until it almost broke my heart. For a light-headed second I thought I grasped the true nature of the religious impulse that resided in my brother Roger—that maybe he did not mean to be inscrutable and scornful, even if he intended to be out of reach. I tried to stay in step with Alessandra Vehemente to "Golden Slippers." We split the ring with elbow swings until suddenly I lost her hand and was paired with Lianne, my darling frightened sister, for "Life on the Ocean Wave," then with Aunt Jackie, cornered by Imonie, for "Mañana." Several dances later I wound up with Mother.

We were all by then in two big adjacent circles, where Mother and I made up the link between the two. Movement between the two circles had become fluid, a grand march, and yet Mother and I somehow stayed where we were, the circles moving through us. I could tell the adults in the room wanted Mother and Daddy to dance together—more, I thought, than they wanted Roger to show. Somebody, I kept thinking to myself, is getting really ripped off here. Eventually, all this marching and honoring we were doing was going to lead to one big circle, then to two lines, a good-time reel, and at last one circle again. At least that was how Sliniak mapped it out for us in exuberant Slovakian-accented patter. We might turn out anywhere in the circle and yet all be together.

You'll make a big ring, he called, *with your favorite little thing.*

As much—as I say—as the others wanted Daddy to have the spot I was standing in, Imonie wanted the spot Mother was standing in. I didn't notice this until I saw Daddy, partnered with his older sister Jackie, advancing hungrily toward Mother and me from one adjacent circle, and Imonie, partnered with Mother's younger brother Jared, marching unquenchable toward us from the other. Couples were swapping and moving ahead, some hobbling like a three-legged pair, others limber with rhythm, and Imonie, if you saw her the way I did, moved like a pink mass of girl you might read about in the newspaper Monday morning who vanished from the middle of a crowded area and showed up three weeks later in a Daytona Beach hotel room, unable to recall a single fact about herself—*Now what did she go and get her self into?* Mother would ask. Seeing my big sister this way, and my little sister Lianne about to flee out the side door, it was like being in the dream where the storm weather is rolling in from below the fields, and while the others take shelter and shutter the windows, you are unable to move, looking out at flat land, the palm leaf of your rib cage splitting down the center.

I wanted some hooch. The music was changing again. Mother was about to end up with Daddy, Daddy was about to end up with Imonie, Imonie was about to spin Moises, Moises was about to star Lianne, Sliniak the caller had the clearest blue eyes, and I was never going to see Alessandra Vehemente again. I puked. I started retching all over the rented parquet floor, a thin streaming gobbling trail. I stumbled toward the side of the room, dripping at the teeth. Corn, wheat, grapes, molasses, bits of pulpy innard soured in my mouth. It was good that there was so much else for people to pay attention to. A small mob of cousins began lighting torches to go out and find Roger, who Daddy, now at the center of the dance, said was shaming us all by being absent. Mother slipped on a black-eyed pea pod. On a bale of hay near my aunt Frieda, I found an empty bushel basket, and I puked some up in that. I might have heard a hora. I think I glimpsed Maxine. Over one record, Sliniak roared into the microphone, "If tonight was Buddy Miley's poker game, we would all be a full house!" I gazed up at the rafters, and down, down even further, between my legs, like a dog. When I raised my eyes, my aunt Frieda looked at me through sunglasses like she knew anyone alive for the first time. We were about the same size. Her hair matched the baubles on her stone-washed jean jacket. Once I had been told that for three years during the War, Aunt Frieda slept in a forest and lived on nuts, but at the time that story had sounded farfetched. Now I wanted to tell her I believed every word and that when I got some money of my own, I would buy her a less mildewed bed for her room on Miami Beach—and better nuts for her crystal bowl.

She said, "What do you know, *liebes Kind?*"

I said, "My name is Chaim, Aunt Frieda. Chaim. You probably can't remember."

People were dancing festively now with white bandannas. Aunt Frieda spoke my name with her Slini-like pronunciation, and I tried not to feel sorry for her, like Daddy had taught me nobody needs from me. In the middle of the room a reel began, and when, at long last, one big circle was announced, which eventually enclosed Roger too, everybody scattered trying to get to where they thought they were supposed to get and wound up more or less where they had started out. Aunt Frieda dipped the edge of a cocktail napkin into a pitcher of water and dabbed around my lips. She knew more than I expected—about lots of things. For instance, who I was named for; also, how I was related to people I had never met.

Two weeks after the Bar Mitzvah, Roger walked in the door from junior high in his I'd Rather Be Davening T-shirt, his *tallit katan* ruffled underneath, with his cheeks swollen and his jaws wired shut. Daddy stood next to him, stroking his hair, so I knew he hadn't done it. By that point, Roger knew so many blessings for so many occasions, you assumed he was always saying one even if you couldn't see his lips move: the blessing over the doorpost, the blessing over the blessing over the doorpost, the blessing over walking through the door after just getting your face bashed in. Mother was still at work. "Rednecks get me, too," Imonie said, jealous, I think, of Roger's bruising, making herself a face at Daddy. Daddy mixed us all a raw egg and honey drink that we sipped through straws. He could be a very tender man.

I don't know why we had money when we did and didn't when we didn't, but there were a couple shining months for us while Roger's jaws were wired. It rained clothes and toys. Books from the Jewish Publication Society. Soft ice cream, too. There was plenty, so much of plenty, it worried you if you worried about that kind of thing. Daddy was always peeling out of the driveway on a spree. "More, more, and more, Mama. My three favorite words" was an expression he preferred. I wore out the tires on my bike and got new ones without having to ask.

In geography, we studied the history of our state. We learned that in 1845, Florida had been admitted to the Union as a slave state in exchange for Iowa, a free state. Mr. Panadero divided us into groups to discuss if that had been a fair compromise, but nobody in our group seemed to know what the expression *a fair compromise* meant. I heard kids in another group talk about *give and take*, and I wondered on this idea. Mainly, though, I gazed at the World Map that Mr. P pulled down from the ceiling every morning—at Iowa and Venezuela and Barcelona (where Lianne vowed she would follow the Vehementes) and New York City (where Roger told me he was going the day he graduated high school, to Yeshiva University, with Maxine his bride) and the Gulf of Mexico (where Imonie said not one of us would care if she sank to the bottom).

I also glimpsed at Tennessee, home of the Great Smoky Mountains, where I thought I might like to go. I suspected that if I ever did make it up to Tennessee, I would find nice people there who'd let me stay with them if I needed to. Cornbread, one of my friends from the basketball court, was from Knoxville, and he and some other kids were going there this summer with the Boys Club to play in a regional tournament. Each day I wanted to ask if he would take me with them as a ball-chaser and a floor-wiper, but I was practicing not talking too much. Cornbread didn't talk much—which made people scared of him, and I wanted to be more like that. That, and call everyone holm j. holmes and make up handshakes. I figured I would just copy Cornbread until I got it. Learning to hold my liquor and making more people scared of me—these seemed like better goals for right now than Tennessee. Of course, if I wanted, I could swipe fare out of Mother's stocking drawer—twenties had replaced NSF slips recently—and ride a train straight to Tennessee (Gatlinburg: 712 miles). But Mother might like to have me nearby the next time Daddy whatevered and siblings started disappearing and somebody needed to carry the eggs. That was something I also considered.

APPLES AND ORANGES

Christmas Eve, 1952—beautiful night in West Oak Lane, Philadelphia: no rain, no snow, lights lit, money counted, *easy*— and Herm Gruber, rattling in his father-in-law's Champion Appliance delivery truck, was carrying with him the new baby girl for his wife's sister Sadie. "Life!" he cried out, and struck the wheel with two hands. "That right with you, cupcake?" He reached over and cupped the back of the infant's head. Sure, it was right. He and Ceil with their two little pishers, four and two, and Ceil once again in a family way; Ceil's brother Mort the doctor and his wife Pearl in Wyncote with their three. And now add a perfectly good new child to the family. One for Sadie. One in the plus column. Coming up.

A little orange-headed lentil. Serene, bashful. Angel in a bundle, lying straight as she was able in her cradle. Head tilted to two o'clock, yes: Mrs. Roder hadn't mentioned that. But not *crippled*. She was going to be fine. Better than fine. Trouble was having to bury your infant daughter, your only girl, as his mother had done. On the scale of catastrophes it had not been much. And yet Herm had watched Baby Goldie's coffin drop into the baby hole, had walked three and a half miles with his dear, tired mother each Sunday to the cemetery to lay new flowers. Then two winters later, his mother caught pneumonia and didn't get the right treatment. Why, he never understood, but he imagined it was because she didn't speak good English. He never spoke a word of Yiddish afterward, not even in private. Or maybe she didn't have enough money, or maybe the doctor had a personal hatred of Jews, as one of his aunts had said. *The proper serum!* the aunt had wailed, in a saggy white dress of black falling leaves, after the funeral. The following week, he and his classmates wrote letters of sympathy for the Red Cross to deliver to the child victims of a great tornado in the Middle West. *I cannot let this day pass without expressing the sorrow I felt upon hearing of your loss,* he and the other boys wrote in their most careful script. The teacher tacked up a map from the newspaper: REGION STRICKEN BY DISASTER. Arrows through towns showed the path of death.

Yes, the point of life was to make it better. And this little girl was a dream. Look at her! A home run! Apricot complexion, sweet pink lips, blushing cheeks, eyebrows the warp and texture of young rabbit hair, all, in their way, matching Sadie's dark-red features, her serious expressions, that would sometimes break, after she had turned over an idea a few times, into untroubled bursts of laughter. In a carriage, this kid would pass for Sadie and Gilbert's own. Traded for with old Mrs. Roder, a customer of many years, who on collection day before Thanksgiving invited in Herm and told him about a fourteen-year-old niece of her neighbors, a bright tall healthy girl, whose parents were looking to put this whole year behind them. The girl was expecting in three weeks; for now, she was staying with relatives. Herm shook his head yes. Yes was the movement his head made most often when he worked. He offered, offered comfortingly, to take the load off everyone. He told Mrs. Roder he would work something out, don't worry and don't let the family worry, and as he drove away, up Bergen Quarry Road, through woods where nearly all the leaves appeared to have just turned a single shade of yellow—a small forest grove with a soft wet bedding of leaves—ideas came to him about Sadie, more and more.

He had been approached like this once before on his Langhorne-area routes. Four years ago, in Neshaminy, a customer had asked him through a screen door to please take a baby away from here. Ceil told him not to touch that child. There were things to get involved in, things not to. And yet after he found the baby a home—after he delivered the not-too-fair-haired, not-too-light-complected one-month-old to Pinky Marinov in North Philadelphia, a parts distributor, a Sephardic fellow, who attended with his childless wife the old Mikveh Israel congregation—after he did it, Ceil saw the good. He had taken a healthy living creature from their column and put it in ours. Multiplied Am Yisroel. A tiny answer to what had just happened in Europe. And the baby, who had looked pinched and bitter and about eighty-five years of age when Herm got her, in the Marinovs' good hands would grow up happy and provided for, and by God, four years later, she was.

On Thanksgiving night, in the tasseled warmth of their bed, Herm told Ceil he had found the right one for Sadie. A girl—he could sense it. Came on very good recommendation. Ceil frowned. How could he be so sure this baby was worthy of her sister? It wasn't even out. He hadn't inspected it. So he told her all the good things Mrs. Roder had said to him. Then he went back to caressing Ceil's full belly, rubbing his own against hers, walking two fingers down between her breasts and saying, "You going to be the sweet baby girl your dear mama wants?" Ceil laughed then, hooked a foot around Herm's ankle. She had never told him why Sadie, almost thirty-one years old, had not conceived, and Herm felt he didn't need to be told. Gilbert couldn't get the job done. And so Herm kept his eyes open. On delivery and collection routes, he listened to the country girls who begged him to spare a week's due, offered water, offered themselves, launched into stories of abandonment and hard times. He usually stayed in their doorways or sat in a tattered armchair, where he would linger, sometimes stroking the cold wet coat of a dog, while the girl fixed her hair, answered the telephone, smoked and left a cigarette burning at the edge of a table, all the while deciding if her man would agree they needed another item from Herm's father-in-law's catalog, which came with the fairest payment plan available in southeastern Pennsylvania. If she asked advice, he gave it to her, in a nice fashion. And whatever else happened in a day, he loved the babies, loved being around them, even the ones with diapers falling off, mothers snarling threats from rooms with no pictures, peeling walls. German, Polish, Irish, Dutch babies. Babies with curled chins, moony eyes. Babies fenced off in backyards and babies crawling through pumpkin patches, gnawing acorns and grasping at squirrels. Who didn't love a baby? He kept track of all of them. On the way into a house, after unsnapping his rubber-banded stack of accounts and finding the right dog-eared card, he would silently speak the name of each child he might see. That way if there were any problem with stern Mrs. So-and-

So, what nice things he could remember to say about little Val or Emil, who would have grown since last visit, whose smile would be brighter, whose forehead would be higher and handsomer.

Yes, the truth was, and Herm realized it only now, passing the twinkling lights in his neighbors' front windows, the incandescent nativity scenes, then seeing his own brick row house, third from the end of the block: He wanted to give Sadie a baby. Had wanted to since the day in 1948 when he and Ceil had had their first, or maybe even in '45 or '46 when he and Ceil and Sadie used to overnight together in Atlantic City. Back then, Sadie followed the dance bands. She knew all the rhythms. A slight girl. Looked plum in two pieces, reclining in a steamer chair. Herm with his girl and his girl's sister—Sadie an assistant research librarian at the public defender's office, Penn College of Women graduate, talking about books, music, theater, *ideas*, a year older than Ceil—surely he had made many a young man at the shore jealous. Herm, who could carry a combination refrigerator/home freezer up a flight of stairs. Just out of the service. Arms that Ceil adored, that Sadie noticed. The sisters talking about a man for Sadie, the babies they would have together some day.

A promise to this woman had been kept, Herm told himself, and switched off the engine. The heat blowers sighed. He waggled his nose in front of the baby's. Then he came around the truck and lifted out the cradle.

As he swung open the front door and the chimes rang out their familiar up-down, up-down melody of home, the baby began to make its first sounds since Herm had gotten her: ar-ar-ar, hmm-hmm-hmm, ar-ar-ar. Ceil turned off a whirring appliance. Smell of roast turkey. Warm apple sauce. Brown sugar yams. *We are Americans too.* Then Brucie cried out, "Let me touch the feather!" and in his excitement tumbled off the metal stepladder, crashing to the kitchen floor. Neil, the two-year-old, thudded down next to him and started bawling too.

"Up up up. None of that," Herm called. "Who's my Whiz Kids?"

In the dining room, he set the wooden rocking cradle next to his place at the table, the burbling baby facing the spinet piano that Sadie and Ceil sometimes played four-handed.

"You be careful *each* time on that ladder," Ceil told Brucie, crouching and clutching his cheeks, "or I'll never let you climb and sprinkle spices with me again."

Ceil covered the boy with kisses and lifted him to her. She wore a violet dress and pearl-gray house slippers. Neil climbed his brother's back, trying to get some kisses.

When Brucie was freed, he shot to Herm's work hat, which Herm had just dropped on the head dining room chair. Brucie plunged his nose deep into the wool, then stroked the red feather in the band, purring, "Soffft," to his parents' delight.

Then with a display of selflessness, he handed the hat to Neil and began tiptoeing around the skirt of the tablecloth, black curly hair and black deep-set eyes, toward the object he had seen his father carry into the room.

"Bebber, bebber, bebber," the bundled baby was saying.

"A *baby*?" Brucie cried, eyebrows jumping. "Where'd you get it?"

"You're going to meet her," Herm told Brucie, looking to Ceil. "I brought all kinds of good things. I'm a real Santa Claus tonight."

"We don't believe in Santa Claus," Ceil reminded Brucie.

"I know," Brucie said, his favorite new expression.

"Well, do you believe in I give the boy a little taste of something if it won't wreck his appetite?"

"Not wise," Ceil frowned.

"Winesap?" Brucie asked.

"We got a winner," Herm announced, and pulled a lopsided red apple with a small rotten crack near the stem from the left pocket of his parka, as if accomplishing a magic trick. His stocky, callused fingers had motor oil in the design of the fingerprints.

"Don't test my word," Ceil warned Herm. She snatched the hat from Neil and set it on the rack by the front door.

Herm returned the apple to the left pocket.

"What's in the other?" asked Brucie.

"You hear your mother? Nothing. Just a nice little piece of smoked bluefish. Nothing you'd like. Just your favorite."

"Bluefish!" Brucie screamed. "Mine. Mine. Mine."

"Mine," Neil cried.

Herm reached in his right pocket and grabbed the oily waxed paper.

"Put it *back* and stop the games!" Ceil said. "Company's going to be here any minute."

She went into the kitchen to turn off the gravy. He knew her biggest worry: Children should never be confused, and if he wasn't careful, he was going to confuse them, Brucie, in particular. This baby, he practiced explaining to the boys, was from the hospital. Where babies come from. It was Auntie Sadie and Uncle Max Gilbert's new daughter, and he had just brought it home for them, pony express. On the table the baby was talking in a merry, private, slightly cross-eyed language. Was it warm enough in here for everybody? Herm wondered why Ceil didn't give the baby a bottle or change it or wipe its chin. She hadn't even looked at it.

"Where *are* they?" he called.

"Wash up and change," she answered. "You know Max Gilbert is probably running late."

"Where'd you get the baby?" Brucie tugged at Herm's work trousers. "Where's my bluefish?"

"Shah a minute," Herm told the boy. "Let me think."

"You don't know?" Brucie demanded.

Herm leaned down and swatted the boy's cheek. "You're going to listen to me when I tell you." The boy ran wailing to his mother. Neil followed him.

From the street Herm heard carolers. The sound made him feel unwanted. In his blood he hoped Sadie would get here soon. He could hear children and their parents, singing in unison. Still in his thick work shoes, he stepped as lightly as he could on the wood to the little orange-headed dumpling, wrapped in her white blanket. He thought she might like to be held. He put her to his shoulder and patted her a bit, making a little half-circle as he rocked, and she made a kind of *braaaahh* sound, as if this were a great relief from something.

Two knocks came at the back door, and Max Gilbert, all six-feet-one of him, let himself inside, out of breath.

"Ho ho ho," he hailed with one of his big salutes, and began to unravel his fancy striped scarf from around the neck of his fancy topcoat and to hang it on a hook.

Sadie, much smaller, pushed him all the way inside the kitchen so she could close the door behind her.

"Here we are," she said.

The boys ran a dizzy circle around Sadie, greeting and kissing her. "I'm Hans Christian Andersen," Brucie sang. "Andersen, that's me."

Herm placed the baby back in the cradle. He kept patting her, promising he would hold her again, but his touch seemed to agitate her now.

Gilbert wandered into the dining room, sort of dancing in his soft leather shoes.

"What do you say, Max?" Herm bellowed. "Your night of nights."

Gilbert was peeking in cabinet doors, around an arched corner, seeming, as Ceil had, to be not looking at the baby, who was now beginning to cry.

"Wish I knew how to thank you, Herman," Gilbert bellowed back. He was wearing a green-tinged blazer of expensive-looking fabric and a red-flecked collared shirt, and he sounded, as usual, like he was trying to convince a jury of something, though in fact he had never spoken to a jury in his life. He was a law school dropout, and for as long as Herm had known him, he had planned to finish. He also planned to put down 10 percent on a row house in the neighborhood, though he continued to rent an inadequately heated apartment, fifteen minutes away, above a dressmaker's, on Ogontz Avenue. His father, a well-known judge, kept him in work at the courthouse, and if it weren't for the judge—who had given Gilbert every advantage a Jewish boy could be given—who knew what his and Sadie's lives would be? Gilbert lived as if the sidewalk could not any day open up and swallow everything he had. Still, he did what he believed in: improving things for the worse-off, trying to make things fair for all people in the city, volunteering on education commissions, housing organizations, which of course was very good and which Sadie admired. It was just, he was spoiled: a fellow who wants to solve everyone's problems and can't run a comb straight through his own hair. Half hour late to his own wedding, where Herm, at the Mark Hotel, turning to Ceil, had said maybe Gilbert fell in love with his own reflection and decided to marry that.

"You're a father now," said Herm, proudly. "May you and Sadie find the joy you are looking for."

"Well, let's see her," Gilbert said.

The men walked over to the table, where the baby was crying.

"Is that—darling," Gilbert called to Sadie. "Doll, come here and join me. Somebody wants to meet you. She may need a woman's touch."

Sadie clopped into the dining room, eyes low, smiling wryly, in dark red lipstick, wearing a wine-colored jacket and skirt suit Herm remembered from a night back when he worked at the anti-submarine warfare plant, not long after he met Ceil, and he was awaiting orders from the Navy to be sent off for mechanics training. He, Ceil, and Sadie, and one of Sadie's old hopefuls had gone out dancing after work. An orchestra from New York was playing. One dance, the couples danced a switch-off number, where, swaying to and fro, Herm's palm met the smaller palm of Sadie during one stretch of song and returned to Ceil's in the next. Ceil was about his size, her hand was his size, and he remembered thinking that Ceil fit him and that he was going to marry her and that she was going to live a long life, outlive him, and die in good health, not suffering. Sadie had worn this jacket, with white stitching on the collar and a sweetheart neckline. The cuffs had white stitching too, and in them her hands looked tiny, strong, and nimble.

"Hermes the Winged Messenger," she sang, like notes of a door chime. "What have you brought us?"

The pink-faced baby had cried itself almost breathless and blue. The head lobbed, past two o'clock—almost to the left shoulder.

"Aw, look at that," Sadie said, crooking her head, in congruence with the baby's. "A real Chagall masterpiece come to life. 'Wailing Infant with Cradle and Family.' A perfect village rooftop scene. Is she uncomfortable?"

Herm could make no sense of this response, only that it was not the moist-eyed, come-to-me-child one he had been waiting for. He drew forward to Sadie.

"Go ahead. Hold her. She's got a wonderful disposition when she's held."

"I'll be right in," Ceil called.

"Right with you," Brucie added, in the fashion of his mother.

"Right in," added Neil.

The carolers were right across the street now, voices stretching in the night air. They would not stop at Herm's door. They had not stopped last year. Ceil didn't want them. They knew.

Herm searched for a simple sign of joy in either Sadie or Gilbert, but didn't see one. Gilbert was craning his head over Sadie's shoulder, looking at the baby as though it were an exhibit to be rated, and Sadie's eyes gleamed with the dark intelligence of certain successful people—like her father,

Seymour, who nearly always saw behind what Herm saw to a more complicated set of circumstances that had to be mastered. One dry look from Seymour could frighten Herm to speechlessness.

"Oh, did we spend a lovely afternoon in that truck," Herm chuckled. "She asked me all about you both. I told her what a lucky girl she was, to have parents like you."

"I bet you did," Sadie answered. "Let me take her," and folding the orange-headed baby across a forearm, she sniffed its behind and called to her sister, "I'm going to see if she needs to be changed."

"She's got to be hungry," Ceil called.

As Sadie swept the baby upstairs in two arms, Gilbert walked over to the piano in the front room, and Herm found himself unexpectedly alone. He could think of nothing for a short while but Richie Ashburn in the bottom of the ninth, two years ago, throwing out Cal Abrams at home to preserve the 1-1 tie in the pennant game against Brooklyn. Upstairs Sadie was running the faucet in the master sink. Herm had recently resealed the connection between the hot water pipe and the faucet hose, no leakage could be occurring, and he called up to Sadie with confidence, "Got everything you need?" Gilbert's fingers studied the lid over the piano keys. Gilbert didn't know how to play piano any more than Herm did, but he could hold a melody—unlike Herm, whose off-pitch warbling made Ceil laugh at him in front of her father. Sometimes Gilbert sang duets at the piano with Sadie, though not often. He was one you often found suddenly lost in thought, even when it was rude.

"Turn around, please," Ceil said.

Herm spun and over her shoulder saw his boys in booster

seat and high chair, licking apple sauce from spoons.

"How many minutes home before you wash?" she demanded. "I'm *carrying* your child."

By the time Herm stared at his hands, she was pulling herself upstairs by the banister, saying, "I'm counting on you," clutching a diaper and a dripping bottle of formula. Her bosom was plump, her arms filled out the shoulders of her violet dress.

Herm meant to go scrub himself, run wet fingers through what hair he had, change out of these shoes, but he had the urge to ask Sadie something, though he could not now remember what. He thought of a streetlight across the block on which a child had pinned a green wreath. Gilbert was tapping a rhythm on the piano lid. He and Herm glanced at each other, but their eyes didn't keep.

Ceil shrieked Herm's name.

He took the steps in two, then three.

Inside their room, Ceil motioned for him to shut the door. The baby lay between her and Sadie, its knees pointed out. It had been washed, powdered, lotioned, and was lying calmly, taking the bottle from Ceil, who dunked the nipple into its mouth almost backhanded, as if nursing a little found animal, its head resting on a red satin-edged utility blanket, lips swallowing ecstatically. The baby was swaddled in a white blanket that had been used to swaddle Brucie and Neil. A hot, perfumed mist drifted through the room, and Sadie was smoking at the foot of the bed, using the very tips of her fingers. Ceil shook with confused fury.

"What did you bring my sister, Herman?" she asked, almost with wrath.

Sadie set her cigarette in an ashtray on the bedspread.

"Answer my question," Ceil said. "You got this . . ."—and she didn't know what to call the baby, so she left a stammering space in the sentence—"from my father's customer, Florence Roder, in Langhorne?"

"*Near* Langhorne."

"*Don't* raise your voice to me—"

"You know where," Herm said meekly. "Out past the Metzger bee farm. About two miles west of that old rubble-wall church with the great rummage sales, where I get you—"

"Well, you're going back tomorrow and you're telling Mrs. Roder you're exchanging this one for one that works. Or *returning* it. I really don't care which—and neither does my sister. But first, you're calling my father and telling him *not* to come over for dessert *or* tea at eight o'clock. You've ruined this night. Do you understand that? What am I going to tell the boys?"

Ceil was somehow shouting, but at a volume that only people in the room could hear. Sometimes when she got this way, when every thought she had made the next one worse, you could calm her just by listening, nodding, following her with your understanding eyes. Herm was doing that. But she was getting more enflamed.

"For this *disfigured* infant," she hissed, "you're giving one of my father's customers *half-off* a new *Kelvinator electric range* with *lamp and oven-timer control?* You think that's smart? You think that's going to make my father want to sell you into the business someday?"

"She didn't want a range, nobody wanted a range, all she wanted was to help," Herm told her. He didn't want to stoke her anger, but he didn't wish to appear cowardly either.

The truth was, Mrs. Roder had scoffed today at his offer of a discount on a new Kelvinator range, which he had priced for her at $99.50, down from $219, to be paid over five years at absolute lowest possible financing. *Just be good*, she had said, transferring the cradled newborn to his arms, and Herm, seized with gratitude, wanted to give some gift in return that would not be rejected, but he did not know what, so he left a simple sealed white envelope in her mailbox with five dollars cash for the girl's family. He drove a half mile up Bergen Quarry Road, happy with the baby, happy beyond happy, then turned back and rubber-banded to the envelope five dollars more. With a snap of his blue Champion Appliance ballpoint pen, he drew a Christmas tree on the envelope.

"Nothing's ruined," he told Ceil, and glanced at Sadie, whose dark-red pencil-lined eyes were cast low. "This baby is a dream. Look at her. She is sweet as pie."

"Herman!" Ceil said. "You're a classical moron."

Herm bit his tongue. He tried to soothe it along the forgiving walls of his mouth. Ceil knew what crippled was, a child who couldn't manage, who wasn't coming back. This baby had all its brains, fingers, organs. Slits of eyes that wanted to know. Everything in a good proportion.

Ceil reached for a cigarette while feeding the baby. Sadie lit her. In Ceil's vanity mirror, Herm saw the far side of Sadie's face, still trying to figure something out about the baby. The baby had been alive a week. What could it tell her? Ceil exhaled. "What deformity does this child have, Herman? Don't tell me you didn't see it."

Herm licked a soft spot behind his bottom teeth and tasted salt, blood, and the faintest trace of degreasing solvent that he used on Seymour's wheels.

"Why do you have to . . . ?" he said in a hushed voice, and his eyes moistened, seeing this constellation of females arranged across his tasseled bedspread. "If it wasn't good, would I have brought it to her?"

Sadie, cigarette at the crease of her lips, took the bottle from Ceil and went on feeding the calm baby. She stared out the window, at the lights in other shaded windows. She had the look of not knowing the most basic thing she was supposed to know in the situation she was in. She sat the baby up and held it against her slight hip. A gesture. An effort. The baby's thin lips feeding made a comic expression.

"See how they go together?" Herm laughed. "So it's a wryneck. You think *wryneck* is a problem? If wryneck is the worst trouble this child ever gets . . ." Ceil rubbed her belly with two hands and breathed deep. "Listen, they got braces, they got all kinds of braces. You just squeeze her into shape. How long— few months? Mort'll tell you how it's done. This girl never did a thing wrong in her life. All she wants is a good family to—"

Sadie hummed a long sigh, a note that unfurled and then disappeared into the warm mist of the bedroom. Somebody on the sidewalk was jingling bells in threes. Ceil looked like she had the feeling Herm had gotten the better of her verbally. He softened his stance. Tasted his dry lips, came over, sat next to her, and caressed her shoulders. She put out her smoke.

"So it's a torticollis?" asked Sadie, stroking the baby's hair. "Do you know if there's vertebra damage?"

She adjusted the baby so that it was comfortable against her side.

"That I would not know," said Herm.

"You wouldn't know plenty," Ceil told him.

"If she needs a brace, Mort'll get her the brace."

"*You* see what you want to see. Sadie and I see what's *there*."

In the kitchen something crashed. A bowl. A plate.

"Ayyy, mios babbinos caros!" Ceil cried out, and with a grunt, hoisted herself up from the bed, not letting Herm help. Sadie accompanied her by humming the famous Puccini aria, which made Ceil laugh.

"I'm not finished with you," Ceil told Herm.

He followed her down the stairs, stopping first to wash so that she could not say that he was still filthy in her house.

Sadie stayed upstairs with the baby.

By the time Herm sat down to dinner—which Ceil would not allow him to call Christmas dinner, though what was the big harm in it? It wasn't as though Christians were breaking down the door trying to convert anyone: if anything, we had one of theirs—Ceil had garnished and set out on the table the sliced turkey and casseroles and gravy and everything else the men would want, complete with nice matching servingware and utensils. In the kitchen, she had cleaned the boys' mess, given them clean bibs, and settled them down to their plates of drumsticks, yams, and broccoli trees, which she cut finely into bite-size pieces and fed them carefully by fork. Herm, now in fresh shirt and house shoes, ate Ceil's delicious cooking with barely restrained belches of gusto while he half-listened to a speech by Gilbert about the city's lack of moral seriousness, about the old cronies and de facto segregators who meted out injustices daily from their comfortable offices in City Hall. The clock next to the brandy decanter on the liquor cabinet showed almost ten of eight—which meant Seymour and Lillian would already be on their way. The baby was not going to be cancelled or exchanged: Herm could feel it.

Jumping up, he announced he was calling off Seymour.

"Don't you think it's a little late for that?" Ceil said.

Herm winked at Brucie as he dialed the wall phone in the kitchen. Just in case Seymour and Lillian *were* home, he dialed the wrong number. With each wrong rotation, he pictured Seymour, a grave, accurate man, difficult to please, given to rare fits of convulsing laughter, wider, it sometimes seemed, than he was tall, always with a wide solid tie that didn't reach his belt buckle, catching his first look at Sadie with that baby, how hard Seymour was going to fall for that kid.

"You're right," Herm said, with a twinge of false innocence in his voice, a sales pitch, that he tried to cover up. "They must be on their way."

"Like a child, you don't listen," Ceil snapped. "And you wonder why I blow my stack at you."

"Toot-toot!" said Brucie, and mocked a train engineer from a storybook pulling a make-believe chain.

"You want a real licking later, eh Del Ennis-Robin Roberts? Eh Whiz Kid?"

From the dining room Gilbert's speech turned to the legal challenge somebody with gumption ought to make to stop the birthday of Jesus from being observed as a national holiday.

"It's separation of church and state," he declared. "He is not *my* personal lord and savior. Why should my tax dollars go to celebrate the birth of *their* messiah, who wants me and others like me to burn in hell if I don't follow his path?"

"That's right," Ceil agreed, with an admiring tone.

Gilbert, this was, who ate Italian pork loin and rapini sandwiches like they were never coming back in fashion. Who spent Yom Kippurs at the courthouse, or at fancy political luncheons with his nonobservant judge-father. Who referred to certain of his fellow Jews—bankers, business leaders, men Herm looked up to—as "the money changers." What was so wrong with Christmas? Jesus wasn't the only thing about it.

"It already *is* a national holiday," Herm called out. "Everybody already knows the songs."

"You're right, Herm," Gilbert laughed derisively. "It should be a national holiday because everybody already knows the songs."

Ceil laughed. Herm rested his fists on the kitchen table.

"What this country could use," Gilbert added solemnly, "is a few extra dashes of secular humanism. Not that we'll be seeing *that* from our leaders any time soon."

Brucie decided this was a good time to ask, "Where'd you put that baby, Dad? Where'd you get it from?"

Herm went back to the dining room. He stood over all the nice plates of food and offered Gilbert more of everything. For a moment he pictured his two sons years from now, sharp as tacks, starting up in professions of their choosing—leasing an office, hiring a secretary, on their way to living in the lap of luxury—then walked over to the front window. *His* window. The street was peaceful. Families were together. He had a mortgage, same as any other man on the block, $34.39-a-month payments, and he had never once been late. A visiting car paced slowly, looking to park. Herm reached into his parka, which hung by his hat, wanting to touch the lone Winesap he had brought home as a treat from J.D. Appleseed orchard near Mrs. Roder's place, just feel it in his hand for a moment, but instead he found the wax-paper-wrapped bluefish, smeared with orange oil, from Joe Lou the toothless monger's in Logan. He licked a flake of smoked fish from his finger. In the kitchen Brucie started to cry. Then Neil cried. They were refusing to eat anything more on their plates.

He heard not a peep from his bedroom.

Just then, shoes beat the front steps. The doorbell rang. Up-down, up-down, replied the chimes, as Herm opened the door.

"Well, well, Grandpa and Grandma! Come in, it's cold out there!" Herm exclaimed, more or less in Seymour's ear, and he gave his father-in-law a warm tug across the shoulder and Lillian a kiss. Lillian, whose smile was always bright and a bit off-center, had some kind of tiara in her hair, and a gown that reached almost to the base of her heels, as if she were going somewhere much more important after this, and bald Seymour, the boss, who was less tall than Herm, was squeezed into a navy sport jacket and wide burgundy tie with an American flag tie clip.

"Hi, Mom. Hi, Dad. Welcome," Gilbert called, rising to his feet, in a voice Herm found insincere and possibly mocking. When Seymour wasn't around, Gilbert sometimes impersonated him telling his life story, as if there were anything comical about a child leaving behind his family in a Russian village, not being able to afford school past the fourth grade, and going out to sell half-rotten fruit on the streets of South Philadelphia.

"I hope we're not interrupting your dinner," Lillian called in falsetto to Ceil, as though Ceil had failed to choreograph Lillian's arrival properly. Herm took Lillian's fur. Seymour stayed behind Lillian, his expression like a bulldog's. He walked with a slow hobble from the gout, no cane out of pride, and Herm quickly took his hand and sat him in the low-backed Catalina chair, plenty of back support, nice upholstery, across the front room from the piano. "You did say eight o'clock, yes?" Lillian asked.

"Yes, yes," sang Ceil from the kitchen.

Herm fixed Seymour a brandy and Lillian a stinger.

"Come here, let me see you," Seymour called to Ceil, his youngest, at just the moment she left the kitchen to come see him. When she reached his chair, Seymour ran his small, meaty hands around the dimensions of her belly, as though it were a mound filled with precious earth. Ceil looked so proud that Herm thought she might throw her head back and faint.

"You like?" she said.

"Why not?" he said. "More the better," and he shot a glance at Gilbert, who had never shown any sense of obligation to produce a grandchild for his father-in-law.

"Clean it up clean it up," Seymour told Ceil, indicating the remains of dinner on the table. "Don't let us getting in the way. We wait."

As Ceil stepped away, out from the kitchen ran the boys to their grandpa, who gave them each a penny and a kiss on the forehead. Their little socked feet stamped the floor with hearty commotion, and everyone was smiling.

"Second Infantry, to the rescue," Herm narrated like newsreel. Upstairs, the floorboards creaked. Tonight, Herm told himself, his house was filled with no less joy than the del Priores' next door or the Moores' across the street.

Ceil got the back of the house in order while the men and Lillian drank. Seymour, inventing a game for the boys, demanded to see who could stand longer like a loyal soldier and salute him, the winner receiving a dime. So with Herm setting their little hands at crisp, sharp, angles, the boys stood and saluted their grandfather, knees bowing slightly under the pressure of performance—and promptly straightened by Herm—one boy on either side of Seymour's short, plump legs.

There was a silence then in the front of the house that said something momentous was about to happen, and then it did. Sadie came down the staircase, holding the child.

"Hooray!" Herm exclaimed three times, and each boy thought this meant that he had won the saluting contest, but Grandpa quickly informed them neither had won.

"More practice," he shouted, and made the dime disappear.

Gilbert extended hands toward his wife, who appeared almost to be floating down from above.

Sadie. Sadie.

The name rhymed with *baby*.

The street was still. Everyone was with the ones they belonged to.

When she reached the bottom of the stairs and Herm could get a look at her, she appeared, unlike earlier, to adore this child—or was this an illusion? His senses, which he never questioned day to day, felt unusually untrustworthy. Sadie had formed an attachment to the baby, hadn't she? She didn't want to return it, did she?

Sadie sat on the piano bench, facing the room, and everyone stood around her like rows of a choir. The boys were closest. They appeared to want to give her something. Gilbert bent low and kissed her on the cheek. Ceil arrived and stood between Herm and her father, one hand around each man's waist.

"And what do we have here?" asked Lillian, with her best

imitation–Society Hill accent and pucker of the lips.

"Meet Marjorie," Sadie said. "Marjorie Joy Gilbert."

Joy! The word had been in Herm's thoughts all day. Had he spoken it to Sadie? Had she *heard* it from him?

"That's *your* baby?" Brucie asked Sadie. "Where'd you get it from?"

"Every baby is a miracle of the Lord," Sadie answered, in her research librarian's voice.

"Nuh-uhh," he said.

Neil shook his head no in agreement.

"Babies come from the hospital," Brucie stated, and grasped the side of the piano bench. "And you can only have one if You-Know-What."

"What?" Sadie said softly. The baby was sleeping peacefully across her lap.

"Aunt Sadie and Uncle Max Gilbert have a new baby just like any other lady and man," Ceil said to Brucie, in a voice that did not invite dissent.

"I know," Brucie answered.

"Marjorie," Lillian sang the word, as if she were tasting it and it didn't taste quite right.

"I think Marjorie is a perfectly lovely name," said Ceil. "But I can't say the same for Joy. It sounds . . . a little too . . . Christian for my ears."

"We don't believe in Christian," Brucie said.

"Well, it isn't Christian," Gilbert retorted. "There are plenty of Jewish Joys."

"Let the grandfather hold her," said Seymour. He had sat himself back down all the way in the Catalina chair.

Sadie set the baby in the grandfather's lap, and the grandfather gazed down at it.

"Come here, you know how she looks?" he said to Lillian. "Like a little Polish, doesn't she? That's how she looks."

"I've got some Polish," said Gilbert.

"You know your mother's people were Polish," Seymour continued to his two daughters. "Ya? These people had nothing. Little village in the country. Not even a village. Farming people's area. You know what her father did? Umbrella maker. Worst kind of business to be in. No rain, no money. Person of no status, no *yiches*. He was always going under."

Suddenly Herm remembered a moment on his first date with Ceil. A string in his heart had been plucked that he had not known was there when she told him that her mother— whom she never mentioned again—died when she was sixteen, and that when her father began seeing another woman only three months after the funeral, she chose to love this woman, Lillian, right away, out of love for her father.

"She's got some Polish," Lillian agreed, massaging the air around the baby's face like she was sanctifying it or being sanctified by it. "But what about that hair. I never knew any Polishes to have hair like that. What do you call that, orange?"

"That's the *Jewish* in her," Herm said, clenching his chin. If only he could phrase a feeling he had about how this baby was the same as everyone else in the room. "Look at Sadie."

"Sadie's red-complectedness she get from her mother's side," said Seymour, as if, now that the memory of his first wife had surfaced, it could not, or ought not, be removed. "The umbrella maker had a lot of red in his beard."

"What about the neck?" Lillian said. "The neck looks like one of those, uh—with the heads turned slanty on the body—

who is that painter? You know who I mean," she said to Gilbert. "The one from Vitebsk."

"Chagall," muttered Gilbert.

"You going to get Mort to fix that neck up?" Lillian asked Gilbert.

"Right-o, Lil," Herm broke in. "Don't you worry about a thing. This kid is 100 percent pure gold. Just like my two. Exactly like Mort's three. No different."

"Mort'll get her in some kind of cast," Seymour said. "That boy of mine knows everyone there is to know in the field of medicine," he assured Ceil, whose expression had become anxious. "It's a good little girl," he said, rocking the baby gently. "It's a very sweetheart."

Pop, went the shot. Hello, Dick Sisler. So long, Brooklyn. Your Philadelphia Phillies. Losers no more.

Amazed by something, the little boys began turning in place, lifting their heads as if they could see every star in the heavens above the chairs, the lamps, the bookshelf, and the mantel. The grown-ups watched, craving, envying the ardor in their eyes.

"I know what these boys would like," said Sadie, a bit starry-eyed herself, and she lifted the piano lid and lightly touched the keys, a simple up-down, up-down melody Herm had watched her figure out by ear one evening from the Danny Kaye record she played for the boys on her and Gilbert's phonograph. It was a song in rounds. She led.

"Never before and never again."

"Never before and never again," they answered.

"Never before and never again," added Gilbert.

"No two people have ever been so in love."

Been so in love, Brucie and Neil were supposed to answer, but they were giggling so loudly, almost collapsing into each other behind the piano bench, that Sadie had to remind them to come in on their part or the song could not be sung.

"And I'll have to put you up for your bath," Ceil warned.

She was keeping a watchful distance from this merrymaking, as though any blessing that was given in her home must immediately be met by some counterweight of disapproval.

Sadie led the boys in song—"Inchworm, inchworm, measuring the marigolds, you and your arithmetic, you'll probably go far"—Gilbert made inchworm motions with his fingers, Seymour's chin shook like jelly as he swayed to the music, and Herm began to feel a bit useless. He could not hold a tune. He did not have a part.

"No Christmas songs in this house tonight, right Gilbert?" he said loudly, fraternally, and drank another brandy.

"Right you are. Only secular humanist wisdom for us," Gilbert answered, with more mirth than Herm expected. At family gatherings Herm often felt himself competing to be the less disliked son-in-law of Seymour, but for some reason not now.

Sadie reached over and squeezed Gilbert's hand. Ceil glanced at Herm with contempt. Sometimes she liked to look at him that way, it just came natural to her and nothing could be done about it, but this, he sensed, was not one of those times. She did not approve Marjorie Joy. And wouldn't—not until she got to love her. After all, Marjorie Joy had just stepped out of the woods. Out of the orchards, the rubble-wall church! Ceil didn't know these places as he did. She didn't know how many good people were there, far more than the ones who muttered *dirty Jew bastard* as you approached their doors. He wandered to the back of the room, wondering what he could check on. You couldn't make everything right at once. He thought he might go down to the basement for a minute to check on the furnace, the whole forced-air heating system. Ceil liked a warm house. Seymour liked a warm house. Sadie played and Gilbert joined her on the bench. The boys sang.

I SHOULD HAVE, BELIEVE ME, ALL THIS,
THE WAY I'M DOING IT NOW

Gee, you want to hear a real story about those times, I'll tell you, I'll tell you the one time I met Ella Fitzgerald, I was looking for Errol Garner backstage. This was back, gosh, I don't know exactly when, not so long ago I guess, but there were all these corridors leading everywhere and I ducked, I must have heard, I don't know why I poked my head in the door, and there was Ella in purple there standing by herself. And I said, "Excuse me, could you tell me where Mr. Garner is?" You know, cause I was there to see Errol and I was looking for where he was. And Ella, she was in a dress, she was taking off some makeup and all like you'd expect, but you'll never believe what she said back to me when I asked her that. You won't believe this. She said, "How the fuck should I know where he is?" Was like a sailor talking. Can you imagine? You know, I'm talking about Ella Fitzgerald now, the queen, in other words, the queen of American popular music vocals. She sounds like such a sweet innocent girl for the most part on the records, but really she wasn't like that the time I met her.

But that was already—no, yes—that was already when we were back here in San Francisco, before she, it all, everything. When you were asking, we were still in Sweden. Gosh, there's so much appreciation among those Europeans. You know the Swedish people in addition to having such an appreciation for American music and jazz and all that, they're very decent. They're fair, I'm talking about. You know, I could support myself and my wife over there for the most part playing piano in a club for five years. Of course that's unheard of in America unless you're, you know, some kind of rock music outfit with explosions and lasers and all that business.

We lived all over Europe when I was working and playing. We thought, at that time, we thought we would stay in Sweden possibly forever, those sweet, either Sweden or go to Japan, because my wife, you know, as I think I was telling you, my wife was Japanese, and she always wanted to go back there. Probably if it wasn't for my mental illness, I would've gone to Japan with her, you know, if I wasn't on Social Security all the time.

Probably would've been terrible for her if I'd become manic over in Japan though. She really would've lost face. You know it's one good thing about this God-forsaken country, you can be anonymous. Too anonymous, that's why half the country's being abducted, half the country's living with somebody else. You know it's ridiculous, really! It's almost, well. Anyway, but anyway, in Japan it isn't so. Everybody's on the registry someplace, and all the family—if that happened all her family would know about it, and it would be very embarrassing if that happened.

Gosh. We finally found a place to live in San Francisco after they sent me back to, oh they know me real good over at SF General in particular, that one. They know my wife, too, of course, from visiting me, you understand, at that time. But our place was grand, by golly. It was on the top floor of one of those new high-rises over there on Russian Hill. Her parents helped us, just, you know. I should really sit down, when I have the chance one day and write a letter to those people, her father and mother. They never turned their back on their child. I have a lot of respect for people from the Orient. From the East, I'm talking about. They're more concentrated, generally speaking. They're more, yeah.

Gee, that apartment with the big long window over the bay. Around Polk Street somewhere. But anyway, I was going to say, yeah my wife, I remember. Do you like Jelly Roll Morton? Have you ever heard his band, and the Seven Hot Peppers or something? You, I mean, you can't sit still. It's so good, it's so hot, I hate dancing. Basically, I hate to go out dancing. But if I hear that, you know, I just feel like struttin'.

No, I can't do justice that way when I play it, it's just a recording, but boy it's good. Anyway, I'd put on that record, that player piano stuff and just a few minutes into it I'll say, Gee, and she was in the kitchen, pulled back the curtain, and like this was the expression—and just then when she started dancing, you know, it was spontaneous, not any regular dance the way she did. I should have done that more often to her. This kind of playing that I'm playing for you, you know, I should have, I could have done it so easily, you know?

I did it once in a while but, just have the whole, you put the candles on, just have her sit down cause she loved to listen just like you do, and just play only for her, and not just the renditions of "Summertime" or something but do real far out improvisations of, of haunting melodies like the one I was doing before. That would have meant so much to her just to, just to listen all night, I know she would have loved it, no one loved it more than she did. Ttch. Boy, I feel, I know how to live now, but it's too late unless I could find someone with—

You know, after she died, what I should've done. This was my first mistake. You're a student, you study things, right? I mean, in a manner of speaking, isn't that what a student is? Okay, so afterwards, after she died, I should've done it, I think I told you, while I was away, off the roof of our apartment building. One story above our story. Eight stories. A little boy watched her jump. Told the police what happened, but I'm sure the police could've figured it out. I mean, this was a beautiful, this was, I'm talking about my wife.

But okay. So I should've, if I was smart I would've allowed myself one or two months maximum and got it firmly in my mind that I couldn't do anything for her, that I couldn't undo, never, could never undo those things. Except that you should be able to, see I could've been able to mourn and live at the same time. It's what she would've wanted me to do. When I still had her stuff too, and the piano, what I should've done is find another Japanese woman, another Japanese woman. Kept gigging. Get out of bed at the very least, right?

Ho, but I don't think I have to tell you what it's like to be depressed. So fucking. But did I tell you—did I tell you what he did after I got evicted? I told you how we lived in that apartment that overlooked the bay, Gee, and shared a bedroom—wow, I'm telling you San Francisco's a beautiful city when you get out there and see it—cause after she died, you know, I stayed in bed for ten months in the same clothes and of course they threw me out, what would you expect them to do?

What would you do in that situation?

I was in the hospital, mind you, at this time. Stuck in there, couldn't get out. I begged them to let me out because I knew that son of a bitch brother of mine was up to something. It's always been something with him. He taught Mother the language to use against me, I mean, he gave her the vocabulary and turned her against me because it didn't used to be that way when we were young. Mother favored me, I think, and he plotted. Oh, he was plotting even when he was six years old, I bet. How to get Mother to hate me and love him more. Well, it finally worked. Look at me. Cleaned out. One suit. Donation for the disadvantaged.

I don't know why I stopped playing, it sounds nice, doesn't it? You can make yourself happy playing for yourself and one other person. Just for yourself, really! It's not as if I would necessarily have to love it. You know, you can bring yourself a lot of pleasure playing for yourself, you can surprise yourself, for instance. That's one thing that often happens. You'll be playing a flatted fifth like in that one piece, Monk, before, remember? You can, it's all mood, how you're feeling at that moment in other words. You can put that flatted fifth anywhere, pile up the notes you want, you're making trees, really, with your fingers and your fingers are the branches. You follow, right? Yes, playing can make you feel, gosh, like no problems today, fella. Grab your coat, get your hat, all that stuff.

Oh, but after she died, that was the end of the music until now, talking to you and so on. Because you care about the music like she did. She had favorite songs, too, you know. Oh, they were the most beautiful of all. "Say It Isn't So," "You'll Never Know," "Isn't It a Lovely Day," "Just Friends," "No Moon at

All," "Little Girl Blue." You know, you can learn a lot from the changes in a sad song. There's always that half-step drop, like in "Lover Man." "But I'm feeling so sad." Minor to major, major to minor, drop a half-step, pick it back up. I mean, that's life, right? That's how it goes. You fall down and, well.

See, he took the, yeah, he threw away all the cassettes I had, including cassettes going back to Europe, you know, you could see they were valuable, the only ones we had. And they were in the cupboards, you know, he just dug them out, including I have three cassettes that were encased in plastic, obviously protected, those were thrown out, with my voi—with my wife's voice and singing on it. One of those tapes we made in Sweden when we were living there, in Europe, you know, and he didn't miss a single thing, the son of a bitch, and then he took the tape recorder with him. The tape recorder isn't there. And yeah, yeah, you know: "Your apartment wasn't guarded very much and so I figured somebody would come in and be tempted to, if they'd come in they'd be tempted to run off with your tape recorder." So he took it himself. You know, but I still, in other words: "I felt your tape recorder might be stolen so I stole it myself" is what he was saying.

See, he's, my brother's very smart. He's an accountant. So he didn't, and he's, he's economical, he doesn't waste his time, like this one time he could get me and finish me and finish it, everything off altogether. He knew I'd never recover from having, he knew I'd either be manic or depressed and that losing all my, coming home.

Mental hospital.

I, that's why I was gone. He's, he volunteered to, said he'd go up and straighten it up, since I'd been evicted, since it was such a mess. So he knew when I came home to find nothing that sooner or later he'd just wipe me out and he did. But I—

I should have had the recorder going. I should have had the recorder going all, believe me, all this, the way I'm doing it now, for you, this is the way I should practice, you know, if I'm ever going to—do you think it's too late for me? I'm very old if you think about it. Look at all these fingers, you see all the nails eaten all the way down to the bottom. Not very attractive, eh? She used to hate that. She'd say, "Don't do that to your fingernails, Arthur," as if she really meant something like, you know, "Stop doing that to yourself, Arthur." Because I am my fingers in a way. My fingers are the branches of my heart, and I hardly even know how to use them properly, the way I should.

Gosh, when I had it still the apartment, not to mention the wife, in other words the tape recorder—nice Sanyo tape— the kind, you know, it's the—and with the detachable speakers, good speakers, next to you. Anyway, back to the practicing. What I should have been doing, is playing, is taking an idea, a basic musical idea, something simple that you can't resist, and just play. And if you listen to it on tape, and then after about a half hour, stop practicing, play it back, listen, it always sounds so great when you hear yourself back on tape! Especially when you're alone. It's amazing, it's like nothing you can play yourself.

I should have practiced like that after she died, would have been the right thing to do. Oh, I know that's true from past experience. You have to take advantage of it, it's so stupid, I know. The idea would be that after you play it back, just spend an hour following an idea: say what, what would, what was the effect, of say a minor second in a certain position? Too gloomy? Not gloomy enough? Then, the thing to do obviously is to expand as much, practice, not play, just expand the ideas, playing with the ideas, in a composition notebook up there, making up it doesn't have to be exact, just make a few notes, like you do on a special pad. That would have been the logical. See, I know the logical things to do but I haven't been doing them.

I've known for many years, for example, that what Leonard Bernstein said of course is true, you know, that the best tool a musician has for expanding or playing better is transposition. If you're able to play equally well in every—a simple thing, play it in every key on the piano, spend the whole day, that's what you should do. I've known that for twenty or thirty years! And haven't done it. Why? Can you tell me why?

Oh, but gosh, I really shouldn't be talking to you like this, should I? It's really not nice, there are so many nicer things I could—you were asking me before about the old times, weren't you? Things were always hard but they were never crazy like they got crazy later. Even when I was a boy—it's rough. For kids growing up now, I see they have no chance. You know, kids are not kids really they're just little, little people, right? Little people that have to be guided to a certain extent but basically they just have to be adjusted to you like you would to any other person, you know, which means not hitting them and so forth. I don't know how people justify it. Total hatred. But that's all—

When I was a boy, all I wanted to do was sit in the living room after school and listen to Julie London come on the radio. Gosh, it would make me so happy. I'd be sitting on the back of the big chair waiting and when I heard her, I'd spill over the back of the chair. "Just friends, lovers no more." That's how I guess you could say we are now. The story ends, it ended, it ends, she's back in Japan, you know, her parents paid for her body to be shipped back there and frankly, to my knowledge, I don't know what happened to her after that. They didn't deal with me, they dealt with—I don't know who, but anyway, they got her and she's there now. And here, well, I'm trying to, you know, keep from, but I think I told you that already.

A CERTAIN LIGHT ON LOS ANGELES

I met her at a 7-Eleven in Chinatown. She was at the counter, digging through her orange Guess bucket purse, trying to find some cash to buy a bag of jalapeño-flavored potato chips. I was next in line. How much do you need? I said, and pulled out my wallet. Here, I said, and set a twenty-dollar bill on the counter. Go get yourself a bottle of water too. When she turned around to face me, my knees almost gave way. She was that beautiful. She had a pair of pink-tinted sunglasses perched high on her head and was wearing a zipped-up Aeropostale sweat jacket and black leggings. She had bright, tender eyes and dimples at the edges of her smiling mouth. She was tall—almost my height—with wide shoulders, long arms, tapered light-brown fingers, medium-sized breasts, and a generous rear end. I wondered if she was Chinese.

I ran over and got her the biggest bottle of water they had.

I want to pay you back, she said.

I want to take you on a date, I said.

She didn't seem to understand.

A date, I said. Let me take you to lunch.

That whole week we texted—or rather I kept texting her and she would get back to me hours later or the next day with brief, guarded answers. Her name was Jeeranun. She was Thai. She had been in the U.S. three years. Her job was casino. Sorry her English not good. Okay, let's have lunch.

I went to pick her up the following Saturday at one p.m. in front of the Albertsons on the corner of 3rd and Vermont, in Koreatown. I didn't know why she wanted to meet outside a giant supermarket, of all places, but I had decided to go along with the plan. I live off Fairfax, south of Pico, in a neighborhood that, a generation or two ago, was mostly Jewish but is now Ethiopian/Eritrean and mixed professional. I like Koreatown. It's got vibrant street life and good restaurants. When I arrived at the supermarket, she wasn't where she had said she was going to be—in front of the lawn and garden center—and I immediately got the feeling I'd been had. I pulled into a yellow-striped No Stopping zone, flicked on the hazards, got out of the car, and began casing the outside of the market. I texted her. A minute passed. Two minutes. It was a clear, sunny day in January, one of the best times of year in Los Angeles, a day after rain, when the city smells green and you feel at ease, as if you're being warmed and cooled at once. I gave fifty cents to a young panhandler whose eye sockets were ringed yellow; he was leaning back against some cords of firewood. Two-inch black plastic pots of succulents were out for sale in front of the lawn and garden center.

Finally, Jeeranun came out through a sliding glass door, sunglasses on her head, the orange Guess purse over a shoulder, a plastic bag in the other hand. She was bouncing with excitement.

I came over and lightly kissed her cheek. She seemed as touched to be with me as I was to be with her.

She asked where I had parked.

I pointed to my car, a nice German two-seater.

When we got inside, she offered me a cold sixteen-ounce bottle of coconut water. I had never seen such a thing.

It Thailand, she said.

I unscrewed the lid and tasted the drink. Not my thing exactly but I said that I loved it. She showed me the contents of the plastic bag: eight navel oranges and six green mangoes. I kissed her on the cheek again.

Who's all that for? I asked.

You and me.

Do we really need eight oranges and six mangoes? I asked.

She told me she didn't like to buy just one of anything. She liked to have lots.

She had on a tight red ribbed sweater, white pants, and tan wedge sandals; her lips were plump at the middle, her long eyelashes curled up slightly; this was the best-looking woman ever to look at me as though we might have a future together.

I couldn't help but think of Delaney Rubin, my ex-fiancée. Delaney and I had met fifteen years ago when we were juniors at UC Santa Cruz. She had been a women's studies major and when we were first getting to know each other, she was always pointing out ways that women in our society are objectified, taken advantage of, and underestimated by men. When I would reply to her with what I thought were simple truths, such as, "Why deny it, every man's goal is to obtain the most beautiful woman he can," she would blow up at me, saying that's not man's nature, that's the way men are socialized. If men were taught proper respect and value for women from infancy, they wouldn't think like that. Delaney, like me, had been passed over for a good-looking face. She wore her fine black hair in a pixie cut, which, though flattering, made her head look slightly too big for her body. She worked at a taqueria and played the saxophone. She smoked a lot of pot, loved obscure British female novelists of the eighteenth century, and took forever to come. Even though Delaney had become less fiery in her views over the years, I could still imagine her seeing me now and informing me that the balance of power between Jeeranun and me was tilted way in my favor and that I was out with this woman only because of how she looked. Or maybe, like many other men on the planet, I was looking for a kind, pleasant, nurturing woman who was insecure enough that she could be made subservient to me.

I asked Jeeranun how old she was.

She said thirty-nine. She looked twenty-four. I was thirty-five.

What kind of food would you like for lunch?

Up to you, she said.

No, up to us, I said.

You want Thai food? she said.

Yes! I said.

I was so happy to be out with this lovely woman, elated really, that when I pulled out of the supermarket parking lot onto Vermont Avenue, I didn't notice an oncoming orange Metro bus barreling up the right lane. Honking loudly, it screeched to a halt instants before it smashed into the side of my car.

Careful! Jeeranun shrieked.

The driver shook his fists at me.

I whipped the car around and floored it.

Minutes later, she had me turn left onto Hollywood Boulevard. Suddenly we were creeping through Thai Town, with its dingy assortment of mom and pop groceries, noodle places, dessert shops, souvenir stands, video stores, and old apartment houses with Z-shaped iron fire escapes and open casement windows. Jeeranun pointed out a four-shop strip mall, where I pulled up in front of a liquor store that bordered a restaurant with Thai lettering on the sign. The restaurant was called Two Thai.

Inside, a waitress greeted us and said something to Jeeranun in Thai, then sat her and me next to the large window at a table that had four kinds of chili out in round condiment jars. Jeeranun asked if I liked hot. I said I did. The food came out one dish at a time. First was a tom yum soup with shrimp in a flaming metal bowl. Jeeranun ladled me a cup of this, with its slivers of lemongrass, galangal, and cilantro, and set it in front of me. Then came a hot spaghetti dish with chili paste and clams, which she served me with fork and spoon. Then came an eggplant dish and then a pancake and finally rice noodles in a thick, black broth that I would later learn had pig's blood. We ate ravenously, smiling at one another, sucking down noodles, and glancing back and forth.

You've got quite the appetite, I said.

She didn't understand.

You're hungry, I said, and she nodded happily and sucked down a rice noodle. I was clearly going to have to simplify my English to make communication possible.

What were you doing in Chinatown the day we met? I asked.

Study English, she said. My school.

What school?

She told me that there is a free adult school in Chinatown that offers ESL. She goes by bus every morning from eight to eleven.

What are you studying right now?

Anne Frank.

Oh. Do you like it?

She nodded.

I'm Jewish, I said.

Teacher Jewish, she said.

Then she told me she had never met any Jewish people before she came to America. She hadn't known there *were* Jewish people.

For some reason, this set me brimming with delight. The world was big and Jeeranun came from a very different part of it than Delaney and I did, a part that struck me as being more authentic, less advantaged, closer in kind to where the majority of the world's seven billion people live. And not just Delaney and I. Jeeranun was bracingly different from everyone I knew— especially the wealthy kids I had grown up around in Hancock Park, not to mention the women I later went on to date. All my life, it seemed, I had socialized with people that had gone to the same plentifully funded schools, the same after-school enrichment programs, the same test prep classes, overnight camps, parties, clubs, concerts, road trips, vacation destinations. We wore the same clothes, went to the same restaurants, had the same weddings. I'd had experiences with other kinds of women. When I was in Germany for five months after my father died, studying watchmaking, I had had a relationship with a local girl from a modest upbringing who worked as a tour guide. But for the most part, I hung out with people who had gone to the same competitive universities I had and who, after graduating from those universities, had relocated for a few years to the Bay Area or New York for some prescribed sowing of wild oats, then returned to Los Angeles and either went into our parents' professions, as I did, or stepped into some other lucrative field in which they had connections—real estate, money management, construction—bought houses, and started breeding. What did any of us know about the hand-to-mouth struggle to survive? We could always fall back on our families and usually did.

Jewish own all the banks? Jeeranun said.

Not exactly, I said, and forgave her ignorance. We all have misunderstandings of other cultures.

I told her that I had grown up in a kosher home—that my mother was an observant Jew—but I had difficulty explaining what kosher or observant meant.

Perhaps better to change the subject.

What job, I asked her, did she have at a casino? I pictured her as a bookkeeper or perhaps as a floorperson or dealer or concierge or, worst of all, as a cocktail waitress in a skimpy, frilly white uniform serving scotch and sodas to obsessed card players with glazed eyes. Whatever her job, I wanted to rescue her from it.

As it turned out, she was a gambler who went to three different casinos a week. She didn't have a Social Security number, which meant there were very few things she could do for money—all under the table. Thai masseuse. Thai waitress. She'd already done both of those, twelve hours a day. The pay was low and the work was hard.

If I understood her correctly, for the past year she had been supporting herself playing baccarat seven days a week. She had taught herself the game. The way she described it, she came out ahead five days out of seven but could only play for a half-hour. After that, her concentration was shot. She put up several hundred dollars to get started and would usually leave the casino up two hundred—she had the discipline to stop when she reached her target—which was enough to pay for food, rent, and entertainment but not too much that she drew attention to herself when she cashed out her chips. When she went to the casinos, she told me, she dressed as invisibly, as boyishly, as possible, her thick long black hair tucked up in a white twill Titleist cap, with a loose-fitting T-shirt and jeans, so that the crowds of leering Chinese men who populated the place didn't pay attention to her. She ventured over to the casinos after ESL class on free buses that the casinos provided. She didn't have a car. No driver's license. If she ever drove a car and was pulled over, the police would turn her over to Immigration and she would be deported. She loved America. She wanted to stay here forever.

I asked if I could join her sometime at a casino and watch her play.

That's a fast way to lose your mojo, she said and laughed.

Mojo! How did she know such a word! Her vocabulary was both limited and completely surprising. She had been in the States three years and had hardly known a word of English before she got here—she had studied English as a child but had forgotten much of it—and yet she knew words like *mojo* and *lark*.

She had come to America on a lark. She was thirty-six and had accidentally gotten pregnant when she was nineteen. Her parents had been very angry with her and made her have the baby and marry the father. But once her son got into high school and was preparing to go off and study medicine at university, she desperately wanted to do something for herself. She had had an unhappy life, being married to a man she didn't love, having to follow his wishes, having to follow her parents' wishes too, which were to raise her son respectably and work for the family's wholesale rice business. Her father also grew longan. They were neither rich nor poor. Jeeranun had gone to university part-time and studied landscape architecture but she never finished and always felt she'd been left out of something. Her parents hadn't cared if she got educated or not because she was a girl. More than anything, she wanted to be free. Free of being a second-class citizen in her country. So one day she hopped on a plane with a friend who was taking a tourist trip to L.A. and never got on the plane going back.

Who knew why it had taken me this long, but at last it dawned on me that Jeeranun was in the U.S. illegally and was probably looking for a citizen to marry. Maybe that was all she saw me as: a mark.

I had never been married—had not found my soul mate—though every few minutes a feeling came over me that my soul mate was sitting right across the table. In any case, my soul mate was not Delaney Rubin. Delaney and I had broken up and gotten back together three times over the past fifteen years, had run into each other now and then at the library, at restaurants, had lived together and split off, courted and recourted, separated and reseparated, which had culminated in my asking her to marry me a year before. It was an awkward ask. Even though I knew Delaney as well as I knew anyone in the world, I had brought a piece of paper with me over to her apartment, a kind of cheat sheet, to remind me of the reasons I wanted to marry her, as if otherwise I might not remember them. When I got to the moment of proposing, I reached into my pocket and realized I had left the velvet-boxed diamond engagement ring in the studio behind my watch shop on Hope Street in the Financial

District. Delaney had cried, and it had taken me more than a few seconds to realize it was because she was happy I was finally proposing. We stayed engaged for twenty-eight days. When I rescinded my offer—I couldn't go through with it—she didn't say a word, just pointed me to her front door. Soon after, she moved back to the affluent community in San Diego County where she had grown up.

The waitress took away all our bowls and plates; I couldn't stop gazing at Jeeranun.

What's your last name? I asked.

Suparat.

Super what?

She said it again. It Chinese.

Your family's Chinese?

They were. Both sets of Jeeranun's grandparents, business-people, had left Yunnan Province for northern Thailand at the onset of the Communist Revolution. Jeeranun's parents' marriage had been arranged. While Jeeranun was growing up, her parents spoke Mandarin with each other but refused to let Jeeranun or any of her siblings speak anything but Thai.

My mother's grandparents' marriage had been arranged, I told her. They were also businesspeople, I said. They spoke Yiddish with each other but forbade their children from speaking anything but English.

Jeeranun smiled and nodded.

I wondered if I would ever be able to bring my mother around to Jeeranun, should it turn out that we were soul mates. My mother didn't believe in soul mates. She thought the idea was preposterous, an illusion, a sentiment of the young. Marriage, she said, was a practical arrangement meant to make daily life more manageable, curb loneliness, and create the right environment for children. She had talked like this for years, in an effort to convince me that Delaney Rubin was the best possible partner for me. Delaney had character. A good head on her shoulders. A good heart. Similar values. What my mother never said was that she had married my father for love and that my father had not always been faithful to her. But I was my mother's son; I had never cheated on a woman and never would. And yet over the years I had worried that if I married Delaney, whom I was only moderately attracted to, I would be tempted to cheat on her. In any case, I could see my mother disapproving of Jeeranun, even if I got her to convert to Judaism. And especially if I told my mother that Jeeranun made my heart beat the way it was beating now. I had been in Jeeranun's company for an hour and already I didn't want to spend a moment apart from her.

I have some more questions, I said. How come I had to pick you up at a supermarket?

She said I was not allowed to know where she lived.

Why not?

She had illegal roommates. If their American boyfriends ever got in a fight with them and got angry at them, the boyfriends could go tell Immigration where they live. Get them deported quick.

And what would you do with your life, I asked, if you ever got a green card?

I asked this proudly, as if I might someday be the bearer of this gift.

She rolled her eyes dreamily.

Go back and forth to my country, she said. See my son.

But what would you want to do here in America?

Have a business, she said.

Like what, I said.

Real estate, she said.

But the language of real estate contracts is so difficult, I said.

Sell property to Thai people, she said.

Oh, I said.

Manage apartments, she said.

You're nothing if not ambitious, I said.

She smiled.

So, technically, you're still married to the guy in Thailand.

Yes.

And presumably you'd like to marry a guy here.

I marry here already.

You did? Who?

Thai guy.

What she then said was—or at least I thought it was—that within ninety days of arriving in the United States, she had given a Thai guy, an acquaintance of an acquaintance, $19,000, almost all the money she had in the world. He married her legally, then when he received the money from her, he disappeared—to Texas, she had heard, with another woman—before he could take Jeeranun through the process of acquiring a green card.

Fuck, I said. People are such assholes.

I'll marry you, I almost said.

Why haven't you gotten a divorce? I asked.

When you're married, she said, it's harder to deport you.

Do you want to go out with me again? I asked.

She nodded and her plump lips formed a buoyant, irrepressible smile. I leaned across the table and kissed her forehead. She said she wanted to split the bill.

I couldn't stop thinking about her all week. I pictured her in her ESL class, discussing the hopes and desires of Anne Frank with a roomful of immigrants. I pictured her sliding chips along green felt baccarat tables in Commerce, Gardena, Bell Gardens. I tried to text with her three times a day but she was never in any hurry to get back to me.

The following Saturday morning, at 5:45, I went to pick her up in front of the Albertsons. Again, she was not outside at the appointed time. But this time I wasn't worried. She was probably inside buying something for our date. Which turned out to be true. She strode out of the glass doors, sunglasses on her head, with a bag full of smoothies, energy bars, muffins, and chocolate, along with coffee for me. We were going to the Los Angeles Flower Market downtown, which she had heard about but had never been to. This was the distribution site for cut flowers citywide. It opened to the public at six a.m. The entrance fee was $1. She had told me she loved flowers, so our plan was to stroll through block after block of fragrant stalls. To reach into buckets of clean water and pluck out stems tied with string.

When we arrived at ten after six, the last of the traders, a middle-aged man with a waxed moustache and his assistant, were taking off with hundreds of sunflowers that they had just shoved into the back of a van. Inside, several vendors had dedicated their stalls entirely to long-stem roses. Others to white carnations and blue hydrangea. Yet others to silk bushes and fake bonsai. There was a scattering of shoppers, mostly older Mexican women, who were examining the flowers with meticulous care. In celebration of the English language, I told Jeeranun that I was going to pick out flowers for her in alphabetical order. In other words, the first bunch of flowers I bought would start with the letter A, the next with B, and so on. ABCDEFG.

And that's what I did. I put together an enormous bouquet for her of amaranth, bouvardia, campanula, delphinium, echevearia, freesia, and ginger, which she rested happily against her shoulder. She said she was going to bring it back to her apartment and look at it every day. Share it with her roommates. I then held the bouquet as she went around assembling one of amaranth, astilbe, and anemones for me. A was for Adam. Afterward, we grabbed some pancakes at the Pantry, then drove over to a quiet part of Griffith Park, above Vermont Avenue, and took a nice, strenuous walk uphill. By the time I dropped her off at the Albertsons, I had our next three dates planned in my head.

But the dates ended up taking on their own shapes. For our next one, we went back at six a.m. to the Flower Market, where I bought her an alphabetical bouquet so big it took both of us to carry it. As we walked back to my car, past vendors hosing down streets and a couple motorcycle cops standing in front of a shop that sold stuffed animals and balloons, Jeeranun pointed out that even though it was light out, the moon was large and visible; above the buildings it looked like a nearby parkland. Seeing the moon this way, I realized that she and I were already establishing patterns and traditions; weeks, months, years from now, we were going to connect the time we were having then to the time we were having now.

Over lunch, in a booth at Langer's Delicatessen, we talked about exes. Although I fancied myself the first person in the world to truly appreciate Jeeranun—and maybe I was—she had in fact already had two American boyfriends, both older, a pipe fitter and a limousine driver, each relationship lasting about a year.

That was not including the Thai guy she'd married, whom she had spent time getting to know so that they would have a unified story to tell Immigration when Immigration checked to make sure their marriage was not a sham. And then there was her husband back in Thailand, a banquet waiter who later went on to open an imported spirits store with Jeeranun's younger brother. Had she really not loved him? I asked. She didn't answer.

And what about the two American boyfriends? What went wrong?

She said she had tried cooking for them and cleaning for them.

I told her about Delaney. I said that Delaney worked with troubled girls ages eight to eighteen. I said that Delaney was Jewish. I said that I had had other, brief relationships but that Delaney was the main one. Even though Delaney and I had been very intimate at times and even though I had told her on countless occasions that I loved her—and meant it—when I described her to Jeeranun, I made it sound as if our relationship had merely been a practice run for the one authentic relationship I was going to have in my life, i.e., with Jeeranun. And in a way, that was true. Until meeting Jeeranun, I had never felt the initial spark that many men will tell you is necessary for forming a lasting bond with a woman. I had never missed someone so much, nor spent so much time imagining a future. Leaning across the table, I tried kissing her on the eyelid.

Don't, she said.

Then she blinked and insisted we go back to Griffith Park. Only this time we wound our way by foot up the busy road that led to the observatory. I couldn't contain myself: I placed a hand on her lower back (she didn't reciprocate), I took her hand (she didn't reciprocate), I kissed her ear (no response), I kissed her shoulder (no response). It was a cloudless day. We caught a glimpse of the chalk moon. When I kissed her goodbye in front of the Albertsons two hours later, it was again on her forehead.

The following week was Valentine's Day, which, along with Christmas, is my busiest time of year at work. I had as many orders as I could handle and was working in the studio till midnight. I have chosen not to expand my business and train workers to make my watches for me. This limits the number I can produce; it also confers greater value upon the ones I do. I make an entry-level high-end luxury watch called The Alex, which is named after my father, and one called The Emma, which is named after my mother. There are ways one can customize the watches. Different dial colors, dial features, bezels, straps. But the most basic dimensions and components of the watches, the hand-assembled movements, are the same. The Alex has a 40-mm case diameter, the Emma 32. Other than that, they are equally elegant, equally striking. In short, I make a $16,000 timepiece that takes me a hundred hours of highly focused labor. All 177 basic parts are made either by me or right here in Los Angeles or in Germany. My grandfather and my father used to sell luxury European watches (Swiss, German, French, Italian) and do repairs in the small shop on Hope Street where I still do business. I was the one who began handmaking the watches in the studio behind the shop. I got my start when I was four and I disassembled and reassembled one of my father's Rolexes when he wasn't looking. As a child, I identified with artists but wasn't sure if I was one myself. I had a passable talent for pencil drawings but nothing that was going to get me into the Rhode Island School of Design. Once it occurred to me, however, as a boy, that I could grow up and spend my days making watches any way I wanted, using my own fingers, a future began to reveal itself. Still, I resisted that future. In college, I thought mostly about a life of direct service, beginning perhaps with the Peace Corps and then moving on to helping the poor and needy here in America. I looked into becoming a rabbi, a teacher, a counselor, a specialist in helping abused children, a disaster relief worker, an EMT. But I could never really get away from watches. They were, quite literally, my first love.

On Valentine's Day the four women who had ordered watches for their husbands all showed up in the shop at the same time, and I coddled each of them, formally handing over the burlwood storage boxes that contained their gifts. I had Adele on—Jeeranun's favorite singer. Adele sounded as if she had known pain and had made it through to the other side. I was wearing a spiffy shirt, light starch, with cuff links, that had a pattern of tiny multicolored checks. When the women had all left, I possessed $64,000. If you counted my Christmas take, I had made $144,000 in the last eight weeks, a record for me. Of course, I can go six weeks and not sell a watch and I still have to pay my bills, which includes the part-time salary of my shop assistant Helene. Nonetheless, this money was burning a hole in my pocket. I wanted to get on a plane to New York with Jeeranun and stay in a $1,000 hotel room. Buy her a 24-carat diamonds-by-the-yard rose gold chain. Go out for the best omakase-for-two in Beverly Hills.

Instead I picked her up in front of the Albertsons in Koreatown at seven. She was wearing a sleek black form-fitting outfit with leather shoulders and a tiny red heart pinned over her left breast. I had made reservations at a nice, family-owned, candle-lit Italian place in Hollywood. The centers of her eyes sparkled with light. We smiled at each other and didn't speak.

I asked if she had finished *Anne Frank*. She said she related to the story because she herself felt trapped, always having to hide from the police. I reminded her that if she were ever caught and deported, at least she wouldn't wind up with typhus in Bergen-Belsen. She didn't understand what I'd said. My heart felt fluttery. I couldn't explain it, it didn't feel reasonable, but I wanted to possess this woman, to kiss her endlessly. I wanted to take her to gallery openings and concerts, Joshua Tree and the gym. I wanted to latch elbows with her on a wide sidewalk and make her life better. Never stop looking at her face. And what if something happened to her face? What if a lunatic assailant dragged a razor across it, disfiguring her forever? Would I still want to be with her? Yes. Perhaps even more.

I ordered a second glass of Barolo. She didn't drink alcohol, not even a sip. The candlelight was flickering. She was staring at my glass of wine.

Drinking not healthy, she told me.

The opposite is true, I said. Many studies show that drinking moderate amounts of red wine is good for you. As part of the Mediterranean diet.

It no good, she said again. Coffee no good for you also.

You've bought me coffee, I said.

Because you like it, she said. She pronounced "like" *lie*. Her pronunciation was dear to me. I heard it in my dreams.

Can we agree to disagree? I asked.

If you want to be my boyfriend, she said, you want to be healthy.

I told her that four out of five doctors say that kissing your girlfriend is healthy. If she wants me to be healthy, she should kiss me.

I leaned across the table.

She turned her mouth away.

I got an idea.

I asked her to close her eyes. Once she did, warily, I pulled out of my front pocket the simple 18-carat rose gold chain that I had bought for her at cost from my friend Johnny on Broadway in the Jewelry District. I had not wanted to overdo it.

I clasped it around her neck.

Okay, I said.

When she opened her eyes, she looked down guardedly but, it seemed to me, happily. She held the necklace up with her fingertips. She let it drop. She took a compact mirror out of her purse and examined the necklace from different angles.

With my index finger, I pointed to my stomach: I.

I pointed to my heart: ♥.

I pointed to her: U.

Thank you, she said, and, smiling, passed her fingers around the length of the chain.

After dinner, I took her hand and we walked down a long residential street to my car. (I had made $144,000 in the last two months but was still too cheap to pay for valet parking.)

Do you want to come over my apartment for a nightcap? I said at the car.

What's nightcap?

Cognac. Scotch.

Alcohol?

I nodded.

You know I don't drink.

You can have lemonade.

Okay, she said.

My living room walls are painted fire-engine red and crowded with blown-up matted photos of the insides of watches that I have made or repaired. As I gave Jeeranun the tour, I pointed out some of the anatomical parts of watches—the jewel, the rotor, the mainspring, the mechanical movement—and explained what each part did. The photos brought her pleasure. Her life was hard; where did her constant childlike sense of joy come from? The most compelling sight on Earth, I told her, is the 177-piece puzzle of a round Alex watch.

Except maybe the sight afforded by my bedroom.

In our socks, she followed me upstairs.

I have one of those super-expensive, eco-approved, five-star organic coil mattresses that is handcrafted in the mountains of Nepal by raw-textile specialists with enlightened souls, etc., that is indescribably comfortable. Delaney used to call it The Monster because of the way it made her want to jump up and down on her knees and have sex.

Now the lights were off and Jeeranun, the light of my life, was in bed facing away from me with all her black clothes on. Her cheek was resting on her hands, which were on the pillow. I hoped she wasn't sad.

Indescribably comfortable? I asked, nestling up against her back.

More lemonade, she said.

After I had fetched that, I tried enticing her to issue me a kiss. I even reached over her cheek and tried to plant a soft one on the edge of her lips. She squirmed away.

What's wrong? I asked.

Thai people don't have sex until marry, she said. She pronounced "sex" *seck* and "marry" *mally*.

I wasn't trying for sex, I said. Just a kiss.

She shook her head no.

Are you saying you never kissed your pipe fitter boyfriend or your limousine driver boyfriend, who you were with for a year each?

She shook her head yes, as if that were right, and buried her eyes in the pillow.

I had the distinct feeling she was sad. I could not recall ever feeling so much tender concern toward a woman.

We don't have to do anything, I said. I love just being with you.

She turned over onto her back. She looked like a very cute frog.

Ribbet, I said.

When she didn't reply, I realized that I still hadn't talked about her with anyone. She was like a dear secret I kept pressed to my chest.

Twenty minutes later, she fell asleep in all her clothes.

When I woke up the following morning, she was downstairs talking on the phone in Thai.

Like everyone, I am a mixture of cautious and bold. If I could have my way, I'd be less cautious. Presented with a Jeeranun in one's life, who wouldn't rather be wild at love than a mere dependable timekeeper?

The next time Jeeranun was over in bed, and still in all her clothes, facing away from me, I spooned up behind her and spread my left arm across her left arm. My heart was throbbing. From the feel of the back of her ribs, hers was too.

Do you want to talk? I asked. Her hair smelled sweet.

Thai people don't have sex until marry, she said again.

What do you mean by that? I asked. Do you want to marry me? Do you want me to marry you? I know you want a green card. I'm not ready to marry you yet, I said, but I could see getting there.

She turned over onto her back. The chain fell around her neck.

Please let me kiss you, I said.

She shook her head no and dragged an arm across her mouth.

This time, when she fell asleep, I could not sleep at all.

I was imagining what it would be like to be her, a woman, a beautiful woman, who must often draw predatory male attention, who moves to the United States at thirty-six, to Los Angeles, sight unseen, with no family here, not knowing the language, a language that is nothing like her language, with a different alphabet, different pronunciation, not knowing how the culture works, except through whatever pop culture she'd imbibed in Thailand, or visitors' accounts, not knowing who to trust, not knowing how the streets, the neighborhoods, are laid out, not feeling comfortable around many Americans—the mentally ill homeless, for example, whom she could not avoid at bus stops or 7-Elevens—not knowing how to accomplish the simplest tasks, never having taken care of herself all alone like this, with only one friend here who is not a particularly close friend. There are lots of Thai in Los Angeles, so it isn't as if she is getting off a plane in North Dakota. Still, she doesn't have much money, she quickly gets fleeced by one of her countrymen, and all there is for her to do is live in the shadows of a crowded apartment with other illegals, wait tables, and give massages.

And what about those massages? Weren't Thai massage places notorious fronts for brothels? What if, not knowing how else to support herself, she had given hand jobs—or more—day and night to businessmen passing through LAX? And why, really, had she come to the U.S. alone? What was she looking for? What was she trying to leave behind?

She had said that she'd been forced to marry the man who got her pregnant at nineteen, had been forced to have the baby, then had been forced to follow her husband's wishes. Did that include forced sex? Maybe she had gone through years of what Delaney would have considered spousal rape. Maybe she had never had an orgasm. Maybe she didn't know what an orgasm was. What if her two American boyfriends had not pleased her? Surely that wasn't something she'd ever talk about. And yet if I was considering marrying her, didn't I need to understand such things?

Perhaps it was simpler than all that. Perhaps she had come to America to—as every immigrant says—have a better life. To have more gender equality and make a happy, innocent home for herself with a good guy: me. So what if she had left behind a son in high school? If she got a green card, she could bring him over here or go visit him there.

I then had a very unhappy thought. What if she was withholding kisses/sex in order to get what she wanted: marriage. In that case, she might withhold sex after marriage in order to get other things she wanted.

She had an evasive side, it was true. But maybe her indirection, her reserve, was cultural. Maybe it was how she maintained her deserved privacy and dignity. In this regard, she was the opposite of Delaney, whose way was to confront everything, to drive home her points in your face.

Somehow I got used to Jeeranun staying over Saturday nights and us not kissing. I would wrap an arm over her arm, bury my nose in the base of her neck, and tuck my knees inside hers until eventually we fell asleep. Some nights, though, before dawn, when the room was dark, we would find ourselves awake at the same time and would fool around under the covers groggily; I would kiss her hair, ear, neck; embrace her; turn away; then flip back over and re-engage. Some of these nights she accepted my caresses, some not. When she did, I would inhale the clean scent of the skin on her muscular arms (she always showered before going to bed), bring my fingers across her hips and belly (she had a thin scar from a c-section), and scratch her scalp. I would ask permission to kiss her breasts and, if granted, would lift her top up over her head and softly tongue her taut, perfect, chocolate nipples, then make believe in the morning that none of it had happened.

One weeknight evening, she wanted to see me. It sounded like something was wrong. Knowing that I like Middle Eastern food, she had me drive us to a kosher Middle Eastern restaurant on Beverly, between La Brea and Fairfax, about halfway between where I grew up and where I lived now. How had she heard of the place? It was her treat. After dinner, by the light of streetlamps, we took a walk through the neighborhood, holding hands, until she stopped in front of an unexceptional white house from the 1950s, terra-cotta roof, low ceilings, with a small square nine-over-nine window in front. Spanish tile steps led past yucca plants up to the front door. A gate protected the driveway.

Is something wrong? I said.

This house, she said. She wanted to rent it for Airbnb.

I didn't follow.

Airbnb, she said.

I know what Airbnb is, I said.

She then explained that the house had three bedrooms with three adjoining bathrooms. It was laid out perfectly for guests. Nice neighborhood. Good location. Big kitchen. Big living room. The rent was $5,000 a month. Her plan was to rent out the three bedrooms to guests on Airbnb at $100 a night. Which would bring in $9,000 a month.

What about utilities?

Utilities were included. Central heat, central air. Maybe she would even charge more than a hundred a night during peak travel season. She'd base the price on supply and demand.

Isn't it illegal to rent out rooms in a house you're renting? I asked. Does the owner know what you want to do?

He knows. It's okay with him. The neighbors know. It's okay with them.

How do you know the owner? I asked.

He Jewish.

Where does he live?

This area.

Jeeranun's savviness in navigating Los Angeles never failed to surprise me, especially given that her English was hard to understand. She surely made mistakes in judgment but fewer, I was sure, than I would make if I were in her situation.

I asked what her other costs would be. Five thousand a month is a huge overhead, I said. What if she wasn't able to cover it?

You know what? she said, and she tugged at my sleeve with her characteristic childlike joyfulness. She was going to design the whole house. Top to bottom. It was just what she wanted to do. Buy furniture. Buy beds. Put out bagels for guests every morning. Pay for cable, Internet. Plant flower beds in front. Put in security cameras. Make everything remote. She was going to love it!

How much will it cost you to make the house ready for guests?

I already plan that, she said.

But what I don't see you planning for, I said, is what if you can't book all three rooms every night.

Every night, she agreed. That's right. I become Superhost. Always receive five stars.

Well, if in fact you can clear four thousand a month, I said. That would be a big achievement.

I want to do it, she said.

I think you should. It sounds like you've thought it through.

But, she said, and stared over at the front door. I can't rent house without social.

This took a few seconds to sink in.

So you're saying you want *me* to lease the property for you? What, is it a year lease?

I pay for everything, she said. Every furniture. Every decoration. I don't need one dollar from you.

But you're saying, essentially, that I'd be on the hook—I'd be responsible—for $60,000-a-year rent. Plus whatever other costs. So if somehow you disappeared, I would owe the owner at least $60,000.

Disappeared? Where I'm going? I'm doing Airbnb. I just need social.

If she were in my situation, she said, she would do it for me.

I'm sure you would, I said. You're that kind of person. But I'm just getting to know you. I don't know where you live. I don't even know how to spell your name.

She spelled it for me: S-U-P-A-R-A-T.

Supa Fly, I laughed.

Every time I see you you tell me you love me, she said.

That's true, I said.

But what is meaning of love? Is love words? Love not words. It action. Love not jewelry. It action. If my ma want something, my dad do it.

She was getting angry, as if I had just shot down her airship, the one that was going to deliver her to happiness and independence.

What, I asked myself, was the worst thing that could happen if I leased Jeeranun this house? She vanishes into thin air and I have to sublet an expensive house in a desirable neighborhood until the lease runs out. Maybe I end up taking a hit for a few thousand dollars. In the scheme of things, it wasn't perilous.

Or maybe she would get into some kind of trouble with the owner, which would lead to my credit getting wrecked. I wouldn't eventually be able to buy a house.

Would you still go to the casinos? I asked.

She looked impatient with me.

Of course, she said. How else could she make enough money to design the house? But she would have to quit studying English in the mornings. She had too much responsibility now.

I kept mulling it over. What if, late at night, some guests got loud and kept the other guests in the house awake, and then the offended guests left negative reviews on the website and eventually there were enough of these that Jeeranun couldn't rent the rooms? A Hasidic family, young parents and their four children, two in strollers, passed us on the sidewalk, a bit in their own world.

Do you want me to live in casinos my whole life? Jeeranun asked me, tears forming at the edge of one of her eyes.

Of course not, I said, and dried the tears with a thumb. I

want you to be self-sufficient.

Exactly.

I went on thinking about all I might lose if I refused to do this for Jeeranun. She might shut me out completely. I would miss terribly, for example, the green herbal beverage she made every Saturday for me and kept in pitchers crammed into my refrigerator. It was called nam bai bua bok. The English definition was pennywort or land lily juice but I preferred calling it by its Thai name. On weekends, Jeeranun and I would drive to the only place she knew that had the herb in bulk: a Chinese supermarket on Valley Boulevard in San Gabriel. The beverage was made in a food processor with the de-stemmed bua bok leaves and a sugar-water syrup. The texture was thick green, almost grassy. It was quite possibly the most exhilarating, refreshing drink I had ever tasted, a total head clearer, a body cleanser. During the week, drinking it made me think delightedly of her. On top of that, once per weekend Jeeranun usually cooked us Thai food, sometimes with the aid of Thai-language YouTube instructions, using ingredients she went by Uber to buy in Thai Town. She kept fish sauce, bean paste, oyster sauce, and jarred chili in my kitchen. We ate contentedly in silence. We shared our lives.

Finally, I said I could not do it. Five thousand a month. It's too risky. There are too many unknowns. She had never done this kind of thing before.

You don't trust me, she said. You don't take me seriously.

Not true.

If Delaney ask you to sign rental contract for her—no money, just sign contract—you do it?

I considered this a moment.

It would depend on the circumstances, I said.

Liar! Jeeranun shouted. You lie! If Delaney ask you to rent house for her, you rent house. Don't lie to me!

I've known Delaney fifteen years. Delaney has savings.

Take me home! she said. You're not my boyfriend. I have friend help me more than you. Not even friend. People I don't know well. Roommate. Thai people. Thai people generous. I don't know Thai person well, he will help me and my boyfriend won't help me. In Thailand man do everything he can for woman he love.

I want to help you, Jeeranun, I said. If I didn't want to help you, why would I keep dating you?

You're not even good liar, she said. Take me home.

Show me where you live.

Take me to Albertsons.

We got into the car and, as I inhaled the German leather, I revved the engine.

Is Jeeranun even your real name? I asked.

She looked away from me.

I cannot tell you my real name, she said. Much too dangerous.

Then how do you expect me to rent you a $5,000-a-month house? How do you expect me to marry you?

If only my love had been wilder. If only I could have loved her with the abandon some men are capable of. Here was the closest opportunity I would probably ever get to a great, passionate love, the kind of love I used to dream about and crave when I spent night after night with Delaney, squabbling over what percentage of the world's problems were caused by men and what percentage by women, and here I was stumbling over money. Money!

When I called Jeeranun that week, she didn't return my calls.

I still hadn't told anyone about her, my pet, my light, but now that I couldn't see her, I really wanted to tell someone.

I usually had weekly Shabbat dinner at my mom's condo in Brentwood with my sister, her husband, and their two young daughters. That week, I asked my mom if I could bring someone the following week. I then started leaving texts with Jeeranun, saying I want you to meet my family. I'm serious about you.

At last Jeeranun wrote back. Dinner next Friday at my mom's would be okay.

That evening Jeeranun wore a black lace top over a black bra under a black leather jacket with black slim-leg trousers and black boots. She brought a potted violet for my mother.

When we arrived at the door, my mother looked uncharacteristically frumpy for Shabbat, in a Jerusalem 3000 T-shirt and sweat pants with no drawstring. Jeeranun handed the pot to my mother and said, Exacum. It tropical violet. Indoor plant.

My mother looked at me as if she hadn't understood a word Jeeranun had just said.

E for exacum, I said to my mother. E for Emma.

From that moment on, I could see my mother wasn't going to give this woman, this girlfriend of mine, a chance. Either because Jeeranun was difficult to understand or beautiful or tall or lovely or reserved or Asian or not-American or transparently illegal or different or not yet professional-class or not Delaney.

What do you do, dear? my mother finally asked.

She works at a casino, I said.

Can't she speak for herself? my mother said.

I work at casino, Jeeranun said.

Do you have children, my mother asked.

Jeeranun smiled proudly.

One son.

Does he live with you?

No, he live in Thailand with his dad.

Oh, how old is he?

Now he nineteen. He study medicine.

And how long have you been in America? my mother asked.

Three year, Jeeranun said.

I could see my mom doing some quick subtraction. She got a look in her eye: Jeeranun had left a sixteen-year-old boy on the other side of the world. What kind of mother would do that to her son?

Just then, my sister's younger daughter, Alana, who is four, started to cry, and immediately my sister's husband Mark scooped up Alana from her chair and, holding her to his side, began bouncing around the room with Alana and making baby sounds. Mark was always touching my nieces excessively. Clutching them to his side for minutes at a time and talking to them as though he was four too. It drove me crazy. Children deserve to be physically left alone just the same as adults.

Then I thought: What if I had a baby with Jeeranun? Would that make me love her with the right degree of wildness? I had so much love in my heart. Where was it all supposed to go?

Jeeranun comes from a family of businesspeople, I said proudly.

What business? my mother asked.

Rice, I said.

Why don't you let her talk? my mother said.

Longan, too, Jeeranun said. You know longan?

My mom looked at me as though she were being asked to perform an athletic feat that she was in no way or shape capable of doing.

I thought, What if I marry Jeeranun? Eat longan in the evenings for dessert. Canoodle under the covers. She was the dangerous type, the stirring type.

Jeeranun politely praised my mother's baked chicken, tzimmis, roast cauliflower, and homemade challah. Lovingly, I watched Jeeranun's long, light-brown fingers push food around on her plate with the typical Thai utensils: spoon and fork.

Everyone started talking about Pesach, which was going to be held at my sister's house this year. I love Pesach. The gathering of family, the singing of the songs, the telling of the story. As soon as we were out the door, I was going to explain to Jeeranun the basics of what the holiday meant. There is a long tradition of Jews not inviting non-Jews to Seders but today's Conservative and even Modern Orthodox rabbis encourage Jews to welcome non-Jews to participate in the retelling of the Pesach story. Would I want to bring Jeeranun?

A few minutes later we were on the 10 freeway going east, the open moonroof cooling our heads, the heater warming our feet.

Your ma no like me, Jeeranun said, while we were driving through the night. She ask me question, question, question.

I wouldn't say she doesn't like you, I said. She's not always easy to get along with at first. Give it time.

To the extent that my mother may have rejected Jeeranun, it made me love Jeeranun even more.

When Jeeranun and I arrived back at the Albertsons, it was half past nine and a loud police helicopter was circling low in the sky, sweeping a searchlight up and down a residential neighborhood a few blocks southwest of the supermarket. A dot on the copter's underside was blinking red. Some silent police cruisers with their emergency light bars lit were driving toward the scene.

Wait here, Jeeranun said.

Just then, I thought of a saying my mom used to use while I was growing up, whenever I behaved secretively: *You've got to live your life out in the open, where everyone can see you.*

Do you want to come over and spend the night? I said.

The swirling blades of the helicopter were keeping time. Some gawkers in the supermarket parking lot were leaning up against their cars, staring over at the scene. The helicopter hovered, beating its blades, shining down its searchlight. Blinking red. Then someone in the helicopter delivered a loud message by microphone: *Stay where you are. Don't move. Stay where you are.* By now, even more cruisers had passed by.

Most people in this country don't like immigrants, Jeeranun said.

I do, I said, and tucked a hand behind her leather jacket so that I could draw her close to me and bring her lips to mine. But she held her mouth away, refused to kiss me.

If my ma ever need something, she said, my dad do it for her.

What do you need? I asked.

I don't want to sleep at your apartment, she said. You don't trust me. Your ma don't trust me.

Jeeranun, I said. Do you know something? Technically, it's illegal for me to let you stay over in my apartment. Okay? I read it on the Internet: "Harboring an illegal alien is a federal offense punishable by up to five years in prison under the Federal Immigration and Nationality Act." If one of my neighbors, or my landlord, knew you were illegal and that I kept you at my apartment on the weekends? I could go to jail for that. But I would take that risk.

You don't have to let me stay with you, she said. I don't want to marry you.

But you do want to marry me, I said. You have to want to. How else are you going to get a green card?

You're right, I want green card, she said, but I don't want to marry you or anybody. I was married my whole life. I hate married.

I tried to look her in the eye but she didn't want to.

The helicopter now raised its searchlight and shone it straight ahead, in the direction of us. The helicopter ascended and flew away.

Good night, Jeeranun said with finality, and smiled and blew me a kiss and closed the passenger door behind her.

For some reason, I couldn't stand one more night of not knowing where she lived, so as soon as I saw her walk across the parking lot and over to the corner of 3rd and Vermont, waiting to cross Vermont, I got out of my car and I followed her. It was a busy Friday night in every direction: lots of grocery shoppers, lots of couples in cars waiting for lights. Young Asians and Latinos mostly. I stayed a block behind her. She crossed Vermont, then 3rd; I crossed Vermont, then 3rd. She walked west on 3rd, toward Normandie; I walked west on 3rd, toward Normandie. In front of a doughnut/kabob shop on Catalina, an old lady in a shower cap, housedress, and slippers came up to her, shrugged, and asked her something. Jeeranun shook her head and kept walking. When I got to Catalina, I saw that the street, south of 3rd, had been barricaded off by the police. Although some people were staring out their night windows at the lit cruisers, nobody was standing on the sidewalk. After a couple more blocks, Jeeranun turned left. I hastened a bit so that I didn't lose her.

Just before I got to the corner of 3rd and Alexandria, I poked my head around a cluster of agapanthuses on a lawn to see where she was.

Two buildings down, she climbed a few concrete steps and stood at a black iron-grated security gate at the entrance to a four-story apartment house that looked, from the lighting out front, eggshell-colored, and as though it had been built in the 1980s, during a period when tacky design and cheap building material had been prevalent. All the windows facing the street were secured with iron bars, as if anyone would try to scale the apartment house and try to enter it from the outside. There was a parking garage under the building. Jeeranun took keys out of her pocket, turned the lock, and entered.

Once she had disappeared inside, I made my way over to the building. At the black-gated front door, there was a security phone next to a list of twenty-four names and their numerical pass codes. I scanned the list. Of course there was no Suparat. I looked straight up. Burning electric light. Barred windows. Clouds drifting slightly, backlit by the moon. I made myself a promise that I would gradually orient myself toward marrying Jeeranun while asking for as little from her as I could in return. Marriage would be a gift to her, a gift from a good man, a gift she would, when faced with it, be happy to receive. It would give her the life, the freedom, she wanted. It would be a love marriage, thus legal. And if at some point I had to get a divorce, I would get a divorce. People get divorced all the time.

Anyway, there was no hurry. For now, I would just let things take their course.

Over the next few weeks, we gradually went back to seeing each other on the weekends. I encouraged her to leave pajamas and a change of clothes in my upstairs closet and she said she would but didn't. I didn't bring her to Seder. She didn't want to go—was convinced my family didn't like her—and even though I objected, I didn't press it. I didn't want to make her uncomfortable.

Then, one Thursday afternoon while I was at the shop, and she was usually at a casino, I got a call from her. She sounded out of breath.

What, sweet? I said. What is it?

She was losing her apartment, she said. Her roommates were all moving to Las Vegas at the end of the month. Rents were cheaper in Las Vegas—they could live in a big four-bedroom house for what they were paying for a crowded two-bedroom apartment here in Koreatown—and they could just as easily get jobs working twelve-hour days at Thai restaurants there. So Jeeranun could come with them or else she had two weeks to find a new place to live in Los Angeles. She had no idea where she was going to go.

I don't want to go Las Vegas, she said.

You could live with me, I said.

I'm not your servant, she said.

Who said servant?

I'm not your housekeeper, she said.

I clean up after myself, I said.

Your apartment dirty, she said. Your kitchen dirty.

I'll hire a cleaning lady, I said.

I don't want to live with you, she said.

What do you want?

You know what I want?

What do you want?

I want you lease me apartment. You don't pay anything. I pay. You just sign lease.

We're back to this, I said. Not only is it illegal for me to do that. It's dangerous.

I might ruin your credit? she said.

That's right. You might. I plan to buy a house someday. Maybe for the two of us. And our children.

So what I do?

You come live with me. It doesn't have to be forever. If you find another roommate situation you like better, you can do that.

If I come live with you, you can call Immigration come get me any time.

Would I do that?

You might.

You can trust me, I said.

A hundred percent?

A hundred percent.

She sounded as if this were not the first time she'd made an agreement like this.

Okay, she said.

On the day she was to move in with me, I rented a pickup truck. When we got to her apartment building, I acted surprised to finally find out where it was. Before we got out of the truck, she told me the history of how she had ended up in this place. She had moved in following an Immigration raid at a Thai restaurant in Silver Lake. The American boyfriend of one of the undocumented waitresses had tipped off the authorities. The raid had led to a big housing scramble among Jeeranun's friends and the detention and deportation of someone she knew. When we got upstairs, I saw that the whole apartment had been cleared out; on the carpeting were some flattened cardboard boxes, bubble wrap, pages of Thai newspapers, and warnings of overdue utility bills. We put most of her stuff in storage— her large-screen TV, sofa, single bed, night table, cold-weather clothes, bone china (she had a collection that she amassed through eBay), and British porcelain figurines (which she also bought and sold on eBay). We brought everything else to my place—plants, clothes, household items, bath products.

From the moment she arrived, I loved having her live with me. I loved the scent and the moisture in the bathroom after she bathed. I loved that she bathed. I loved that she shaved her long legs in the claw-foot tub. Beauty is its own explanation. Some mornings we woke early and went and worked out. Other mornings we relaxed and had smoked fish on bagels. She had a sweet tooth and would sometimes eat half a box of Trader Joe's macaroons before we left the house. I would drive downtown with her; on the way she would talk to her son in Thailand. I would drop her off at English class and go to work. At the end of the day, after she had gone to a casino and done whatever else she wanted to do, she would either meet me at the shop or we would go somewhere for dinner, sometimes with friends of hers or friends of mine. I put up a photo of her in my studio.

Because we were going to be sleeping in the same bed every night, I expected that we were going to start having sex. I don't know why I thought this. I didn't want to rush her into anything, so I was as gentle about it all as I could be. She would sometimes wear two layers of clothing and a bra to bed, as if to declare that sex was out of the question. Other times, she would dress in very little, which was tantalizing for me, but when I came up behind her and physically approached her for sex, she would just say "Sleep, Adam" and within minutes she was out cold.

One night, before she fell asleep, I asked if we could talk about sex.

Okay, she said.

Do you think you're ever going to want to do it? I asked.

When we marry, she said.

The answer angered me. It couldn't be the truth. She had had one-year relationships with a pipe fitter and a limousine driver. Had she not had sex with them? Was that why they had broken up with her? Or had she broken up with them?

Or did this all go back to forced sex in Thailand?

Or sex work in Los Angeles?

The last thing I wanted was to be an aggressive male.

The following night I said, I have an idea. Let's go to a clinic together and get tested for STDs. That way, if we want to have sex, at some point in the future, we'll be prepared. She agreed.

That Saturday we went to a clinic in Hollywood that dispensed contraceptives, gave pregnancy tests, performed annual checkups, tested for STDs, and did abortions. It had a small waiting area, which was packed—mostly with teenage girls who were trying not to look scared. There were girls of every size and hue, whispering to each other, whispering to themselves, laughing and telling jokes, doing each other's hair, sitting on each other's laps. There was one wall of thick bulletproof glass, behind which sat a receptionist, who gave Jeeranun and me forms to fill out.

While we were looking at a contraception pamphlet, I pointed to the pill and noted its high rate of effectiveness.

Never, Jeeranun said. Not good for my body.

What do you mean? I said. It's safe.

She shook her head. I know some girl it hurt, she said.

I then pointed to a drawing of an IUD.

She shook her head at that too.

Only condom, she said. The only one.

I was called in first. In an examination room, a young woman with dark-brown indigenous-Mexican features wearing plastic gloves and a belly-revealing Guns 'N Roses T-shirt took a blood sample. I handed her a cup of urine. She observed my genitals and anus.

While Jeeranun was inside, I read the clinic's advisement that a man should always wear a condom, no matter what other form of contraception is being used, in order to protect against the spread of STDs. I hated using condoms. But if that was what Jeeranun wanted, I would do it.

The following week, we got the results. I was STD-free. Jeeranun had gonorrhea.

Gonorrhea! I wanted to shake her by the shoulders and tell her I was furious, felt taken advantage of.

Instead, on the ride over to the pharmacist to fill her antibiotic prescription, I asked her in my most composed voice how she thought she might have gotten it.

I told you, she said. I had two boyfriend before you.

So you had unprotected sex with them? You told me you always use condoms.

We use condom.

Every time?

I make them wear it.

So you think you got it from one of those guys?

Only ones, she said.

Do you think one time the condom might have broken or fallen off or something like that?

Yes, she said. Like that.

I didn't believe her but I didn't know what to say. Maybe she had in fact accidentally gotten the STD from one of her boyfriends. But why had she been willing to have sex—repeatedly—with them and not with me?

At the clinic, I said, How long did they tell you you have to take the antibiotics before you're free of the gonorrhea and can have safe sex again?

One month, she said.

That's funny, I said, because when I was reading about gonorrhea in the waiting room, it said one week.

One month, she said.

After a couple weeks had passed and she had gone through the antibiotics and had gotten a clean bill of health from the clinic, we were lying in bed together one night, both on our backs, not touching. I could smell the sweetness of her clean thick black hair. I edged up beside her.

Rather than do what I usually did, which was ask permission to nuzzle up further and kiss her hair or cheek or neck, I leaned into her and placed my hand on her thigh and stroked it gently. I kissed her shoulder.

She was wearing boyish striped underwear with a white elastic band under a short red Juicy Couture nightshirt.

Without asking, I slipped my fingers gently under the elastic band. She put her hand on mine to stop. But I didn't stop. I reached down further until I was touching her softly beneath her underwear. The underwear was damp. I reached in further. Touching her now was like putting my fingers into a pool. I had never felt anything like it. I had thought she was not attracted to me at all but it was the opposite. I almost melted with gratitude and desire.

I asked her if I could put on a cigarette. I had bought condoms at the pharmacy when we picked up the antibiotics and they were boxed like cigarettes.

Okay, she said.

I put on a cigarette, which diminished my arousal.

I slid off her underwear. I pushed up her nightshirt. I kneeled over her.

She lay still, on her back, as if waiting for me to climb on. No friskiness, no kissing, no conversation. Her genitals were brown. Her eyes looked almost dead.

What can I do that will make you happy, sweet? I asked. Anything?

Do what you want, she said. I fell down on the mattress beside her. I reached over and tried to kiss her eyelid.

Don't, she said.

I took off the cigarette. I edged up against her. I was still aroused.

Have you ever come? I asked.

She laughed.

Why people have sex? she said.

But you, I said. When was the last time you came?

She didn't answer this question.

Did you come when you were with your husband in Thailand?

When I met my husband, I thought he was special person. But he not. He the same as most people.

The pipe fitter and the limousine driver weren't good people? Same.

What can a person do who wants to make you come? Touch you with his fingers?

She smiled and the dimples at the edges of her mouth delighted me.

Woman supposed to come first, she said.

I know, I said. Do you want to try doing that now?

She blinked her eyes and shook her head no. I took off my Alex and laid it next to the bed.

I want to go to sleep, she said.

The next night, to my complete surprise, she stroked me off in bed, making a shape I had never felt before with her fast left hand that brought me to ecstasy. But when I tried to touch her in return, she would not let me do so.

Why not? I asked.

When we marry, she said.

Nor would she let me initiate contact with her the next night or the next. Things in bed remained as they always had: kisses on the hair and cheek, some spooning, and occasional innocent late-night canoodling under the covers and pretending that nothing had happened.

Weeks passed. One Shabbat evening at my mother's condo, after my sister and her family had gone home, I asked my mother if I could talk to her about Jeeranun.

We were in the living room. She had her feet up and was sipping iced tea.

I told her that I knew she didn't like Jeeranun but that I was serious about her and was considering marrying her.

I don't say I don't like her, my mother said. I don't know her. On the rare occasions when she comes over here, she hardly says a word.

She's embarrassed that her English isn't better, I said.

I think it's more than that, my mother said. She doesn't seem to know very much. About politics, for example. Where does she get her news?

Local TV, I said.

She doesn't seem to know much about current events. She hardly knows anything about Judaism. She doesn't know much about history. She doesn't read.

She reads the weekly Thai newspaper.

Is she a critical thinker? Is she a curious person? What kind of person is she?

She's a businessperson, I said. She's a survivor.

Survived what?

A hard life, I said.

So you're going to make it easy for her?

What if I told you I love her.

I can see that, she said. It concerns me. Are you really ready to marry this woman? Are you ready for all of your income from now on to be community property? Are you ready to be responsible for all her debts? You don't know this woman. You don't know her family. Her background. It's easy to get married. Not easy to get divorced.

What if I told you I trust her?

I don't know if I'd believe you.

Are you saying you couldn't give us your blessing?

I bless you. You're a good boy.

I want to help her.

Help yourself. Don't marry her for at least a year. At least.

I had never brought up the subject of Jeeranun's immigration status with my mother or anyone else.

Now I said, If I marry her, she can go back and forth to Thailand any time. I can go with her. I can meet her family. She'll be able to launch her own business ventures. Be independent. She won't have to feel hunted by the authorities any longer.

My mom sipped her iced tea and took this in.

It's not her future I'm concerned with, she said. It's yours. If you're her path to citizenship, how do you know she really loves you?

Do you think I haven't thought of this?

She'll be getting an American husband with a lot of loyal customers, a big earning potential.

I think she's the most beautiful woman in the world.

I could see from the way she flinched that she was thinking about my father, who had probably never thought my mother was the most beautiful woman in the world.

I give you my blessing to keep getting to know her, she said. I would like you to have a wife who is there for you. Not just one where you're there for her.

Thanks, Mom, I said sincerely, and I went home to see Jeeranun.

To marry against one's mother's wishes has a long history. For some men, a mother's disapproval is a sign that they should proceed forward with the marriage. But I really did want my mother's blessing. I also saw that I could do without it.

When I got home that night, Jeeranun was on her iPad at the kitchen table, looking at china cups and saucers on eBay. She was wearing her red Juicy Couture nightshirt and I felt impossibly lucky.

She didn't ask me how my family was.

What are you looking at? I asked.

She was looking for collectibles that were underpriced. When she found one, she would bid on it and if she could get it for cheap enough, she would buy it, then re-sell it for a profit, sometimes as high as 150 percent. Now that she was living in the apartment, the bench seats at the kitchen table and the back of the table itself were stacked halfway to the ceiling with shipments of china, porcelain figurines, jewelry boxes, and music boxes. She even brought over some of the collectibles she had put in storage. Then she started buying and selling cacti too, which she lined up in the living room by the stairs and in our bedroom. I take a fairly minimalist approach to home décor, not to mention watch design, but as with many things, Jeeranun was my opposite. Opposites match well, I told myself.

It was August. The summertime streets around my shop downtown were even more crowded than usual with drifters, kooks, prostitutes, evangelists, bankers, oil executives, paralegals, housekeepers, tourists, library patrons, and men living in boxes. The hot still air left grit on your teeth; I thought it would be nice to take a week off and travel somewhere with Jeeranun. Show her some of the beauty of the American West, which she had seen almost nothing of. If she couldn't travel by plane, we could drive to Yosemite or Monument Valley or the Grand Canyon. Or maybe some places that were new to me.

But when I brought up the idea of traveling to Jeeranun, she ruled it out. She had heard that if you leave Los Angeles and the cops pull you over, they search the IDs of everyone in the car. Especially an Asian that can't speak English well. And if you don't have ID or there's something wrong with your ID, they could take you in.

I said, But your roommates all moved to Las Vegas. Has that happened to them?

I don't know, she said.

There's no crime in not carrying an ID while you're a passenger in a car, I said.

She wouldn't hear of it.

Where would you be willing to go?

Up to you.

We agreed to take a short trip up the coast to Morro Bay.

We packed some leftover papaya salad and nam bai bua bok that Jeeranun had made and hit the road.

It was an exceptionally clear day, and once we got into Ventura County and started driving along the Pacific Coast, where the sunlight glittered across the ocean, I could see Jeeranun begin to take it easy. It had to be exhausting to be as worried as she was all the time about getting caught by Immigration. She was not the first person I had known to be living in the United States illegally, but I had never met anyone who seemed more on the run.

We checked into a hotel near the ocean and took a walk along the bay to the great round Morro rock formation that gives the town its name. We circled the 580-foot-high rock and ran our hands along it as if it would bring us good luck. Otters were playing in the water. Also flying about, floating on the water, or resting on the rock or causeway were grebes, pelicans, cormorants, egrets, and bitterns. Thousands of years earlier, Morro Bay had been a Chumash settlement, the rock a sacred site. Today Morro Bay is largely a fishing town, and the following day we decided to go out in the morning for a half-day trip on a sport fishing boat. I didn't know the first thing about fishing, but Jeeranun had done it in Thailand with her father.

In line to get onto the boat, I could see that the man taking our tickets was looking at photo IDs. I glanced at Jeeranun, who saw it too.

I'll just tell him you left your ID at home, I said.

Too risky, she said.

You don't want to go fishing?

I want, she said.

When we reached the front of the line, I explained to the gentleman taking tickets that my wife had left her wallet back home in Los Angeles.

He let us on. Jeeranun broke into a big smile. She was wearing sunglasses and carrying her orange Guess bucket purse.

The boat was a fifty-five-footer and we shared it with about thirty other amateur fisherpersons, most older than we were, and a few deckhands, who helped us set up tackle and get started when we had reached water that was about 150 feet deep. At the front of the boat, a few young long-haired boys in skateboarder attire who had not yet casted were studying the ocean. The sun was warm, the breeze was mild, and you could see a long way up the coast. Sailboats. Paragliders.

The longer we drifted and the more the boat rocked, the sicker I began to get in the stomach. I was embarrassed to be such a wimp, but after a few minutes I had to put down my rod and sit. Before long, I was bent over, having trouble breathing, getting sharp pains as if I was going to throw up. Jeeranun, meanwhile, was in her element. She pulled in three rock cods and a vermilion. The vermilion was the heaviest catch of the day on the boat, so she won the $26 jackpot. A group of heavy-set men all extended their hands and congratulated her. Meanwhile, I had vomited twice over the side of the boat and dry-heaved for a long while afterward. Jeeranun found my nausea funny and didn't come and micromanage my pain as my mother or Delaney would have done. Before we went back to shore, the deckhands cleaned and filleted the fish for us and put it in plastic bags. We were told there was a restaurant we could go to in town that would pan-sear the fish if we brought it to them.

The next day, since Jeeranun was having such a good time, we drove up to Big Sur. From there we went to Santa Cruz—where I spent a day and a half showing her my alma mater and the surrounding areas—and at last we ended up in San Francisco, which she had also never seen. We stayed for four days. We did all the tourist things but I also took her to an out-of-the-way pizza place in the Richmond and a little-known piano bar on Union Street and the bronze and stone statue of Don Quixote and Sancho Panza on their knees before their creator, Cervantes, in Golden Gate Park, which I (whose favorite book is *Don Quixote*) regard as an impossible-to-overpraise example of public art.

Except for the fact that Jeeranun would not get physically close to me in any of our hotel rooms and wouldn't talk about it, we had a great week.

Back home in Los Angeles, I had the impression that Jeeranun was becoming more comfortable with me because, for the first time, she was letting me pay for things. Dinner. Gas. As recently as our trip upstate, she had insisted on splitting the cost of everything, usually paying her share with crisp one-hundred-dollar bills. What more could I do to make her feel close to me?

The following Thursday morning, while we were driving downtown and had almost reached her school, Jeeranun realized that she had left her purse at home. Her phone, wallet, and keys were inside.

Did she want me to turn around and get it?

No. Could I just float her some cash for the day?

That night a big misty orange moon hung behind the city, looking as if it were roasting in the sky. Jeeranun went out to dinner with one of her girlfriends. The girlfriend was going to bring her home.

When I got home from the shop, I saw Jeeranun's orange Guess bucket purse on the kitchen table. When I was a boy and my mother smoked cigarettes, I would sometimes go into her purse when she wasn't around and take out her box of Marlboro Lights and throw it into the garbage. After that, I would comb through whatever else was in the purse—lipstick, compact, aspirin.

Later, my mother would ask, What did you do with my cigarettes?

Now I sat down at the table and stared at Jeeranun's purse, which was cinched at the top.

A few moments later, I pulled the purse open and looked inside. At the top was her phone, a prepaid one. She had changed her phone number once since I'd known her, and a couple times when I'd called her I'd gotten a message saying the number was not in service. I considered not digging any deeper into the purse. But did anyone have to know? It wasn't like she was going to be checking for fingerprints.

Her long blue vinyl wallet, snapped shut, was below the phone, surrounded by a packet of perfumed tissues, a hair brush, her keys, a small notebook that she used for making lists, a crumpled, torn-open envelope with Thai postage that had been mailed to Jeeranun Suparat at a Los Angeles address that was not mine, and a rabbit's foot.

At the very bottom of the bag was a maroon passport.

I knew right away why she would not want me to know about the passport. It contained her real name.

I pulled out the passport, and when I opened it, I was so struck by the photograph, my fingers began to shake. It was not Jeeranun. It was the woman who had existed in Thailand before Jeeranun had come to the United States, before Jeeranun was invented. Strangely, she looked older than Jeeranun. Her eyes squinted, her skin was clenched. Her hair covered more of her face than Jeeranun's ever did. She might be trying to hold back tears.

I looked at her name in Thai, which I didn't know a word of. Not even hello.

Then I read her name in English. It was nothing like Jeeranun Suparat. The first name started with D. The last name had more than ten letters. Only then did it occur to me that on our first date, when Jeeranun told me about her Chinese forbearers, the Suparats, she was either talking about people who didn't exist or people who, more likely, did exist but had other names.

194 ★ JONATHAN BLUM

I closed the passport, and when I did, I realized that I couldn't remember her real name at all, nor did I have any idea how to pronounce it. I looked at it again. It was a stranger's name.

I poured myself a tall glass of vodka and lemonade and stepped out onto my second-floor balcony, which looks out at a peaceful, tree-lined street of old two-story apartment buildings with arched doorways and single-family homes with tastefully understated gardens. The moon had grown paler in the sky but was no less large. It was so lovely, I wished I didn't have to die, because that would mean I'd never be able to see it again. While I was looking down at the shadows on the asphalt that were left by the streetlamps, I realized that Jeeranun's passport was her form of ID. She must use it, for example, when she goes to the casino or to the bank. But she had never used it around me, had avoided using it. Why was it so important to her that I not know her real name?

I made myself another drink, even stronger. Like Jeeranun, I come from a family of businesspeople, but we also have an intellectual streak. On my father's side, we can trace our lineage back to Berlin in the mid-eighteenth century, where one of my forefathers was a pupil of Moses Mendelssohn, the German Socrates. Kant was said to have admired his gifts. My mother's side is the observant one, from Ukraine. Once Orthodox, we are now Conservative. I grew up going to synagogue weekly with my sister and mother, and although I always had non-Jewish friends, there was a time, certainly when I met Delaney, that I would not have considered dating a non-Jewish girl. I didn't break kashrut until I was eighteen. I had a Pink's hot dog with two friends and the meat tasted like cotton gauze; that's how strong my aversion was to tref. Even though I have been known since then to inadvertently eat pig's blood in the company of a beloved Gentile, I am not as secular as you might think. Jewish learning, Jewish customs, Jewish people are very important to me.

An old Nissan with a ding on the right front door pulled up in front of my building. Jeeranun said goodbye to her girlfriend, the driver, and climbed out.

Look who's here, I called out.

Hi, she waved, smiling.

I went downstairs and let her in. I was holding my drink.

What you drinking?

Vodka and lemonade. You want some? It's g-o-o-o-o-d.

I told you. Drinking not healthy.

She saw her purse on the kitchen table.

Ah, here it is, she said, and checked her phone.

I came over, set my drink on the table, put a hand around her shoulder, and kissed her neck. Her hair smelled like hot cooking oil and fried bananas.

How your night? she asked.

I know your real name, I said.

She looked at me as if she had not heard me properly.

Say again?

I know your real name, I said. I thought I was being intimate.

What you mean?

I found your passport.

Where?

At the bottom of your purse.

Her eyes frosted. The muscles at the sides of her face tightened.

You went to the bottom of my bag without permission and looked at my passport?

I shook my head yes.

Why you do that?

I don't know, I said.

I think you know, she said.

Why don't you want me to know your real name?

How I can trust you now? she asked, very calmly.

Because I'm me, I said, raising my empty palms. I'm harmless. I would never hurt you. Never in a million years.

You already hurt me, she said. And you know it.

We looked at each other uncomfortably then broke our gaze.

Drinking, she sniffed.

I took the glass and poured the rest of the drink down the drain.

Did you do other things like this? she said.

Yes, I confessed.

Yes?

Remember the night the police helicopter was sweeping its searchlight around Koreatown near where the Albertsons is? That night I followed you to your apartment building. Your apartment building on Alexandria. I stayed about a block behind you. I watched you walk home. I couldn't stand not knowing where you lived.

She nodded. She exhaled. Then she walked upstairs and, for the next half-hour, performed her nightly hygiene routine in the bathroom. She put on pajamas, tied up her hair, then came back downstairs with a pillow and a lightweight blanket and told me she was sleeping on the couch. Please don't disturb her.

Okay, I said and went up to sleep alone.

On the ride to work the next morning, with the sunroof open, a ray of light caught the tops of my hands on the wheel. I said, We have to get past this.

What that mean? she said.

It means that I tell you I'm sorry—truly sorry—for going into your purse without permission, and you forgive me.

She didn't say anything.

Three days later, at the end of the day, she didn't show up at the shop, like she always did, when I closed at six. I waited fifteen minutes before I called her. No answer. I called again five minutes later. Then two minutes later. I texted. I texted again.

Finally, I texted her saying I was very concerned about her and was going home. Please call as soon as you get this message and I'll come pick you up.

When I got home, almost all of her stuff had been cleared out. She had left the rose gold necklace I bought her for Valentine's Day on the kitchen table. She had left all of her cooking supplies, including a nonstick pan. Upstairs, she had left her two small bottles of shampoo and conditioner, with their sweet familiar scents, and her Aeropostale sweat jacket, which was hanging on a hook behind the bathroom door. Other than that, it was all gone: the collectibles, the cacti, the clothes.

She didn't call that night. I considered contacting the police but realized that that would just be endangering her. She was probably staying over at a girlfriend's place, trying to sort things out. I didn't know where any of these girlfriends lived.

If I had had a wilder heart, I would have tracked her down. I would have waited every day at one of the casinos for her to show up; I would have gone to our favorite Thai restaurants and talked to her friends there, the waitresses; I would have shown up at the school where she studied ESL. I would have bought an engagement ring, gotten down on one knee, and insisted that she marry me. There are plenty of men in Los Angeles who would have done those things. Jeeranun might well be dating one right now.

Instead, I told myself that hunting down a woman who has rejected you because you wanted to know her real name is a bad idea. It had been wrong of me to go through her purse, but was that the end of the world? To her, it apparently was. If I would go through her purse, what else would I do? She wanted to stay in America. She seemed to value that over everything else.

For the next few days, I felt achy, jittery, hoping she would call or text. I must have checked my phone a hundred times during those days. A longtime customer who always greets me by saying, "Hey, it's the Watch Guy," whom I hadn't seen in a long while, came into the shop and, fifteen seconds later, asked me with concern in his voice if I was doing all right. I didn't tell anyone what had happened. I left one phone message per day for Jeeranun and one text. To do more than that would probably just make her more scared and mistrustful of me than she already was.

The High Holidays arrived. There had been years, around the time my father died, when I was sufficiently ambivalent toward Judaism that I didn't go to High Holiday services at all. But I had been coming back around to Judaism, even during the time I was seeing Jeeranun, and I knew it was important to my mom that my sister and her family and I go to services with her.

This year, when I closed my eyes on Yom Kippur, during Yizkor, with the tallit over my shoulders and the blue knit kippah on my head, and I heard the melodies and listened to the prayers, I felt a profound, wordless connection to my father. I found myself wishing Jeeranun was standing there next to me so that I could try to describe the feeling to her, but maybe there are feelings you can never share with anyone.

As the Yizkor prayers continued, I kept moving my body in a slow, davening motion, eyes closed. Who knows why certain people touch us the way they do? I had spent eight months of the past year with a woman from Thailand, who went by the name Jeeranun Suparat. At times, I had felt closer to her than I had ever felt toward anyone. Now I was probably never going to see her again. Though who knew? Maybe she would have second thoughts and forgive my trespasses. Or maybe we would bump into each other years from now at a 7-Eleven or the gym or the downtown Flower Market, with other people at our sides.

On the day after Yom Kippur, I decided to call Delaney Rubin. We hadn't spoken since the night I called off our engagement, well over a year before. I wanted to hear her voice. I wanted to know how she was doing.

She answered on the first ring and immediately said, Adam.

Delaney, I said.

Interesting timing, she said.

How so?

I just got engaged. Twelve days ago.

To whom, I said.

Would you believe a forty-seven-year-old Dutch-Jewish philanthropist named Vincent? We met online.

Her voice was heavy but spry.

That's great, Delaney, I said. Congratulations.

Yeah, it's a good thing, she said.

I'll say, I said. What else can you tell me about him?

He's bald. He has short fingers. He's perfect husband material.

Mazel tov, I said.

You won't be invited to the wedding, she said. Don't be offended.

I won't, I said.

What about you? she said. No one standing beside you at the altar?

Nah, I said.

I had decided not to mention Jeeranun to anyone again, to just try to act as if nothing had happened. I hated the idea that what I had felt for her could be underestimated or misunderstood.

Not even an iron in the fire?

Honestly, no.

That's pretty unusual for you, she said.

I couldn't stop thinking of Jeeranun. This separation was not what I wanted.

Delaney and I talked about family and work and then I was back alone again in my apartment.

I poured myself a vodka and lemonade and went upstairs and sat out on the balcony on a director's chair, one of a pair that Delaney had once given me for Hanukkah. I couldn't see the moon but I knew it was there.

I was trying to figure out how love worked. It seemed like one of those things you never figure out. You just turn the thing around in your hands and look at it from as many angles as you can and hope you're not missing anything too essential.

One thing I was sure of: You don't necessarily love most the people you know best. You would think it's otherwise. I have known a number of people better than I know Jeeranun Suparat. But I have not loved any of them better.

Love also seems to command that you keep its secrets. Once you reveal to your beloved how you've wronged her, memories pour forth in her of other times she's been wronged. Your misdeed becomes much larger. Also, the more you try to tell friends and family about how much you love her, the harder it is when they don't love her too. It can be unbearable. For this reason and others, I wasn't going to be talking with anyone in the foreseeable future about Jeeranun Suparat.

NEW POCAHONTAS

At the time this story takes place, I was living in a two-room apartment with odd-angled ceilings on the top floor of a divided Victorian mansion in the town of Napa. Some months earlier—just after my mother reappeared for the very last time, in fact—I had visited the town with a friend, seen the house on a quiet street called Kite Street near the river, and said to my friend, *I must live in that house.* I was always adding to my list of reasons to leave Berkeley. When I came back several months later to look at the available apartment, it was early March, and the weathered house, with a complex of scaffolding along one side, seemed on the verge of a renaissance: at the very least, someone was about to do quite a bit of painting here. The mossy gables, the exalted peeling cornices and pale shingled walls, the quiet inclining street near the river, all gave the house the appearance of being a kind of calm glorious creature, comfortably set on the land, ambivalent about drawing attention to itself. The house brought me to it in ways I can hardly express. I had recently turned thirty-five. My mother had just died.

The owner of the house was a small-bodied man in his fifties named Alexander M. Culver, who lived in Sacramento. Mr. Culver drove an old gray BMW and kept a weekend unit for himself on the second floor, down the hall from the resident manager, Uzziel. Mr. Culver came and went. He was rumored to own other extravagant, quasi-dilapidated properties in Santa Barbara and San Diego. He would typically bring a different woman on each visit, walk her up the front path, and wave a hand out at the span of mansion between the two thirty-foot-high English walnut trees on either side of the front porch, as if he were dream weaving. He was always thudding up and down staircases with these women, explaining a dozen or more intricate restoration projects he had in mind—for the lobby floor, the main oak banister, the fireplaces and mantles in each unit, and so on. I think he liked the glamor of owning a mansion more than the obligations of it. When no woman was around, he and the manager Uzziel quarreled about repairs and improvements that Uzziel insisted the house needed and which Mr. Culver said could wait. Mr. Culver spoke to Uzziel those times as if he were a naive, headstrong local with no business sense, though he often ended up taking Uzziel's suggestions. When Uzziel was speaking, Mr. Culver liked to hold his head away, cross his arms, and make a disregarding expression that had the effect both of making him look smaller and of accentuating Uzziel's vanity. Uzziel tended to treat Mr. Culver as a cheap, slovenly intruder who happened to be his landlord. I had a real affection for both men. I can't tell you exactly why.

Uzziel was used to having his way in the house. For one thing, he lived there. He was also competent—an immaculate groundskeeper. He planted the garden, shopped for fixtures, swept and dusted compulsively. It was he who had built the scaffolding and otherwise organized the complicated task of repainting the house, according to a design he had adapted from Mr. Culver's book, *Classic California Victorian Restoration Schemes*, which Mr. Culver kept on a pedestal in the lobby. When I first visited Napa with my friend, I had left my card with Uzziel; it was he who called, showed, and rented me the odd-angled apartment directly above his. Uzziel was in his mid-twenties with jet-black hair. He was from the nearby town of Suisun. His father grew olives. He was a bodybuilder, bicycle enthusiast, and aspiring computer programmer, of Greek descent, who looked, to me at least, as if he had stepped out of a Rogers and Hart song. At dinnertime, he would listen to bossa nova jazz on his state-of-the-art sound equipment in black Spandex shorts. He made perfect chai. The two women in the building (a chef and a baker) were homosexual, and I assumed Uzziel was too. Then not long after I moved in, I began to notice, week after week, what a crowd of lady friends Uzziel coaxed and attracted. At the end of nearly every day, on the front steps, there was one bosomy girl or another from the neighborhood waiting for him to come home. On top of that, there was a supermarket cashier from Browns Valley, a preschool teacher from Calistoga, and a tasting room manager from Atlas Peak—all female, of various ages and figures, none unappealing—whom he passed evenings with and who, if appearances are to judge, were entirely infatuated with him. Because my bedroom was located where it was respective to his, I have lasting memories of the sounds produced during some of those evenings. Late on a weekend, one would hear him come in from the microbrewery with a laughing date, or two, in tow. I remember a high school girl, Shelley, was always leaving notes with me for Uzziel and then running down the block out of breath. At some point, I began to have dreams that I saw all of his women and girls together in his apartment, directly below, in a twisting conga line, dancing and reveling and feeding him from grape bunches like an emperor. As far as I knew or could see, he had never been in love.

One Friday evening in early August, while it was still light, Mr. Culver arrived at the house with guests, a woman and her two small children. From my third-floor window, I saw the boy slam his door shut and race around the car to meet his sister, then just as quickly, run the other way. I remember that Mr. Culver was carrying a stalk of feathered pampas grass from the backyard and tickling his own chin. For some reason, being with this family made Mr. Culver look extremely bachelor-like. He tried to help the woman drag her large blue duffel bag inside, and finally she let him. The woman was tall and plainly dressed with long black hair, and did not resemble the other women Mr. Culver typically brought to the house, all of whom, it was my impression, might have held season tickets, in the same row, to the Sacramento light opera. The children were about seven and six. The girl wore pink clothes, pink slippers, and a pink plastic handbag, all bearing a logo from the Disney movie *Beauty and the Beast*, popular that summer. The boy wore a variety of athletic clothes and a baseball cap tipped jauntily to one side. The family stayed in Mr. Culver's unit.

When I passed the woman in the hall that first evening, I saw that she was very pretty, northern Chinese possibly, with high cheekbones, about my age. She nodded politely and turned one side of her face away. For some reason, I wanted to see that side, and I arranged to run into her again, the next time I heard her leave Mr. Culver's unit. Passing me along the curved oak banister of the main staircase, she lowered her face again and turned away, and this time I saw that her left eye socket was bruised a terrible dark purple and the eyeball was moist-red like the flesh of a plum. My throat closed and swallowed. The boy was flying around the lobby below in circles with his arms extended, saying *vroom vroom*, kicking Mr. Culver's pedestal on each revolution.

The girl's eyes immediately met mine and she said, "We know. He's very undisciplined."

An hour or so later, I saw Mr. Culver pacing in front of his unit in one of the tweed blazers he typically wore when he was going to take out a woman for dinner and cocktails in his BMW. Tonight, though, there was a romantic ardor to his movements, a lift to his chin. I dare say there were stars in his eyes. The bruised woman came out the door in a flowing rayon dress and bright lipstick. She seemed to look at everyone including her children as remote strangers. She clung to the banister when descending the staircase. The boy was raucous, which hardly seemed to stir her. Just as Mr. Culver and they were leaving, Uzziel walked through the front door. The boy kicked him in the knee.

"Stone," the girl said. "This is a person's house."

"Stone-yeh," the woman snapped, and pulled her son back by the fingers. She then raised her free hand and nearly brushed Uzziel's Greek triceps.

Mr. Culver said to Uzziel, "I'll be having guests here for a while. Be careful," and marched straight out the door with them.

The phrase arrested me, I don't know why: *for a while.*

Uzziel said to me, "Did you see that woman's eye?"

The following day, Mr. Culver came upstairs with a bit of puff in his chest to tell me he was taking his out-of-town guest, Xiao Mei Cheng-Ominsky (he spoke these words as if she were internationally renowned), for a special dinner tonight at Olivier's. This dinner was something she deserved—he emphasized that. Olivier's, a Continental restaurant in the downtown district with a striped awning, was known for its candlelit platters of beef bourguignon, veal cordon bleu, that sort of thing. His question was whether I would babysit.

I should say here that I like children very much, and that generally speaking they like me. I do not, on the whole, expect people to like me when they meet me. But I do expect this of children. I don't know why. Maybe I have just been lucky with them. I am an uncle eleven times over. The O'Connors multiply. I would rather spend time with an ordinary child than with most extraordinary adults.

The children arrived at my door at seven, as if we too had a date. Stone the boy was rambunctious and difficult to settle down. He dashed through the two rooms of my apartment assessing the odd angles of the ceiling and walls and cabinets, then putting his hands out in the air like a mad Cubist trying to abstract those shapes. His sister Daisy was a talker. We got along like old friends. She wore a yellow party dress, yellow tights, and yellow patent-leather buckle shoes. I told her I liked her style, and she blushed, saying she didn't know what my style was.

"Just remember," the boy interjected, "all right? We kick from LA. That's why we got so much flaves."

The boy was like that, silent for minutes at a time, staring at us with fixed jaw, or making shapes in the air, then bolting out with sentences like, "Your beard is weird" and "Get off the pipe, crackhead."

I asked the girl what she would like to do tonight.

"Let's just talk," she said gaily, and crossed her canary-yellow tights and smiled at me as if we were settling in to tea.

Her favorite foods, she told me, were mashed potatoes and salad. Her favorite subjects were vocabulary and counting. She liked Whitney Houston, Mariah Carey, and En Vogue. No rap. Stone liked rap. Stone liked Ice Cube and Cypress Hill—"and whoever sings that song 'Poison,'" she said. His favorite food was Fatburgers. They both liked piñatas. Their mother grew up in Taiwan, she said, which was why, he added, "she talks like that." Their house was in Leimert Park, Los Angeles. On Third Avenue.

"It's not near Disneyland," Daisy said, as if that would answer my next question.

"And Tonio's who gave her the black eye," Stone said. He made a fist. "After that, he put a .38 to her head."

"He's her boyfriend," Daisy clarified.

"Not anymore," Stone said.

"Yes, he still is, Stone," Daisy said.

I told them that I had once lived in Los Angeles—in Echo Park, on a hill. I told them all the places I had lived, in order, beginning with Pocahontas, Iowa.

"Would you like to go to the movies while you're visiting?" I asked.

"Yes," Daisy exclaimed. "We'd love to. We love movies. Right, Stone?"

"Just not *Beauty and the Beast*," the boy said. "And that's the only one she'll go to."

Mr. Culver knocked on my door again the next day, a Sunday, to see if I would babysit the children for a few hours. He said they had requested me. He confided a look of heroic concern. He wanted to take his guest on a tour of the Wine Country. It was her first time seeing our valley. Xiao Mei (he spoke the name today as if balancing in his fingertips a tender flower) was a business associate of his sister's in Los Angeles. She was a bookkeeper. She had had a rough experience in Los Angeles, and he did not want anyone in the building to inquire about it—"just you all leave her be," were I believe his words. "She's in good hands now." From my doorway, Mr. Culver kept looking back across his shoulder as if someone were standing there about to vanish. He said, "Being up here is making her very happy." He shook some bills in my hand and took off down the steps.

Outside my kitchen window, summer was in bloom and the house painting had commenced. Predictably, Uzziel and Mr. Culver had squabbled in recent weeks about paint costs and color variety, but as I understood it, the matter was settled. Uzziel's twenty-one-color design (seven colors for each story, with "punch colors" mustard, maroon, and sylvan green on floors one, two, and three) had prevailed. Uzziel was up on the third-floor scaffolding now, a few feet from my window, painting with the usual combination of fervid concentration and possessiveness he had whenever working on the house. He wore scant, tight apparel. Latex paint cans surrounded him like an exotic musical instrument. One level below, in bikini tops, were the Calistoga preschool teacher and one of the neighborhood girls, also with paintbrushes. The sky was blue, the day was hot with a pleasant breeze, and I could see slate-colored gabled roofs, green trees, and the jagged tops of lava-formed mountains behind Uzziel. We waved.

When the children arrived, Stone didn't want his mother to leave. He made up stories of what could happen if she never came back. She assured him, in a voice that sounded entranced by something high and away out the kitchen window, that she would come back and they would have dinner. Good dinner. Daisy assured him too. She's going for a drive. She'll bring you back treats from the Napa Valley. The boy told his mother he didn't care if she came back. And don't bring him anything from this valley. This valley doesn't exist. Who cares about this valley? Mr. Culver said to the children, Don't you think you should tell your mother she looks lovely today? He stepped closer to her. The children's mother wore harshly applied lipstick and a wrinkled dress, with a silver necklace that lay awkwardly enough on her collarbone that I wondered whether this was her first time in jewelry. The swelling around her left eye had gone down since Friday, but, in my view at least, the effect of this on her was to make her look more downtrodden and confused. Stone shot Mr. Culver a glare and kicked the back of my rocker about knee level. The woman wandered over to the window, as if it were more than she could do to stop herself.

"Hey, Xiao Mei," rang a crystalline tenor voice from outside the window. We saw nobody from where we were. "You've got to get out of the house and enjoy this day,"

The woman raised her hand as if she might wave, then stopped and said to Mr. Culver, "You have a very dedicated manager."

Mr. Culver trotted to the window, budged the woman aside, and craned his head out. When he brought it back in, he looked damp and ruffled. He muttered something vaguely mythical about a peacock who one day was blinded by his own reflection.

He and the woman drove off in the BMW trailing bubbling gray smoke out the muffler. The boy's mood picked up shortly and we knocked on the baker's door; she gave us each a tart made with pears from our yard. The chef cut us slices of warm artichoke quiche. The children and I waved hello to the painters, then took a walk along the river.

The children enjoyed the town. We poked around the tannery and the abandoned mill. We made wishes and threw pennies into the river. We watched a matinee of *Beauty and the Beast*, ate crispy tacos, strolled past the climbing rose bushes that cover an old white house near the Episcopalian church, then came home and set out a blanket on the front lawn. One could hear the neighbor across the street, playing showtunes on the piano. For a little while, Uzziel and his girlfriends joined us. We played "Who Am I? What Are You?" and "Aardvark, Zebra"— Daisy's favorite friendship games.

Perhaps I do not need to tell you in what state Mr. Culver and the children's mother were when they returned late in the afternoon from touring the champagneries and free tasting rooms along the Silverado Trail. Mr. Culver's nose and cheeks bulged bright red, and he wobbled up the front path looking as jolly as I had ever seen him. The woman, weaving in no particular direction, though generally away from Mr. Culver, had an enormous smile on her lips; the rest of her face looked stoned. Daisy ran to her mother. Just before she nestled under her mother's arm, Mr. Culver took the woman around the waist and planted a little kiss on her shoulder. A moment later, he wrapped his arm around both of them.

I had never known Mr. Culver to stay at the house past Monday morning, but that weekend he remained in town an extra day. His gestures were benevolent and fatherly. The sight of new paint on the face of his mansion pleased him. Light poured into the vast lobby of the building all day, and on one occasion I saw him stand on the main staircase with his fists raised high in the air as if thanking the heavens for all this grandeur. He bought Daisy a small, instant camera and Stone a loud pocket video game. During a brief exchange with Uzziel he was chummy and peaceable. In the evening, he came up to my apartment to let me know he would be away and to ask me—somewhat cryptically, I thought—if, as the most mature person in the building, I would look after the family staying in his unit, "just in case."

I work out of the home and I take good company where I can find it. The following night was the chef and the baker's night off, and on that night, Tuesdays, my two neighbors sometimes threw impromptu dinner parties for their partners and confrères, all Napa Valley chefs and bakers as well. Naturally, these are the sorts of dinner parties one hopes to be invited to, and now and again, Uzziel and I would be asked to come down. We were tonight. Xiao Mei and the children too.

This was high summer in Northern California: evening candles, tablecloth. Red wine glass stems. Urn of cosmos. Scent of lemon and sage. A woman from elsewhere, socked in the eye in front of her children, a pistol put to her head, a few nights later is eating roast quail with morel reduction over mashed potatoes and curly mustard greens. Drifting bodies, holding in small circles. Confident laughing friends. Reflections on a bay window. A large fired bowl filled with fennel and beets.

Still lightly bruised and eye-mottled, and with a kind of fearlessness, Xiao Mei held the floor for much of the later evening. It was more than merely the presence of a stranger: everyone, I think, was fascinated with her. She came to life. One felt as if one were seeing her for the first time. Charming and light-handed, she told stories about her upbringing in Taiwan— her father's secret wife on the mainland, the family's densely close apartment quarters, a shy adolescence, joy of slurping e-fu noodles and studying television commercials for American phrases. She had acquired a nursing degree at eighteen (though she hated nursing) so that she could leave home and come to the U.S. Her one relative here, an uncle in Orange County, had put her out on her own after less than a week.

A strawberry clafouti slathered with whipped cream appeared. Xiao Mei stepped back into the crowd. She stood in a corner of the room with Uzziel, spooning compote slowly into her mouth, nodding, face flickering and brightening in the candlelight. With large hands, Uzziel asked questions and leaned into responses. Xiao Mei dipped down to wipe Stone's busy face with a napkin. I think she stood with Uzziel and Stone for a flash photograph by Daisy. Or maybe I took the photograph and imagine myself as Daisy. The baker and chef each gave Xiao Mei a warm hug. As I recall, Uzziel and I walked the family back to Mr. Culver's unit. Xiao Mei still had a smidgeon of sugared strawberry glaze in the crease of her lips. We said goodnight. I continued upstairs.

No later than nine o'clock the next morning I encountered Uzziel in full mountain-biking attire, clopping up the main staircase toward Mr. Culver's apartment. He looked—and there is really no other word for it—irresistible. He opened his side bag, eager to show me what he had carried back from his father's orchard in Suisun for Xiao Mei and her kids: cherries and apricots, the most perfect I have seen and perhaps shall ever see. Each fruit gave off a warm, muted glow and seemed as though it had been plucked from the readiest portion of the choicest bough. The pouch smelled like nature itself. Uzziel, it appeared to me, had every right to be pleased. If there was a little quickening in his breath from the morning's ride and the summer glory, I thought, why not?

The next thing I recollect, he and Xiao Mei became inseparable. Here I feel I must add that at the time this story takes place, I very much wanted to believe that my decision to move to Napa had been a good one. A relentless optimism, you might say, had begun taking hold in me. My mother, as I have mentioned, had reappeared for the last time that year. She had been doing this, disappearing and turning up in different places, beginning when I was five. This last time, she had gone and turned up not on a ranch in Oklahoma or off a highway embankment in Canada but in an emergency room in Cupertino. She was sixty-two, broke, with a gangrenous right foot and 33-over-16 blood pressure. She had been missing for four years. We children charged her successive amputations (the first above the right ankle, the second below the knee) and bypass surgery to our credit cards. She seemed to revive. Her spirits rose; she did not drink and was not nasty to my eldest sister Erin. A girlfriend of hers from New Mexico came to stay with her, and they took a small apartment in San Jose. Then two weeks later my mother had a massive frontal-lobe stroke and died. I think at first we children were all a little relieved, but then you put your mother in the ground and realize that she is in fact dead, and the way is not so simple. In any case, here I was, thirty-five, in a new town, a new region, trying to start fresh, keep clean, possibly even plant roots, all the while suspecting— as those who have moved around, I think, often do—that one does not ever leave behind anything. No encounter or move is coincidence: Like attracts like. You make your own peace.

I do recollect clearly that Uzziel's expressions, beginning that morning on the staircase en route to Xiao Mei's (that is to say, Mr. Culver's) door, filled with the lines and dimensions of what I can only call spiritual love. His youth, his innocence effulged. Hope lit his cheeks, honor deepened his dark brown eyes. Scarcely had I known Uzziel to look upon even himself with such tenderness and curiosity. He seemed genuinely in awe of some power or vulnerability he saw in Xiao Mei. She padded across the wood floors of the mansion on small carpets he wove and spread before her feet. Together they reminded me of two slightly awkward high school kids from very different social milieux— more awkward in a pair than either was on his own—trying out gentle, innocent rites in the halls. I never heard a peep from Uzziel's bedroom. All of his gestures seemed aimed to put Xiao Mei at ease; all of hers at not deterring him from this course. At least this is my memory. Whatever Uzziel's feelings in fact were for her I have no doubt they improved him. Uzziel airplaned Stone around over his head with one hand, wrestled him to the edge of the privet bushes, letting the boy prevail now and then, winning and re-winning his affection. With Uzziel around, Xiao Mei paid more attention to the boy. She belted his baggy jeans, smiled less nervously. Her eyes did not wander so. Daisy began calling Uzziel "Uzziel, Prince of Napa," and though she may have meant this ironically, I think on some other level, she was entirely serious. Uzziel was an uncle, a nephew, a sweetheart.

Most of my memories of Uzziel and Xiao Mei from this time are in warm light. I was happy for the woman, I can't place exactly why. I rooted for her. When I picture her and Uzziel together on the third-floor scaffolding, repainting the beaten shingles of the house and its hand-carved millwork, the kids far below in the grass, Mr. Culver away, I picture her willowy arms and prominent brows—how determined and resilient and reluctantly pretty she seemed—on a platform high above the earth, black wisps of hair across the eyes, in a world, between worlds, ghosted, alive. Whatever she had seen of life, she did not seem to have seen this. Uzziel might have been in tenth grade, his profile was so true—she stands against the shouldered overhang of his ambitious physique. Beneath a gable with paintbrush, he whispers into the ear of our 125-year-old insurance man's family dwelling. Purple mountains behind them. Blue sky. World suspended by days.

Daisy came up to visit afternoons without Stone, jittery. We blended fruit yogurt drinks and held conversations with our legs crossed, our feet rocking. A breeze danced. As I say, she now referred to Uzziel as "Uzziel, Prince of Napa" and used this term frequently, anxiously, as though she had made a perfect fit and the perfectness unnerved her. One afternoon she arrived in all pink with pink rubber bracelets, her bangs clipped straight across her forehead, her ends trimmed in back.

"Did your mother give you that trim?" I asked. "Because you look very smart today."

Daisy boasted that her mother trimmed her bangs and ends, and her own bangs and ends, and cut Stone's hair, and Tonio's, but not her father's any more, except sometimes, if

Tonio was in Riverside, with his brother, but not usually, and we nodded at all this cutting her mother did and did not do, as if it were a two-handed feat her mother could perform.

Daisy peered at a group of old black-and-white photos of my sisters and me that I had put out on an end table when I moved to Napa. I was certain that she had noticed them before, but she had never said anything. It was just as well: I hadn't wanted to draw attention to the photos by putting them out so much as to be able to look at them and have them be looked at, which I had not wanted for some twenty-five years. My mother was in one.

"She's beautiful," Daisy said.

"She was," I agreed.

"People stay beautiful," she told me. "My grandma in Taiwan is beautiful. I like old people. I've never met her. She doesn't speak English. That's you," she pointed.

I nodded. "When I was seven."

Daisy's eyes lit with terrible excitement.

"You were seven . . ." she said, and her tongue seemed to plug her mouth from excess of astonishments.

"You know seven," I sighed. "Seven in the summer."

"Did you like it, Gregory, when you were seven in the summer?"

"Oh, we did what we could," I said. "Things got worse, things got better. There wasn't much to look forward to really in Pocahontas—unless you count the circus."

"Circuses are fun," Daisy chided, as if this were a point I had never considered. She crossed and recrossed a pink denim leg pocketed with a stitching of Beauty and the Beast. "Arsenio Hall says they are."

"Well, our circus was dreary," I said. "Fun it was not." With a straw I took an emboldening hit from a tall blended yogurt drink and returned the drink to a coaster. "The fun," I said, "was how my grandmother loved to walk my sisters and me through town to the circus grounds in our new circus clothes. She was a very polite, sturdy pioneer lady, my grandmother, who liked to do things a particular way, and each year, on the Saturday before the circus arrived, goodness knows why, she liked to take us to the Rough Rider store on the square and buy us one new article of clothing. For the Big Top. Sometimes a hat too. It was a custom for her."

"After Thanksgiving dinner, my grandmother Lillian from Long Beach takes us on the bus with her to Laughlin for the All-Night Roulette Roundup. We stay in the Kid Center. We like it."

"Well, then, you know just the sort of thing I'm talking about."

"But why was it dreary if it was a custom?" Daisy asked.

"Each summer when we walked to the circus," I said, "dressed in our new circus clothes, my three sisters would always say to our grandmother that this circus was not only going to be better than last, it was going to be great—the best circus ever. They would invent all kinds of new attractions that we were going to see there, and I, the littlest, would believe them, just as I had the year before."

"And was it? Was it better?"

"Oh, I would get my hopes so high, waiting for how great it was going to be—all of us strolling together through town in our new plaid shirts and boots—but I'll tell you what: that circus never really was anything but smelly animals and clowns."

Daisy giggled and laughed. She had a nice, strong, white set of teeth. It is easy to tell my favorite children. They are the first to put on sophistication, but really they are delighted most by stories in which a terrible stench comes into the room or someone injures himself by slipping.

"The monkeys stank. The elephants sloshed up dirt and manure. When the elephants tromped around in a circle, little patties of brown stuff flew up onto our new collars and sometimes in our mouths. I left that town as soon as I could and never looked back."

"There's a lot to do in L.A.," Daisy said. "You should try it."

"Yes, I know, remember? I've lived there, too."

Apparently, Mr. Culver had a hard time reaching Xiao Mei in his unit while he was away, because he phoned me more than once, out of breath, to pass on messages to her saying when he would be returning to Napa. Then that day would come, and he would call again out of breath and say a different day, and then would not come that day. After a while, I stopped forwarding his messages.

A dry heat moved in. The shingles outside my kitchen window blazed with new-minted seven-color beauty. Uzziel was refreshing the house, one now saw clearly, from the top down. Under his direction, a pair of workers scraped and washed the tar-black gabled roof of moss and various residues. Xiao Mei and the children pulled weeds, husked sweet corn, walked to the open market. Tuesday evening at pink sunset, all residents of the house, along with the workers, gathered at the backyard table and ate basil and tomato from the garden, dripping with olive oil from Uzziel's father's orchard, on toasted slices of the baker's sour batard. The chef brought out a cold squid salad. More than once I told myself, This valley could be home.

One unsettling episode involving Xiao Mei occurred that Tuesday at dinner. I have thought about it often, as a dark cloud over what was otherwise a bright stretch of time for her. Xiao Mei, Uzziel, Stone, and the workers were seated on one side of the backyard table; Daisy, I, the chef, the baker, and a couple of their friends were on the other. Xiao Mei was shooting quick doe-eyes at Uzziel, and Uzziel was casting sidelong glances of strong-chinned chivalry at her. It was neither here nor there. I would have paid the flirtation, or whatever it was, little mind, except that at some point during dinner, Daisy reached across my hand for the butter dish, and after bringing it toward her, patted my hand affectionately (indeed, politely, since she had reached across my hand for the butter). At which moment, Xiao Mei, nudging against Uzziel's shoulder, announced to the table that Daisy had a big crush on me.

At first, Daisy protested, denying that she had a crush on me of any size. I expected, hoped the matter would drop there. Then Xiao Mei announced that Daisy had *told* her that she had a crush on me: *a big crush*. Daisy became embarrassed (I know I was too), and the more embarrassed she became, the more Xiao Mei repeated that Daisy had a big crush on me, adding that I was the love of her life, and so on. Xiao Mei even told me that if I waited a few years, she would marry Daisy to me. Daisy blushed and deflected her mother's remarks. In all likelihood I blushed too, all the while wondering whether this line of talk by Xiao Mei was part of some coded ritual that she had going with Uzziel. Perhaps I was being oversensitive. But as I say, Xiao Mei continued speaking this way for some time, telling us how fast her American daughter was growing up, and how much Daisy liked to wear lipstick and sexy clothes and attract men, and I thought I could see from the faces around the table that the others, including Stone, wished she would stop too. There was a ferocity that came out in her. Pushing, pushing. You could practically see her in the ring with a spirit. No one knew what to say to her. Her laughter came in attacks.

Mr. Culver showed up at my door on a Saturday at midday wearing shorts and loafers and a pair of old bifocals that did not hold straight on his nose. He reminded me immediately of an advisor I had once had in college in Massachusetts who, during the summers, would go to great pains to convince others how at leisure he was. Mr. Culver's expression, to me at least, showed no awareness that he had been away from our house for nearly three weeks and that however he had left things here, they could not possibly be that way now. He was holding out the pocket video game he had given Stone, which he said he had found just now in the backyard under a chili pepper plant. The sliding plastic cap over the empty battery compartment was missing, and Mr. Culver was sure that Stone had willfully broken and then discarded the game. I insisted this was not so. Stone had done virtually nothing but play that game, I said. It was a third hand to him; he never stopped bleeping.

"Where is he now?" Mr. Culver asked.

I told him that Xiao Mei and the kids were out boating with Uzziel on Lake Berryessa. He asked if I had informed Xiao Mei that he would be coming to town today, and I said I had not.

When I next saw Mr. Culver, he was outside on the lawn, inspecting the bold new story and a half of paint, along with hoses, ladders, vents, scaffolding, the feathered stalks of pampas grass, indeed every inch and item of his property. He looked—and I mean no generalization of character by this—more than a bit off-kilter. He was scribbling notes on a yellow pad, what appeared from his expression to be some vast and intricate form of accounting. He kept pacing the lawn, running his hand through his hair, not patting down the hair he had displaced.

Some time near dusk, Uzziel, Xiao Mei, and the kids pulled up to the house in a silver pickup driven by one of Uzziel's weightlifting buddies—a ranger, I happened to know. Everyone's cheeks were pink. The kids, in the back, bounced around a couple of new rubber-animal lake toys, little rafts. It was the most their age I had ever seen them look.

Stone was first to react to the BMW on the drive. It was as if a bottle rocket had been set off. He flew across the lawn against his mother's call, dinged a rear hubcap with his toe, then mowed his hand along the heads of some purple agapanthuses along the front of the house, sending florets spinning. Uzziel caught up with Stone; he squatted to look the boy in the eye, and Stone shoved him in the chest. Uzziel reasoned with his hands. Stone made fists. Xiao Mei moved toward her son like an old woman without grace. When she finally reached him, she shook her head no, seized him by the neck, and dragged him up the porch steps wailing. "Stone, remember how happy you've been," I heard Daisy say. "Just keep being happy the way you have been. You can."

A stupor fell over the house that night. Two bottles of wine were drunk in Mr. Culver's unit, the green empties posted along the wall outside the door. Stone's piercing wails desisted. Perhaps for the first time since I'd known Uzziel, he appeared at a loss. He sat alone at the back table in the dark under the pear tree, smoking clove cigarettes. Later, when the air was still and the insects made their spry, buffeting sounds, you could almost feel something beneath the house hit the kind of quiet bump that makes people hold onto whatever is most precious to them.

The next morning, fairly early, I heard voices outside on the lawn. I looked out and saw that sprinklers made rainbows in other yards; sunflowers stood at attention; porch swings lilted. A family of Hispanic evangelicals with attaché cases walked up the sidewalk, whispering into each other's ears. Standing back from the house, Uzziel was speaking to Mr. Culver in even measures, solemnly defending his twenty-one-color paint design. His ankles were locked, and he was quoting verbatim from Mr. Culver's book about Victorian renovation, from the chapter titled, "Treatise on the Artistic Use of Colors in the Preservation, Ornamentation and Glorification of Your Latter-Nineteenth-Century Home." He appeared to be delivering a kind of mild, transcendent oratory. He cited illustrations, plates, references, a passage on the value of completing difficult tasks. Mr. Culver, roving between Uzziel and the house, fired back, saying that he had agreed to fund painting of the street side exterior with three colors only: mustard, maroon, and sylvan green. All the rest of this hysterical handicraft—the nectarine around Uzziel's bay window, the aquamarine of the millwork—had been a fantasy of Uzziel's, an outburst of delirious narcissism. Did Uzziel have no self-control? Was this his boyish sense of entitlement? One peacock in the house was enough, Mr. Culver said, without the house being turned into a peacock in the peacock's own image.

I could see that Uzziel was provoked, and I expected him to fly into a proper Mediterranean rage: *I will pay for it all myself!*

I am doubling your property value! Who is the Narcissus here, sir! etc. I expected the usual escalation of passion, the usual battle, with Mr. Culver demanding the last word and the young man's will ultimately prevailing. Instead, Uzziel stared at Mr. Culver with what I saw to be a wholly new emotion in him, a grim resignation, a weariness, as though he could see no way to stop from feeling sorry for all of us. He looked like he might cry. I listened for the woman's name to be spoken. Uzziel bowed his head slightly. A blue rental car drew up and idled along the curb, tourists on the way to the river, gawking and pointing out their window at our half-repainted mansion.

The next day, a Monday, Mr. Culver and Xiao Mei took off in the BMW without telling the children where they were going. I found this out at half past ten when from my window, I heard Daisy shrieking at Stone, who was flying around in the middle of the street with his arms spread wide, fingers firing imaginary gunshots, *pop pop*, at the rooftops. Cars had stopped in both directions. An elderly neighbor (the one, if I am not mistaken, who played showtunes on the piano) was trying also to coax the boy to the sidewalk. I knocked on Uzziel's door: not home. I took the staircase at a speed I did not know myself capable of. On the porch a young woman I vaguely recognized from town leaned against the railing in the shade, as though she didn't mind waiting all day in oblivion to glimpse Uzziel and have him walk right past her. I told her to go away, there was nothing here for her and never would be.

Goodness knows how, Daisy and I convinced Stone to stop shooting rooftops and walk with us to the skate park. At first, the boy looked at us from the middle of the street as though our suggestion were the craziest he had ever heard. He sniffed the air just in front of him; even in open space, he could seem in a corner.

"You like skate parks," Daisy reminded Stone.

"It's a sanctuary for our disaffected youth," I added, trying to strike a note of levity.

The boy shuffled off the asphalt with exaggerated style.

"You talk so weird," he said to me, "it's amazing you're not dead."

At the skate park—a row of subterranean paved hills steepening in grade, cut out of the earth opposite the cinema parking lot—the kids were flipping about on their boards, listening to thumping music in small tribes. Some dyed-hairs in black make-up and dog collars milled by a sanctioned graffiti wall. We three sat on a concrete bench and looked in different directions. It was one of those moments like in the dream when you lift the neighbor's johnny jump-ups out of the ground and there's a dim cave underneath lined with scrolls containing all the secrets of the town, but when you climb down to read them, you can't crack the code. Daisy covered her ears, I think as a protest against the aggressive song lyrics. The violent rhythms tranquilized Stone, almost like a lullaby, for about ten minutes. Then he said he was leaving to go see if his mother was home.

At the house, Mr. Culver's apartment door was wide open, and Xiao Mei was on her knees at the foot of his bed, stuffing her blue duffel bag. I could not see her face. "She wants to leave," Mr. Culver was repeating, pacing the floor.

The children ran to their mother and tucked themselves under her arms. The woman continued windmilling garments into the bag.

"Take me, take me, take me," they said.

"Just when she's getting better," Mr. Culver cried.

That evening, a little while after I heard him come in, I paid a visit to Uzziel. He was alone, unboxing a bossa nova jazz record that had arrived from one of the several CD clubs he belonged to. We stood at his kitchen counter. The ashen mountains and pasture lands of East Napa were still, their obsidian glitter darkened. Some swallows outside the window were swinging behind each other, repositioning themselves on a wire. I told Uzziel how Xiao Mei and the kids had driven off today with Mr. Culver, how I had said goodbye for him, and he nodded with an expression reminiscent of the one prescribed to old Chinese men in the movies, a possessing-the-inscrutable-wisdom-of-the-East type of thing. I mentioned that I missed having the kids around and that the house felt a little spooky. He nodded again. He made lemonade, and we sipped it.

In the weeks that followed, Uzziel's silences deepened. His groundskeeping tapered in quality and breadth, becoming as spare as, I think, his natural dignity would permit. He and Mr. Culver did not speak; I transmitted Mr. Culver's phone messages to him, and when Mr. Culver visited the house, he and Uzziel exchanged notes on sheets of yellow lined paper. No agreement between them was reached about finishing the paintwork, and after a point, the latex cans on the scaffolding crusted in the heat, and the house began to look as though it knew it were condemned to spend its next term of life wearing a set of sadly flamboyant, mismatched pajamas. In October, two contractors came round and, of all things, began laying down plastic and loudly sanding the main lobby floor! I had to take this as an indication that Mr. Culver did not mind driving Uzziel to madness—though, in fairness, one had to applaud Mr. Culver's impulse to refinish the fine herringbone inlay. Uzziel dug in his heels. His melancholy persisted.

About a month later, at one of their Tuesday dinner parties, the chef and the baker announced at dessert that they were both going to marry their longtime partners. Wild cheering erupted, along with a chant of "When When When When." "Right now," the chef declared, and she brought out from the kitchen door a lady minister, and a wonderful double ceremony was performed and we were all witnesses and the meringue was exquisite and I wondered if the mood in the house might at last become less somber.

It did and it didn't. It was the time of year when grapes were being harvested all over the valley, and the night air was pungent and dark with the odor of ferment. One smelled pumpkin bread at dawn. I remember that the relentless optimism that had taken hold in me and carried me to Napa, that had been carrying me for nearly a year, relented some, and I began to catch glimpses that there was a way of viewing things that I had not perceived before: something apart from optimism and pessimism, hope and despair, involving a faculty more immediate, morning to morning. I was falling in with a social group, some ceramic sculptors who had gone to art school in the Midwest and had moved out to California a number of years earlier to build a twenty-five-foot anagama kiln into the side of a volcanically formed mountain. A handful of men and women of various ages, in love with fire. I liked how they lived.

It was the Saturday after the chef and baker married. I was

packing to go to an all-night firing at the mountain when Mr. Culver called. He was out of breath, he was choking on breath.

"I want you to deliver a message to Uzziel," he said. "Not that he deserves any favors from me. But I know he'll want to know. I know he had feelings for her."

Mr. Culver moaned. He said that Xiao Mei had been killed yesterday. In her living room. By the guy who had roughed her up over the summer.

"She brought him right in the house," he said. "I fly her back to Los Angeles, and she invites him right in. Rolls out the red carpet for him. But you saw her in action. You saw the willful streak."

I could hardly open my throat. Dear goodness God, I said.

"Animal was staying with her for at least a week before it happened, they're telling me now. Meaning, she was keeping it all on the side. As if nobody gave a shit. And we kept up with her, too. Believe me. I never gave up on that woman. Somebody else might have, but I didn't."

And the kids? Where were the kids? I asked.

"That I don't know," he said. "The detective told me it all went down about an hour before they came home from school, but who exactly found her, I don't know."

Neither of us knew quite what to say for a moment after that.

Collecting myself, I told Mr. Culver that I thought he had acted well. I told him he had nothing to regret, even in the face of this awful kind of thing.

I remember using that phrase: *this awful kind of thing.*

"I would have put her kids in goddamn private school up here," he said. "But she courted it. She let it right in the door. Not a goddamn angel could have protected that woman."

I said that I was very, very sorry.

Mr. Culver was silent now for a long while. He whispered again that he knew Uzziel would want to know. He whispered again that he knew Uzziel had had feelings for the woman. I suggested that it might be nice if Mr. Culver called Uzziel and extended, so to speak, the olive branch. We still had the house. I said I had suspected for some time that there had been mixed feelings between them about the woman.

Such a call took place, though I don't know its substance. Uzziel flew to the funeral—neither he nor Mr. Culver ever mentioned to me seeing the other. After Uzziel returned, he dropped his computer programming courses, gave the house a thorough cleaning, borrowed the ranger's pickup and moved out. Vanished, really. I have been told that he now lives in an East-West vegetarian meditation village somewhere in Humboldt County, but I don't know if that's true. The burial seemed to have made a profound impression on him, though he described little of it to me. About twenty people attended: friends of Xiao Mei's, coworkers, the ex-husband. None of Xiao Mei's family. The gravesite ceremony, arranged by the ex-husband, was presided over by a rabbi and conducted almost entirely in Hebrew, which nobody there spoke. The boyfriend, I take it, the killer, was already in jail. Uzziel said he tried more than once to speak with the kids, to listen, say anything, but they did not acknowledge him. Daisy, her face empty, at the hip of her paternal grandmother, stood straight at the open grave, staring at nothing. Stone, in dress-up clothes, ran circles around a cypress tree nearby, repeating to a second-grade friend the same few gory details about his mother's manner of death.

Eventually, I guess, we all moved out of Mr. Culver's house, kept moving north: Uzziel to wherever he went; the chef and baker and their wives to the area up past the old Greystone Cellars, where they have the Culinary Institute now; and me to this farmhand's little white house on a terraced Syrah vineyard above Pope Valley, on a piece of property collectively owned by my friends, the ceramic sculptors from the Midwest. As I say, I like the way these people live. They take care, and they're not fooled by tomorrow or the next place. The group's leader, if I can say such a thing, is the sculptor Armond Grandbatteau, who grew up in this county. He brought the others out. It was he who built the twenty-five-foot kiln I have mentioned, handpicking and setting each stone in a formation I am told has its origins in three-thousand-year-old Chinese climbing-dragon kiln design, though it looks to my novice eyes much like a silo that has toppled over and become embedded in the foot of the mountain. A smokestack rises off one side.

Armond is my age; he works every day in the studio with a commitment I have never seen. His work is explosive, gorgeous, personal, public, and there is constantly more of it: bullet-holed slabs, spheres with missing sections, obelisks of clay dug from old mining areas an hour northeast. During the summers, he and the others operate a youth ceramic camp they established on the property. This, too, was his idea. You apply to the camp with slides and writing samples, and to be admitted you have only to be between twelve and seventeen years old and very weird—a freak, to use Armond's favorite word. Armond lost his sister and mother to suicide young, and of course AIDS has taken its toll. His zeal is of the art-is-salvation variety. When he and the others go through the camp applications, he laughs riotously at the self-portraits and poems the kids include, kissing some, holding others against the sun. Whatever he sees in these troubled drawings usually will make him drag on a cigarette, sigh dramatically, and exclaim something like, "Oh, Terrence," (that is, to Terrence, his imaginary lover) "what are we going to do to keep *this* train from flying off the tracks!"

Also in the group are Karen who lost a breast and Gabriela with the housefire burn-scars and Kemper from fourteen sets of Texas foster parents, and on and on, the stories are not less or more remarkable than anyone else's. Some sell their work in San Francisco and New York; others at travelling shows; others work entirely for their own satisfaction, giving most of what they make away. And they have their day jobs—waiting, gardening, teaching, sales—but these twenty-four-hour fires they get going, this pit, this furnace, firing to more than two thousand degrees, this stone oven, crackling casket of flame, pairs adding wood in all-night shifts, dozens gathered, in sleeping bags, under the fresh night sky, under the sun, in canvas tents, air uncorked, smokestack swirling, billowing, glowing molten-red, smoke whipping the face, brick trays of a thousand pots and urns, shapes turned and cast and set in the earth, bowls, cups, oranging in the casket, glazing, ashing, transforming through the night . . . Who is to say nothing is redeemed? The kids in the summers love this, even the ones who insist they are not freaks. I have brought my homely sister Emily from Davenport and her Born-Again husband Bruce to see a firing, and they too are astonished. Their oldest daughter Cara, now a bookish adolescent scholar of anagama technique and a devotee of Armond's, writes postcards to him from Iowa: THE RANDOMNESS OF THE GLAZING MAKES IT SO YOU *HAVE* TO LIVE FOR THE IMPERFECT! The morose goth teens and arty high school outcasts join us when they like. We will send notices to Daisy and Stone when they come of age. Someone is always recommending someone who will benefit from the camp. Twice a year—after crush and before planting—the group holds a big show in Napa to raise money to bring in kids from other places. Shows are staged along the river in a tin warehouse once used for dynamite storage. The work sells out; people buy what they can. These are memorials, markers, figures, vases, also beautiful things with no purpose.

PANELS

1

[Before she left, she gave him]

Before she left, she gave him three little yellow wild roses. "Where'd you get these?" he asked, and she said, "Found them in a field. Behind the Sandovals' property." Now the petals had dried out but they weren't so dry that they didn't stick to everything in their house—the desk, the rug, the handle of the sauté pan, the kitchen counter, the furnace. She dealt with the separations better than he did. Of course, she was always the one leaving. Separating was almost her nature. And yet he, who craved frequent physical touch, had always liked this about her. How isolated she could make herself. What it was to yearn for her, to long. For days after she left, he could feel the touch of his fingers on her backbone, the sensation of her hair brushing his cheek.

He peeled all the petals off of everything they had stuck to and put them in a small bowl in the kitchen window. This was the digging in. It was going to be email now and phone cards for a long while. They weren't married, and he doesn't know what she would say if he asked her. He's not going to ask her.

He has friends in town, which helps. Unlike her, he has no vocation. His vocation, to a great extent, is her. He has helped build a studio behind the house where she can do her work. He performs the tasks she prefers not to do herself. He takes pride in her. He no longer worries, as he did when they first met, that she does not regard him as an equal. Nor does he worry that if his illness returns, she will abandon him. She makes him wonderful, simple gifts. She always comes back. Things have never been better.

[He loved her penmanship]

He loved her penmanship, so he tried to invent ways to get her to write to him. But the harder he tried, the less she wrote. Then he tried not trying. After that, she didn't write to him at all.

[What can she say to Jean]

What can she say to Jean, the mother of the child who has just died. It is after the funeral, and Roni is standing over a large plate of sliced meats. She works at an office with Jean. They are not close friends but it was important to her that she go to the funeral. She herself is unable to have children, and a part of her thinks this makes her less fit to speak to Jean than are other women who have, or can have, children. She's had thoughts like these for many years now. Less fit. Less able. No one here knows she cannot have children. And what is she doing thinking of herself, rather than Jean?

She used to think there was something to say for every occasion, but as she's gotten older she's questioned that. It would be best if there was always a right thing to say. Then you'd know it and you'd say it, and the person would receive it in the way you had intended. The boy was eight, and it was the end of a long illness. Jean and her husband, Mike, also have a daughter, twelve. The three of them are walking around the busy house, welcoming guests, refilling plates of bread, fruit, and sweets and starting coffee. If a stranger walked in the door and surveyed the scene, would the stranger think that an eight-year-old child had just been buried?

Maybe the thing is to lighten up. After all, she should be doing what she can to make things easier on Jean, on all the mourners, not increase the suffering in the room. But she feels very sad herself, and her sadness is increasing, so much that she doesn't know whether she will be able to say hello to Jean today before she has to wave goodbye.

[After the play, she drove him]

After the play, she drove him back to his car, but instead of letting him out, she double-parked and turned on the overhead light. It was their third date. He had wondered if this moment was going to come. He was about to take her by the hand and turn in to kiss her when he noticed choppy scars on the inside of her wrist.

"I must not have wanted to see them," he said.

"I was so young," she said.

"When I was twenty," he said, "my mother swallowed a bottle of painkillers, then called me to rush her to the hospital."

"My husband found me," she said. "I wish I was still in touch with him. He knew me so well."

"I told her I'm not driving you to the hospital. I shouldn't even take your calls."

"He didn't take it personally," she said. "That was the amazing thing."

On their first date, they had walked through a public garden, trying to follow a map, but they kept getting happily lost together. On their second date, they tried following computer-generated directions to a restaurant and ended up in another neighborhood entirely. They ate there and the food turned out to be delicious.

"I don't know if I'd want to keep dating you," he said.

"I'm not surprised," she said. "You seem like a coward."

He leaned over and softly kissed her lips.

Then they began to talk about the play for a while, which had had a large improvisational component.

[They met in Taos, over live country music]

They met in Taos, over live country music, in a hotel in the center of town. She was on an artist's residency; he was on vacation by himself. He asked her to dance; she refused. She was drinking ice-cold Pacificos with a couple other artists from the residency. He sat down next to her. After each new song started, he bowed slightly toward her, smiled, and asked her to dance. He liked her small hands, which, he could see, were accustomed to physical work. Her face had a working-class cast. After a few songs, she said okay. They danced awkwardly, he wanting to press up against her, she wanting to keep a distance. Then they both switched to frozen margaritas.

Six months later, in the dead of winter, he visited her at her home in County Kerry, Ireland. Before long, he was irritating her with his thin blood, his indifference to dogs, his unfamiliarity with horses, his inability to tie a knot in a piece of rope, and his all-around softness. The sex was good. Three months later, they met in Texas for the wedding of one of his childhood friends. She liked Bob Wills on the CD player, Gruene Hall. But, to her annoyance, he kept asking her to make a commitment to him. Three months later, she visited him at his home in Los Angeles. By the end of the first week, she missed being away from her sculpture studio. She didn't particularly like Los Angeles either. Some days it felt like a parking lot. Others a giant suburb. At least it had birds and trees. She cut the visit short by a week. Two weeks later, she sent him a handwritten note from an island in the Inner Hebrides, off the coast of Oban, Scotland. It said, I'm probably cut out to be alone.

He went back to dating women on the Internet. But he didn't stop thinking about her. She had never married. The one man she had ever gotten really close to, a Cypriot, had died at 46. Her father had also died at 46. She was 46 now. He was a few years younger. Maybe he would be the one who drew her out of her isolation. He didn't hear from her for nine months. When he did, it was to say sorry she had been out of touch. First she had gotten Lyme disease, then her brother had been involuntarily admitted to a psychiatric hospital, then her sister had gotten Hodgkin's Lymphoma. Do you want to see me again? he asked by email. She didn't answer. He started listening several times a day to Buck Owens singing "Under Your Spell Again."

A few months later, he began seeing a dark-complected Bulgarian paralegal. In some ways, she didn't hold a candle to the sculptor. Not nearly as interesting nor as well-put-together. But after a few nights of holding hands, drinking whiskey, and kissing in cars, he saw that she liked him and wasn't afraid of getting involved. No more long distance! Yet if he committed to her, he would have to close the door on the sculptor, who was—oddly—sending him frequent, optimistic emails. Life with the sculptor would never be boring. But wasn't she also squirmy? What if he visited her one more time in Ireland? While he was considering how to settle on the right woman, he didn't consider that he might lose both.

2

[It's pomegranate season, and every evening]

It's pomegranate season, and every evening at the language school he brings her a firm, bulging, red pomegranate, which he quarters on break with a small knife. The pomegranate always sprays red juice in her direction, so before he begins to cut, she makes a show of holding up two sheets of loose-leaf paper in front of her, so that she will not get juice on her blouse.

They met three months ago at the school in Van Nuys. She had been studying there for half a year; it was his first day. He entered the room quietly, looked around, then walked over and sat at her table. There was an empty chair between them. The teacher asked him who he was. He said Hayk Grigorian. A minute later, the teacher saw Hayk glance across the table at Lilit Stepanyan and blush.

Hayk and Lilit sit at the same table every evening; on breaks, they crowd around in the halls with six Armenian classmates. They all leave at the same time each night. One Saturday, the group drives to Malibu beach for the day. They are in their twenties and early thirties, most smokers—though not Hayk or Lilit—the men with shaved heads under baseball caps, the women comely, all on student visas.

The teacher gives a take-home assignment. Write a story that could take place only in your home country. The next evening, each student stands before the class and reads his story aloud. One takes place on the Armenian holiday of Vardavar. Another is about a persecuted Baha'i in his forties who flees Iran to

Turkey on horseback to reunite with his family. Finally, Hayk reads his story, but his pronunciation is not good and the teacher can only make out the words *love, special, woman,* and *home.* The class politely applauds, and Hayk, blushing, walks out of the room. Thirty seconds later, he reappears with a dozen red roses and puts them in front of Lilit. Everyone hurrahs.

Three weeks later, the teacher conspires with Hayk to surprise Lilit. He shuts off the classroom lights as if he is about to show a grammar video. Instead, in a video made by Hayk, a cartoon of a pulsing heart on legs appears. Armenian music plays. Then photos come on of Hayk and Lilit climbing rocks along the Pacific coast. Of them dancing. Using English subtitles, Hayk declares his love for Lilit. After the video ends, Hayk stands at the back of the class holding two dozen red roses.

A soft-spoken young man who rebuilds engines, Hayk goes on making these displays of love for Lilit, and it's not always easy to gauge her responses. She smiles. She nods. Once in a while, she laughs, as if relieved. She holds an M.D. and is studying for some tests so that she can practice medicine in the U.S. She has always seemed older than Hayk. One evening in the computer lab, clutching three dozen red roses, she glances at the teacher. She appears content and yet unsure if this is her moment. Hayk's displays are big. They are familiar to her. He is doing what he is supposed to do.

[Speaking has always been hard for her]

Speaking has always been hard for her. Now forty-two, she is almost completely unable to do it. Words get jammed behind her face, caught in her throat, and she tries to start sentences but almost always swallows the sounds before they have the chance to form. This embarrasses her, which makes her cheeks redden and her eyes get wet until she is almost completely engulfed in a loneliness that at one time her boyfriend Gavin was able to penetrate and solve. She blames herself for not being able to get him to stay, though at times she can admit to herself that one doesn't make the best case for oneself as a partner while one is undergoing chemo and radiation.

To Gavin's credit, he waited until she was free of cancer before moving out. And he is still paying the rent on their two-story love/work space—as they used to call it—though she isn't going to let that go on much longer. She will move out.

He is seven years younger than she and co-owns a restaurant where he is head chef, and where, until breast cancer, she waited tables. He works fourteen-hour days, so there wasn't much chance he would meet anyone, except at work, and that was what had happened. He found the new girlfriend the way he found her: she was a customer.

He had been a junkie when they met. He still credits her for helping him kick it. They were together almost eight years. She had never wanted anyone else.

She is determined to stop waiting tables and do something creative. She has given up on sculpture, which she studied in art school. She could not stomach the reviews, when there were reviews—*uncertain flights of whimsy* was one phrase a tiny East Bay publication had used to describe the playful, painted clay forms in her first solo show, whose opening Gavin had catered. Now she has an idea to make high-quality bib aprons out of cotton and hemp. One blue stripe across the pocket will be her stamp. She has a friend who makes a thousand decorative ceramic balls per month for Williams-Sonoma; another travels the world designing store windows. She had been getting health insurance through Gavin's restaurant; now she has none.

Gavin's new girlfriend, Ariella, she has heard, is perky and makes dangling silver earrings, which she sells at shops on Piedmont, College, and Telegraph Avenues. Ariella is four years younger than Gavin and, she has heard, wears cream-colored sheer blouses and long, gauzy skirts. Pat is not only never going to step inside Gavin's restaurant again, she's going to avoid that whole stretch of Grand Avenue, above Lake Merritt, where the restaurant is, lest she run into them.

To get her apron business off the ground, she is going to have to speak. She is going to have to cold-call potential contacts, distributors. But her friend who makes the ceramic balls will help her do that. They have known each other since art school. Once he sees she's serious, he'll get behind her. She's banking on that.

[Robert's friend Shelli called. Something had happened]

Robert's friend Shelli called. Something had happened to their friend Lyle. Late the previous Saturday night, Lyle had been walking down a side street in West Hollywood after visiting a gay nightclub, when he was grabbed by two strangers, shoved into the back of a van, beaten almost to death, and left bloodied with a fractured skull in a parking lot in Norwalk. He had just been released from the hospital with a plate in his head. Did Robert want to go visit him with her?

Lyle was more Shelli's friend than Robert's. Robert usually kept a distance from gay men. When, a couple years ago, Lyle had rented out a downtown loft space for his fortieth birthday and brought in pulsing electronic music and shirtless male go-go dancers with low-slung shorts, Robert had felt uncomfortable and left after half an hour.

Now Robert felt something different, something strange. He felt as if he himself had been attacked. But he did not go with Shelli to visit Lyle.

Days passed, and Robert kept thinking about Lyle, a gentle soul from the Midwest with a receding hairline, who worked for Disney as an animator and never had a bad word for anyone. At last Robert called Lyle and asked if he could come over. Lyle sounded surprised; he said of course.

Lyle unlocked the door of his bungalow in Burbank. His head was shaved; a crack zagged down the top of his head where he had been sewn up. An eye socket was bruised. He seemed in good spirits. What a lovely temperament he had! Robert had never had a long-term female partner; he was aware that some people, including Shelli, suspected he was gay. Shelli sometimes dropped hints to this effect but rather than deny he was gay, which Shelli might construe as protesting too much, Robert let the hints go unanswered.

They sat in Lyle's living room, where Lyle told Robert everything he could remember about the incident, starting with the two white boys in Skechers sneakers, not older than nineteen, who had dragged him into the back of the van and beat and tortured him until he blacked out. Later he woke up in the hospital. As Lyle spoke, Robert stared at his lips. They looked wet and innocent and full. Robert could imagine putting his lips to Lyle's lips. This was not a thought he wanted to have.

Lyle could use a glass of wine. Did Robert want to join him? Robert declined. He was getting uncomfortable even though Lyle wasn't doing anything to make him uncomfortable. Lyle didn't even seem to care if Robert was gay. Robert said he would have a glass of water, if that was okay. Lyle said of course it was okay. Then they sat with their different drinks and talked and listened until Robert needed to leave.

[*Just before dawn, he smelled smoke*]

Just before dawn, he smelled smoke. This was it, he thought. The thing that was finally going to break them. He kissed her soft hair. Then he crawled across the bed, opened the blinds, and looked out the screen at the street. Nothing. Nothing but a burning smell that seemed to be originating outside.

"Come back," she mumbled, and reached for him.

His skull felt like it was in a clamp. He had moved out here last year for a job after getting his Ph.D., and now that she had her B.A., she was making sure she wanted to join him. The age difference was big. But what he wasn't telling her was bigger: That he couldn't see having children. Couldn't see getting married. That he could be turning into his father, who, at the same age, with dark bags under his eyes and almost unable to speak, had gone away for eight months to a psychiatric clinic in Kansas, then went back to Kansas four years later.

Tears started rolling down his cheeks. The medication wasn't working. And anyway, he didn't always take it because it interfered with his sex drive.

"Where are you?" she said.

They were living in a four-story brick apartment house that had gone up in the 1920s. There was another just like it next door. Across the street was a Chinese preschool called Mind Champs. Was the school on fire? How come no sounds?

And why couldn't he always remember that this girl was more perfect for him than any he was ever going to find? When you love someone this way, this one time, you must cast aside every doubt and go for it. He came back over and kissed her hair.

Groggily she sat up and put an arm around him. "Just because there's smoke," she said, "doesn't mean something's wrong with us."

He crawled over to the window and looked outside. It was daybreak, and in front of the building next door, people were silently congregating in the street, staring up at their building, in pajamas and bathrobes. Then a hum began to rise. As if from a hive.

"The building next door's on fire," he said.

"Come back," she said. "They'll put it out."

The buzzing grew louder, the smell of burning mattresses, burning clothes. By the time sirens went up, who knew how much would be lost?

He felt as if he were in an interview where he couldn't understand the questions. A white sky was about to tear open.

It had happened to his father. It was coming for him.

[She'd been married twenty years, and for the last nineteen]

She'd been married twenty years, and for the last nineteen they'd slept in separate rooms. They'd tried sex after marrying, while they were still living in China; she could not remember what it felt like. She was not sure they had done it correctly. These days, if she thought about sex at all, it was as something vaguely disgusting, base, which, if accompanied, as it often seemed to be, by strong emotion, would cloud one's entire outlook for the worse.

She met the Jewish man at a corporate communications conference in Chicago. She worked for a utility in Southern California; he was at a commuter railroad in New York. He had an unlined face, youthful, but with white hair and a white moustache and thick progressive eyeglasses that intensified his direct, green eyes. After she'd sat next to him on a panel about crisis management, he asked her to take a cab with him to Pilsen. "Oh, but you must have great Mexican food in Los Angeles," he said. And she said, "I won't tell my husband."

At dinner, she confessed to liking Jewish people; many seemed touched by genius. Mental illness is more like it, he said, and she laughed at this remark, which, if it had been uttered by anyone else, would have been a conversation ender. He told her that Chinese culture fascinated him. The silent shapes of the characters. The vastness of the cuisine. He had once attended a *guqin* concert at the Asia Society in which a young female musician had played songs that were five thousand years old. "Makes Judaism seem like a Johnny Come Lately," he said.

Two nights later, they were dangling their feet off his big white hotel-room bed and talking about divorce. You should try it sometime, he said. By the third night, they were under the covers. What's the big deal with sex? she asked. He unbuttoned her blouse and kissed her neck, collarbone, breast. He passed his fingers down her belly. What are you doing that's making me feel so good? He named what he was touching. Am I the same as every other woman you've been with? Is there anything wrong with my body? Afterwards, while she was still trembling, he whispered that he had never felt anything like this.

They spent every day and night of the conference together. She even slept over the last night and woke up, panicked, at six a.m. and rushed back to her room. Where can we meet next? he asked at breakfast. When they said goodbye, tears were flooding her cheeks.

The next month, they met in Chicago and didn't leave the old brick hotel all weekend. The following month, the same. When he asked why she stayed with her husband, she told him he was her only family. He offered to be her family. She told him her life was in Los Angeles. He offered to move to Los Angeles. She told him a person doesn't just get rid of a twenty-year partner for a man she just met. He said, But can't you see what a life we could have?

At one meeting, she tried pot with him. At another, he put her on her knees and entered her, to her exalted pleasure, from behind. Immediately after that, while he was cradling her in his arms, she told him that she and her husband were horse and horse and that she and he were horse and camel. He objected. She insisted, so much so that when she got back to L.A., she stopped taking his calls and returning his emails, which were now coming in three times a day. There were things she could not change. Her husband spoke her native language. His nieces and nephews were hers. Impossible as it was to explain, she preferred sleeping alone.

BOCA

The night the mayor of Miami gets locked in solitary, I arrive in Boca. The mayor, they are saying on the late news, has hit his wife on the head with a canister or something. A man captioned as The Mayor's Spokesman says, "The mayor plans to post bond tomorrow morning and resume running the city in a normal and timely fashion." Meanwhile my stepfather Leo pounds the tangerine leather sofa, shouting, "Ruining the city? Ruining it? Speak English. Bunch of goddamned schmucks."

My stepfather Leo, a retired golf course developer, is seventy-five (nineteen years older than my mother) and has been dying of different forms of cancer for the past three years. He beats one form and another pops up a few organs away; it's like the doctors are playing the old Club the Weasel game at the county fair. His scalp is freckled and slicked with silver hair at the sides. He actually looks good for a man in any condition. He's got a pencil-thin moustache, and he wears stylish pants around the house. On a given Sunday, when I call from Seattle, Leo will tell me that this morning he thought he was looking in the mirror at the morgue itself, the morgue on two legs, worse than the goddamned Dolphins last week—or that he lost another foot of colon Wednesday, and while the doctors were inside with the lasers and vacuums, they pulled out a few other choice portions of him, lymph nodes and reproductive items and so forth, *so as to keep everything evened out in there, I guess.* But then the next time I'm in town he'll look hale and pink and start telling me stories about an old showgirl he ran into at his club, a girl he dated fifty years ago. Leo has builder's hands.

My mother married Leo right after I finished high school, fled Miami, checked out of the world for a while. He's her second; she's his third. They fell for each other on the first date, I've been told, and she moved straight up to his house in Boca with my sister, now a dancer in Orlando. Leo's house is very large. It's at the back—the ritziest section—of the Boca Starre, an "exclusive-living development" in West Boca composed of the Boca Starre Estates, where Leo and my mother live, the Boca Starre Gallerie, a shopping arcade developed by Leo's friend Ed DeVecque, and the Boca Starre Country Club & Golf Course, which Leo developed. At first it was too weird— to come home and see my mom and sister living in this large house on a cul-de-sac named Verdadera Terrace in a security-gated neighborhood in Palm Beach County. My mom had become rich. Also, Leo's grandkids were about my age, and we were all expected to fraternize, go out for smiling amberjack Caesars at the Whale's Rib in Deerfield Beach, shooters at Wilt Chamberlain's. I'd long had it, by that point, with my mother's men and their offspring. And, to be sure, I was unfair to Leo. I cursed him every time I opened my mouth practically— for being a chauvinist and a patriarch, a racist developer who displaced disadvantaged minority communities to build shrines to leisure and shadily acquired wealth, who destroyed the native habitats of Florida wildlife. I was enrolled in the University of Washington then. Environmental geography with an ethnomusicology minor. And was taking money from my mom, too—via Leo—to pay for it. On visits to Boca, dressed in black T-shirts with anticorporate messages, I would attack my new stepfather using all the progressive social ideas I had been exposed to the semester before, while he in a polo shirt would squint at me with sad, indomitable smiles like I was a nice boy riding the Space Shuttle far, far away.

Now, back in Boca, seeing Leo get up from the tangerine leather couch, virile and ailing Leo, I see he's been a good man to my mom these last twelve years, and where have I been? My mom herself is beginning to sag and creak.

"Your mother is very happy to have you home," Leo tells me. He stands himself carefully, arches his back. My mother is giving the dog a biscuit. "She's been pissing herself for days. Of course, she would like to see you more often. But we enjoy your regal presence whenever we can get it."

We hug. Above the Duraflame fireplace are Leo's golf course development plaques from various city and county entities; nailed to the wall are framed letters that thank him for generous contributions to Democratic causes.

As Leo releases me, the news changes: A group of black voters who filed suit against the governor and secretary of state for having violated their civil rights last Election Day now are filing a new set of suits, alleging even grosser misconduct.

Choked with microphones, the governor defends himself, then praises the great citizens of Florida for their sense of fair play.

"YOU are SO FULL OF SHIT," Leo says and clicks off the screen.

In the kitchen, Leo has pills to take. It's late. But still he manages to look as if Manhattans might be served at any moment and, if so, he will down you two to one. He walks slow, holds himself lightly at the gut. My mother and I split a grapefruit.

The next morning Leo wants us all to take a drive. As a family, he says. Donald Trump is doing something with a golf course up in West Palm, near the airport. Bee-yoo-ti-flee landscaped. Would I like to see?

"Steve might want to drive to the Everglades, wouldn't you?" my mom says.

It's where she and I always went, when I was a boy, to get away.

"Maybe we can do both," I say.

It's my one day in town. My first in two years. I've squeezed it in after a business trip to Sarasota. I now install website tracking software and stuff.

"Ach, you go with your mother," Leo says. "Joey's coming over to see me. I'll see Joey."

"We can all go in one car," my mom says, putting out plates of breakfast for Leo, then me.

"You'd like to see Joey," Leo says to me.

Joey is Leo's favorite grandson. The last time I saw Joey, he was refusing an offer from Leo to start him in real estate, which Leo insists is Joey's true calling. Joey is a bouncer and assistant manager at Nooky Teasers, a five-story dance club in Fort Lauderdale.

"The wood storks are nesting," my mother says, as if she's

offering me seconds on something.

"Christ, I love those birds," Leo says.

"You've been seeing the wood storks nesting right off the Turnpike, haven't you?" my mom says to Leo.

"They're everywhere."

"Has Leo told you about his eyes?"

From his seat at the table Leo leans up and kisses my mom's cheek. My mom blushes. I know that we are all going to go somewhere together today, and I don't mind.

Leo scratches the dog's ears.

"A curious thing," he says.

I have heard the story of Leo's eyes but I like hearing it and Leo tells me it again.

"Since I first got the cancer," he says, "my eyesight has actually improved." My mother sits down by the bright patio door to bask in the light of the telling. "The doctors have come up with no proof, of course—my personal opinion is: they have their work cut out for them not stepping in their own shit half the time—but I repeat: I have never seen better in this life since I first got that cancer."

My mom nods. She really does, by all accounts and evidence, love Leo.

"Just the other day, in fact," Leo continues, "while driving across 75 toward Naples with your mother, I looked up into one of the big bald cypresses out there. You remember this, Natalie. Your mother thought the tree was dead," Leo says. "I said, 'It's not dead: It's winter. It's bare.' And up in that bare tree, way out on the other side of the canal, in the sawgrass marsh, I spotted a little yellow-crowned night heron in the tree. Just perched there, thinking."

"Heron," my mother repeats.

"And I tell you what. I could make out every colored feather on him. *Every* one. It was like I had a telescope. Then, later on—"

"He's not kidding," my mother says.

"How many colors were there?" I ask.

"Several," Leo says.

"He can see the littlest things," my mother says. "Meanwhile, get to the dog."

"Meanwhile," Leo continues, eating, "this dog of ours, Sandy—this overpriced two-year-old pedigree bitch spaniel thing has developed cataracts. I'm sure you already noticed. Look at her pupils."

Leo grabs the spaniel Sandy by the collar and drags her to my feet. I look at her pupils. They are clouded at the centers with a spot of blue film.

"Can't see a goddamned thing—not even her own water bowl," Leo says. "Me, I see everything. What do you make of it?"

Just then, the bell rings.

Echoing from the front of the house I hear Joey yell in, "Are you dead yet, old codger? I need that inheritance."

Joey and Leo kiss. Joey and I clap backs. Joey's got a pair of shoulders—and a bouncer's haircut, long in back. His face has gotten wider. He wears a charm around his neck that must be from a girl. He scratches the dog's ears, then starts telling us all about a new friend of his who's been running a game, a game and a half actually, getting oldsters to buy nice new concrete aboveground cemetery vaults and then sticking them in cut-rate polypropylene models. Hundred-plus percent return on investment.

"Guy's cleaning up," Joey says.

"Surprise," says my mom. "Funeral home fraud. I just hope you're staying away from it."

Joey grabs a bagel and spreads shmear on it.

"So how are you, Stevie," he says. "Good to see you, bud. You still doing your ethno-music stuff? I liked some of that stuff you played me that once. Oh, that's right, you're selling computers now."

A sweet guy. Why am I such a long-faced asshole when I come to Boca? Always expecting the worst. Not taking part.

"We'd love to see you a little more often," he continues, affable.

"Now that Steve's a national business traveler, we just may," Leo says.

"Oh, and hey, I heard about your girlfriend taking the walk on you," Joey adds, pounding his chest once for solidarity. "Man, I. Am. Sorry. Believe Joey. It's happened to all of us."

"I think that's called intruding-into-other-people's-personal-business-without-letting-them-bring-it-up-first," my mother says to her step-grandson. "We've discussed that."

"Whatever," I say.

"Whatever. Exactly," Joey says. "That's what you say when she comes crawling back six months later. You feel me?" He puts out a hand for low-five. Then, to Leo, "Did you say on the phone you want to go over and check out that new Trump course together?"

"Or we could all go out and look at the wood storks nesting," my mom says.

"We also have to factor in lunch," Leo says. "We ought to have a nice lunch somewhere today."

"I know Steve likes the Whale's Rib," my mom says.

"Whale's Rib would be fresh," Joey says. Then, "Wait a second. Back up, back up." He fingers the charm around his neck, weighs it in his palm for a moment. "So Stevie's in town for one day, and you guys want to go take a drive right now, all of us together, and look at freakin' *birds*?"

Ten minutes later, Joey is waiting for us, idling in his white Lexus at the bright grassy edge of 30680 Verdadera Terrace. As we walk down the driveway, he revs the engine and Leo picks up his step: "I'm coming, you son of a bitch." His loafers clap the pavement.

On the radio, the spokesman for the mayor of Miami is explaining why the mayor is still in jail this morning. Reports are being aired now about the children's calls to 911.

"Have you been following that story?" my mom quizzes Joey from the backseat, as Joey switches the station to some kind of booty music and Leo shouts across the front seat to turn that crap down.

"That's your hometown, bud," Joey says to me.

"Decision time," Leo interrupts, now leaning over the burgundy leather bucket seat toward me, his lips and pencil-thin moustache slightly atwitter. He looks like a distant relative of Jackie Gleason in the later years, or a game show host at the end of a long successful network run. "You got one day to enjoy," he says. "What'll make you happy? We'll do it."

Leo claps Joey on the shoulder. Joey's still got a few zits on his cheek.

"Where are the wood storks again?" I say.

"Christ, they're everywhere," Leo says. "I see them at the

toll plazas even. Way up over the pond trees."

"See, I never see any there," my mom says.

Joey cruises. He checks out girls in the left turn lanes, in the ATM driveways. We have not formed consensus; I have not done my part.

After a few minutes in the air-conditioned Lexus, I realize that we are heading not north toward the Donald Trump-developed golf course, nor west toward the cypress preserves, where the best birds are. Nor are we driving south toward Miami. My hometown. We are driving east. Toward the Atlantic. Toward the rest of Boca.

"Oh, shit," my mother says, and covers her mouth. "Aunt Bella's in Boca Community. She was having chest pains yesterday—and they brought her in for tests. They said they were going to keep her overnight. They thought she may have had a small heart attack."

"Don't you think we should visit her?" I say.

"Is that how you want to spend your one day?" Leo says.

"It would be the right thing to do," my mother says.

"I'm just dropping you guys off then," Joey says.

"You don't visit *me* in the hospital," Leo says to Joey, "you get Zilch."

"Are you Bella?" Joey says.

We take the elevator very very slowly to the fourth floor. We've brought Aunt Bella, my grandmother's widowed sister, whose two sons live in Japan and Argentina, a small box of schnecken from Flakowitz Bakery, which Joey and I have already half-finished.

As we rise, Leo informs all riders of the elevator that he does not belong to this hospital. This hospital is run by criminals.

This hospital is a dump. His face looks strangely sallow in the dull elevator light but his jaws flash with charm. My mom straightens his shoulders.

"My plan," he stage-whispers to her, "is ten times better than Bella's plan."

"I know it is. Let's just be there for Bella," my mother says.

In the front of a partitioned room, Bella lies with her eyes closed, her curly wig pushed half over her forehead, wisps of gray around her neck. A tube is in her left arm. Near the foot of the bed an exhausted-looking nurse in scrubs writes something on a chalkboard. Letters and numbers. Some kind of medical code.

"What, are you majoring in hieroglyphics?" Leo says to her.

Leo smooths his moustache. Steps a little closer. The woman has a foreign accent.

"Where you from, sweet?"

The nurse is from Romania. She has square, pretty features. Hard. As Leo speaks, she begins to laugh. Her expression calms. He finds out that she has four children, ages twelve to seventeen. No husband.

"Lucky for the rest of us," he says.

"Life is easier here than in Romania," the woman laughs.

"These kids," Leo harrumphs. "They don't have the first idea."

My mother is talking to Bella now, stroking her shoulder, getting the updates.

Joey, holding out the box of schnecken, says to Bella, "You want these?"

"No, you," Bella says, pushing a hand. She's hoarse and looks scared.

I think of Shark Valley, the spot in the Everglades west of

Miami where my mom and I used to drive when things in our apartment got rough with my dad or whoever. A wilderness. A walking path filled with tourists; other times empty. At sunset, an insect stillness. Heady odor of marshland. My mother and I had known how to be close then. Who we were at least had been who we were. No?

"Yeah," Joey whispers to me, musing, as if he is picking up a conversation we've been having for hours, years. A cart of food trays rolls past. "That one CD you turned me onto with that ginormous guy from Pakistan who taught at your college," he says. "Chicks like that CD."

"Nusrat Fateh Ali Khan," I say. "He died, unfortunately."

Joey sighs and swallows. His hulking upper body tenses in the crowded hospital half-room.

"Come down to Nooky Teasers tonight, I'll set you up," he offers, nudging my elbow lightly, then holding in his breath as if he is taking a bong hit.

Sometimes everyone in the world has a tenderer heart than you do.

"I wish I could," I say. "But I'm flying out first thing in the morning. I just stopped down really to say a quick hi."

Joey throats a laugh. "Lives at the exact opposite end of the country if you can believe," he bellows across the bed to the Romanian nurse, who is now taking Bella's blood pressure. "And he's just stopping down to say hi."

From behind the partition, a man brings up sputum. My mom looks sad, and I would like to take her somewhere.

"Bella," Leo shouts. "You racing me to the morgue?"

Under the best of circumstances, Bella's face does not suggest positive coherent interior experience; today she looks like the last one on at the back of a bus.

"It is possible," Bella answers.

"Don't say that," Mother scolds.

"She's right," Leo corrects himself. "Plenty of good things ahead for every one of us."

Leo is wearing a pants and collared shirt outfit in three shades of green.

"Actually, I don't know if I can hang with you guys all day," Joey says. "This place is starting to make me a little physically ill in here."

The Romanian nurse glances at Joey.

Bella is telling my mom that we don't have to stay. She is telling my mom how nice it was to see us.

A technician at last sees to the man who's been bringing up sputum. Above us, ordinary citizens on television are offering their opinions about whether the mayor of Miami did or did not strike his wife on purpose in their kitchen.

"I thought you guys wanted to go see birds," Joey says.

Back in the white Lexus, gold rims, burgundy interior, Leo says, "Well, we wasted an hour and a half of a perfectly good day, but it was the right thing to do."

Leo's freckled scalp is pink.

"Are you hungry?" my mom asks me.

To our right and left, in the palm-tree-landscaped mall parking lots of Boca, the seniors stroll and weave, pulling out from wallets deli coupons and multiplex discount cards. Visored and besunglassed, they wander in small white flocks through congested traffic lanes toward the covered shops. Lines of Cadillacs and Mercedes wait to pull into spaces.

"You know what that nurse told me?" my mother says to Leo. "She hasn't been able to get her certification yet to practice nursing in America, but since they're having such a hard time getting qualified nurses at Boca Community, they let her practice anyway."

"Like I say, a first-class dump," Leo answers. "My plan would never allow—"

"What are you talking about, Pop?" Joey says. "What about that unlicensed Haitian guy who took your blood that time and left you black and blue on your forearm?"

"Let's not speak that way, please, about the Haitians," my mom says.

"Why not?" Joey says.

"Because it's prejudice, is one."

"It's not prejudice! The guy was unlicensed and incompetent."

"And such hard lives, that's why. It's not for us to judge. Let's just stop judging."

My mom looks at me, wants to know that I agree with her, but I can't look at her. Why? Why? What is my problem?

On a dime Joey says, "We've got a new ten-room Virtual Play Station over on Powerline we could take you to. Oh, but you must have better where you live. Baseball club owned by Nintendo! Hey, let me ask you a question: Does Sir Mix-A-Lot still live in Seattle?"

Out the window I see no wood storks—only roofs and banners and spangled handbags.

Joey's head bobs. He starts to turn up the booty music; Leo slaps his hand.

"Do you still enjoy living out there, Steve?" my mom leans

in and asks. It is a simple question, posed in a quiet, undemanding tone of voice.

Why can I not look my mother in the eye?

Softly she says to me, "You loved her. We know you did."

I can tell she wants to touch me, clutch my elbow or something, as she would have when I was much younger, when we knew how to perform such simple gestures for each other.

"You don't ever think of coming back and living closer to where you come from?" she asks.

Leo's head is bobbing slightly now, in unison with Joey's, to "Back Dat Azz Up."

"This is a time, I guess, for rigorous self-examination," I say, with what feels like sour strips of cloth in my cheeks.

"I'm just the chauffeur, folks," Joey cries back. "You say where and when."

To our left is a golf course. More shopping plazas on the right.

"Look out your window, hon," my mom calls up to Leo, "and tell Steve what you see. You won't believe what he sees driving up the street on an ordinary day."

"Oh, for Christ's sake," Leo points ahead, as if he has just spotted a heron on a home furnishings store billboard; then he spins toward my mom with lights in his eyes. "Your mother's yahrtzeit is this Saturday, remember? We got to go check on that plaque we ordered for her."

"You wouldn't mind that," my mother says to me. "That would be something memorable for you to take back to where you live."

"I. Am. Not. Going. Inside. Any. Freakin'. Temple," Joey says, blasting the booty music again for one short moment until Leo clicks it off entirely and rubs a fist of knuckles in Joey's hair.

When we get to Temple Beth Adon HaOlamim, word in the business office is, the mayor of Miami is still in jail. His spokesman, we hear on a clock radio, is saying that the mayor "is the victim of a cold-hearted media assassination attempt." Leo grunts. The mayor, it is then said, "looks forward to running the city again as quickly as possible and to putting this event—which is of a strictly private and personal nature—behind him."

"You are a LYING SACK of hoo-hah," Leo says to the clock radio.

Just outside the office entrance, Joey stands with his arms crossed, examining his musculature. But he is here. I see, perhaps for the first time, that the world is divided into those who excel at loyalty and those who do not.

A small woman in a checked shirt named Felicia Groder appears and takes us through doors into the theatrically vast sanctuary to see the newly installed memorial plaque for my grandmother. There is a golden hum of refrigerating air inside.

"Felicia, I don't believe you've met my son, Steve," my mom says as we walk down a side aisle past velvet seats.

Leo's eyes seem to comb the walls for something—memories, a good joke.

Felicia, chewing gum, says, "Where ya in to Flah-rida from, Steve?"

"I live in the Pacific Northwest," I say.

Felicia looks at my mom: Does Not Register.

"He lives in Seattle," my mom says. "Does computers."

"Smart," Felicia winks at my mom. "That's the future right there."

The sanctuary, in fact—I've been trying to place it—feels like the inside of a whale. The ceiling is vaulted with great concrete ribs, and the Holy Ark of pine looks like, if opened, it could swallow strays and wanderers whole and disgorge the unfaithful through a rear lit exit door. I imagine that the net worth in this room on Rosh Hashana exceeds that of several small Caribbean nations.

Craning their necks, my mother and Leo find the plaque they have ordered, which is taped over with felt for the Saturday unveiling.

"You may look," Felicia says, and brings out a stepladder from behind a door.

Leo ascends first, reads. Then my mother.

Joey, I notice, is not in the building.

"Although I did not know her," Felicia says to my mother, who now is bucking up her chin, eyelids trembling, no longer looking at the wall of names, "I can tell just from seeing you and your son today that she was a great lady."

"She was," Leo says, and touches my mom's back. The yahrtzeit board, with its tiny electric lights, spans several yards of wall. "We owe them so much," Leo says.

Felicia, chewing gum, whispers, "They live with us. They live in our hearts."

I stand alone, separate from Felicia and Leo and my mom. I did not come home for my grandmother's funeral. I cannot even remember why.

In the temple parking lot, we find Joey groping a thick bunch of roots that hang from a twisting old ficus tree branch. He swings from the roots, lets go, and swings again. Behind him, across the street, is the walled entrance to a housing development called Lifestyles of Boca.

"Also an Ed DeVecque," Leo points out in my ear.

At the car my mom says anxiously, "Are we losing our day? Look at the sun. I feel like we keep getting distracted."

"What," Joey asks. "You planning to visit a mausoleum next?"

We are parked in the section of lot where every space is painted MEMBER.

"It's my fault," I say. "I'm the one who can't decide."

"Allow me, then," Leo says, with a large, almost magnificent lift of the hands. "I would like to take all of my family here today for lunch and a drink at my club."

My mother looks slightly embarrassed. I have declined every such invitation Leo has ever made me. Sneered at it. At him. Now, it strikes me that I have never been to a country club and golf course that Leo developed—that anyone developed. And that this is like having shared part of your life with a shoemaker and never having seen him with a pair of shoes.

Joey flies into the driver's seat, as if this latest decision might be revoked any moment, and cuts a back way to the Boca Starre Country Club & Golf Course. We pass through three guarded liftgates. Joey tells Leo, "You're not going to get shitfaced, just cause you can drink free, right?"

At the top of a valet parking circle, we enter a shimmering glass lobby where Leo is greeted by a bevy of friendly staff people in polo shirts and khaki shorts. His club is busy, successful. We are shown seats out back, under a white cabana on a gleaming pool deck.

Much of what I expect, I see. Old Jewish men lounge in groups, on pool steps, rings on heavy fingers. Cute Boca waitresses mill in body-permed hair. A dark-brown man in a bowtie carries bus pans of ice, ties bags of dripping garbage.

But here is something I don't expect: Leo is more relaxed here than I've ever seen him.

And my mom, in sunglasses, looks proud of him.

This is their life—and the life they will live until the one weasel pops up in Leo's insides that the doctors can't club fast enough.

Out past the gleaming deck and the umbrellas and the mounds of shirtless retired entrepreneurs is the golf course, rolling green fairways filled with Leo-only-knows-what-material that creates hills—hills in South Florida. Lone Spanish oaks dot the course.

"Exclusive living indeed," I say, and regret immediately that I have reverted to being the snide Gen Xer from Seattle with my mother's dying husband.

Joey's feet in expensive basketball sneakers are up on a rest. What awaits us?

"You know, when I moved to Florida in 1952," Leo says to me, "you could count the number of Jews in this part of Palm Beach county with your middle finger."

"What made you come?" I ask.

"I just had a feeling. I needed to get away from West New York. Where I was from. I just had to get away, and I thought, this would be a good place for that. Of course, I got here, tried to get work in construction, started doing a little grifting on the side to make ends meet—well, I'll just tell you this: they didn't like Jews in the area. But I showed them."

"You remember Doral Country Club in Miami," my mother says to me. "No Jews."

"So now we have our own great big country clubs," I exclaim. "We exclude just like everyone else. A great American achievement, and I'm glad to have been able to bear witness to it."

I am like a machine with a sock in it.

"I don't think that's what Pops is saying, Steve," Joey says.

"What's he saying?" I say.

My armpits are sweating. I realize that I stink.

We are all drinking frozen strawberry daiquiris, except for Leo, who takes a double Manhattan, up. Four fleshy men in unbuttoned guayaberas play cards at a nearby table. Golfers in carts glide silently up the lawns.

"When Leo's father came to this country," my mother says, "he didn't have two nickels to rub together."

A waitress brings us toasted club sandwiches on rye.

"I know, I know all about it," I say.

"Doesn't matter," Leo says. Draws a circle with his pointer finger in the center of our table. "Let's just enjoy *this*. There's no substituting for family."

A weighty body splashes in at the head of the pool. Leo drains his Manhattan. With longing he stares out at the greens. Joey, who has been conversing with our waitress, pulls his shirt off and shows her the new tattoo on the back of his shoulder—a girl straddling a stripdance pole. My mother and I do not quite look at each other.

Behind us someone flicks on a radio: The mayor of Miami has just been released from jail. The mayor himself is now saying that he has done nothing wrong, that he and his family have been made into victims. When one reporter points out that the mayor's wife has a golf ball-size lump on her head, the mayor answers that a fair and independent investigation will reveal the true nature of all the incidents in question, and for now, he looks forward to getting back to the business of running the city.

Leo spits on the deck.

One of the men playing cards shouts an obscenity at the radio.

"Couple a more sidecars?" I hear a cocktail waitress ask.

"Our nation's presidency: decided here," I say.

As I glance at my mom for her response, Leo grabs her arm and rasps, "Look, Nat—see?" and she and Joey and the waitress and a few other men on the pool deck and I all face out at the golf course at the nothing we have been looking at already, some of us for many years. Trees. Sand. Grass. Flags.

Leo points to one Spanish oak, maybe a thousand feet away, beyond a pond, near the eighteenth hole, and my mom shrugs.

Just then the tree shakes slightly and a cloud of grackles lifts from the green tuft of leaves and flutters about, chattering above. It is as if the hundred or so of them who have been nesting there or congregating in branches suddenly have formed a thick black-dotted dialogue bubble over the tree. Wings flap. The chatter gets louder.

"You speak grackle?" Leo asks me.

"I don't believe it," my mom gasps, and squeezes Leo's hand.

A warm breeze crosses our table. The grackles, who flash an iridescent purple in the balmy sunlight, swoop as one and fly off upward like a wave. Disperse.

"Well, there you have it," says Joey, stretching out his legs as if all is now in order. "You got your birds."

A little while later, just when the sun threatens to disappear, Joey has to get ready for his shift at Nooky Teasers, and he drops us off in Boca Starre Estates. Verdadera Terrace.

"Any time you need to get away from that weather out there," he offers, clapping my back, his charm swinging into my chest.

Leo goes and walks the blind dog.

On television, attorneys, reporters, citizen groups, and political operatives clamor on the steps of the Miami courthouse debating in at least two languages the mayor's alleged assault of his wife and the price he ought to have to pay.

Alone I sit and watch. My mother walks through the tiled halls of the house—large halls, monuments to Leo's campaigns—straightening and putting away. Her sandaled footfalls echo.

When she glimpses a woman on the screen, a women's health advocate, the first woman we have heard comment since the mayor got locked in solitary, my mother comes in and stands in front of the tangerine leather sofa, and immediately I ask her, "Do you remember anything? Do you ever think about how things used to really be with us?"

My voice sounds ugly, out of line, like that of a pious TV personality, grilling someone because he can; and I flush with shame—to speak to my mother this way, my mother to whom I can hardly tender an honest word—but I want to know.

The voices on the courthouse steps ring out with calls for justice.

Joints cracking, cheeks swept with years, my mother sits and turns to me and says, "I remember," and we begin to talk.

WEEKLY STATUS REPORT

Greetings Scrabble Club #1781 Members,

This week we had 39 players playing 63 games, which is slightly above our year-to-date average of 36 players playing 61 games. After three rounds, the only 3-0's were Emily Mordent and Steve Pasternak. In the final round, Emily beat Steve 511-332 to earn the $5 payout. This is Emily's fifth 4-0 of the year, highest in the club, and her third in five weeks. Way to go, Emily.

Emily Mordent also had the high turn of the night with COVALENT for 152. Also earning payouts were Gail Kotter, who scored 140 with MONSTERA, Joe Greenberg, who scored 110 with HRVYNIAS (anagram VARNISHY!), and Marvina Graves-Whitehurst, who scored 101 with BEDTIMES.

High loss for the evening, 472, went to Carl Grove, who was bested by (guess who?) Emily Mordent. Emily, as most of you who read this newsletter know, increased her rating to 1904 six weeks ago at the Las Vegas Classic, only the sixth player in the

39-year history of our club to top 1900. Can she reach 1950?

Speaking of tournaments, the San Diego 3-Way is coming up the last weekend of the month. Jillian Walpole is organizing the carpool brigade. Thanks, Jillian!

And now it falls to me to report some very sad news.

Longtime club member George Fry passed away on Saturday. He was 91.

George, whom many of us called Gentleman George, or just Gentleman, was, for the 24 years that I've directed this club, a solid 1000-1100 player. He played for the fun of it and to keep his mind sharp and not to bring glory to himself. His humble disposition endeared him to many, and he was not infected (if that's the right word) with the highly competitive nature that many of us in the club have. So if you were inclined, you could actually relax your mind a little while you were playing him and enjoy the game.

His last game at the club, this past Tuesday night, was a loss against me. I jumped out to a big lead, bingoing quickly with BIPOLAR and FORLORN, then bolstered that lead with ZYGOMA and CYLIX so that after thirteen plays, I was up by 270. Gentleman then played ROADERS to bingo. ROADERS is not acceptable (though ADORERS and DROSERA, which were both playable, are). As I say, I was beating him by 270, there were nine tiles in the bag, and for some reason, I didn't want to drive the knife in further; however, by not challenging ROADERS, my year-to-date scoring average would go down, my average score against would go up, and I would be pitying an honorable opponent. I challenged ROADERS off the board and won by 345.

Gentleman George, we will miss you.

In other club news, Anders and Carlotta Pertain, who met at Club #1781, will be celebrating their seventh wedding anniversary this coming Tuesday.

For the record, that's seven couples who have met at Club #1781 and subsequently married. (Fellow singles, take heart!) Of those seven, five are still together today.

And three cheers for Andy Weintraub, whose original Web comedy series, The Scream, begins airing on YouTube this week.

In addition, let's all put two hands together and congratulate Olla Ferguson, whose granddaughter Bethany was accepted to Caltech, where she will study mathematics and physics come fall.

Now I must clear the air of all mirth.

As if the passing of Gentleman George Fry was not sad enough news for one week, Scrabble lost a great lady this week. Sue Kararuk passed away after a sudden illness. She was 51.

Many of you have known Sue for as long as I have, and I don't think any of you will disagree when I say that her name is synonymous with Scrabble excellence and graciousness. A lovelier person has never drawn seven tiles at the Artemis H. Therme Community Center, Room B, in Mid-City. Since hearing of her passing, I have not been able to stop thinking back to the good times we all had at Club #1781, particularly those that took place before Sue met newcomer Jack Goldstein, started going on Scrabble wilderness retreats and Scrabble cruises with him, and eventually married him, resettling in Aliso Viejo with their two young children and founding a new club. There, just last year, Sue achieved her peak rating of 1857, which placed her among the top 75 Scrabble players in North America.

I will never forget the Tuesday in August, seventeen years ago, when Sue first showed up at Club #1781. Standing 5 feet 2 inches with bangs that fell just above her eyebrows, freckled lightly across the nose, she was wearing a lacy white blouse, a pair of khaki short-shorts and some open-toed sandals with blue painted toenails. Her unassuming appearance bespoke comfort with self. I asked if she had ever played at a club before. She said she hadn't. I asked if she knew NASPA Official Tournament Rules, which we play by at our club. She said she didn't. I told her where she could procure a copy of them.

For the first game, I matched Sue with Delia Kraal, whose rating was less than 700. After finishing my game, I walked by Delia and Sue's board just to take in the sights and noticed that REDOWAS and HEREINTO had been played. Given Delia Kraal's word knowledge, it was clear that only Sue could have played these words. My heart skipped a beat. Plays such as REDOWAS and HEREINTO, which are Type I Seven-letter and Eight-letter words, will not impress an expert (1700+), or near-expert (me), Scrabble player, but coming, as they were, from someone who had never played at a club, they made a mark. Sue won her first three games. Then Joe Greenberg came along and eviscerated her. I remember asking her if she would come back again sometime. She said she would.

Sue came the next week and the week after, and as the weeks passed, she never missed a Tuesday night. Naturally, people began to wonder. Where did she live? Did she have a husband? What country was she from? English, you could hear, was not her first language.

During her first couple years at the club, Sue made plenty of beginner's mistakes. I can recall games she and I played fifteen years ago when she laid down common phonies such as FREON, INTERNET, and ORALISE. I can recall her challenging non-obscure plays of mine such as LINGUAE, AVOWERS, and TYIN. She did not manage the clock well.

However, during her first couple years at the club, it became apparent to those of us who pay attention to such things that Sue Kararuk was studying and, in the process, getting better. She began playing three-letter words that most noncompetitive Scrabble players don't know, then putting front and end hooks on those words. She gained command of the High Fives and the JQXZ non-bingo words. She methodically learned her Type I Sevens. (The first time Sue beat Emily Mordent at the club, as none of us will ever forget, she played ISATINE, NEMATIC, TOXINES, RONDEAU, CASERNE, and LATHIER for an all-time club-best six bingos!) Then she set out to ace her Type I Eights, which is a multi-year study project that most of us never complete. (Not knowing SORICINE, SEPALOID or SEPTARIA, for instance, can be the difference between a 1693 rating and a 1704.)

By now, several years had passed, Sue had started to play in tournaments, and we at the club had come to know that she lived in Altadena, worked as an actuary, had a non-Scrabble-playing boyfriend, and possessed a wondrous memory for words. Also, that she had grown up in Chiang Mai, in the Scrabble-loving nation of Thailand, where grade school children play Scrabble as part of their English curriculum. (At the last six World Scrabble Championships, five of the twelve winners and runners-up have been Thai, including World Champions Panupol Sujjayakorn and Pakorn Nemitrmansuk.)

We learned that Sue had come to L.A. her junior year of college to study statistics at USC and returned for graduate work two years later. Her mathematical mind, which was so adept at spotting numerical patterns, would prove to be one of her greatest Scrabble assets.

One of my fondest memories of Sue from this time involves a parlor-style game that she, Emily Mordent, Joe Greenberg, and I used to play on Tuesday nights after the crowd had gone home. (I speak only for myself when I say I never wanted these nights to end.) One of us would draw six tiles. Then the rest of us would try to find all the six-letter words contained therein. After that, we would add a blank to the six letters and look for all the seven-letter words we could find. Then we'd add another blank and look for all the eight-letter words.

I remember one especially lively night Emily Mordent drew BELOSW.

Joe Greenberg and I cried out, "ELBOWS!" "BOWELS!" "BELOWS!"

To these six letters we could then add any letter we wanted.

I rushed to exclaim the obvious: "BELLOWS." "WOBBLES."

Joe Greenberg did the same: "BLOWERS." "BOWLERS."

From there, Joe said to Emily, "BLOWSED is good, isn't it?"

Emily, our usual adjudicator, nodded.

Sue still hadn't said a word.

"Penny for your thoughts," Joe Greenberg said.

"BOWLEGS," Sue then said in her calm, tossed-off way. She was always making the words we loved best.

On we went to the eight-letter words. BELOSW plus two blanks.

"COWBELLS," I remember saying, hoping to impress Sue.

"BESTOWAL," Joe said, with possibly the same intention. "STOWABLE," he added.

"WOBBLIES," I said.

"SNOWBELL," Joe said. "Is SNOWBELL good?" he asked Emily.

Emily nodded. "SNOWBELT too," she said.

Finally, Sue said, "SOWBELLY."

"SOWBELLY?" Joe said, with a loud, stop-everything laugh.

"Don't know it," Emily said.

We looked it up. It was good.

Joe and I shook heads.

Emily was already a rung or two above us; now Sue was on her way.

Indeed, who will ever forget Sue's breakout first-place 22-9 performance at the Boise Big Sky Showdown ten years ago when she climbed out of the 1600s, never to return? So many of us, including yours truly, who get stuck in the 1600s either are not willing to put in the study hours, reach the limits of our abilities, or—and in my case it might be all three—don't perform well in tournaments. Sue never saw her own limitations. Maybe she didn't have any. Like many top Scrabble players, she had a talent for not dwelling on losses. Even a tournament's first place winner will likely lose 30 percent of her games. Sue understood this. She approached every game with composure and sangfroid.

After Sue met newcomer Jack Goldstein at the club and had children with him and moved an hour south to Aliso Viejo, we here at Club #1781 saw less of her, and I know I speak for many when I say we missed getting to see her every week. Nevertheless, she continued to improve her game in her new circumstances. In fact, she improved as never before. I know from the Tuesday nights when she did come up to play at our club and from the times I ran into her at tournaments around the country that she was gradually mastering her Type Two and Type Three Sevens and Eights, her -INGS's, her UN-'s, her RE-'s, her OUT-'s, her OVER-'s, and her MIS-'s.

I remember seven years ago, at the Portland Golden Pioneers Tournament, Sue, wearing her usual game face, played OUTWILED on me at a decisive point in the game. You idiot, I thought to myself. You should know this word! How long have you been playing Scrabble? How long have you been directing a club? Why don't you know all your OUT-'s? Sue knows all her OUT-'s. The play must be good. At least I was smart enough not to challenge OUTWILED, which was, of course, good. Sue felled me by 106.

Perhaps Sue's particular Scrabble genius expressed itself best in the weekly study sheets she started making three years ago, which she would generously email to anyone who was interested, including fellow 1700+ players Emily Mordent, Joe Greenberg, and Marvina Graves-Whitehurst, as well as to me. Sue would whip up hundreds of these word lists off the top of her head, either at the office or after the kids went to sleep or on the weekend, words that connected to one another either directly, as in our old parlor game:

HUSBAND + L = BUSHLAND

RANPIKE + D = KIDNAPER

SCOTTIE + I = OSTEITIC

HELICON + R = CHLORINE

or (and these were even more beautiful, at least to me) indirectly, as in:

DEVOUTER OBVERTED OVERBITE VERBOTEN
BEVATRON

ICH LICH CHIEL LICHEN ELENCHI

ARMILLAE LACRIMAL MALARIAL CALAMARI
MARTIAL

AUREOLE EARLOBE ESCAROLE OVERSALE
PAROLEE

Such ecstasies of wordplay gave you glimpses into how Sue Kararuk approached a rack of tiles, by what means she was able to come up with a winning play late in the game, as she did against me countless times, with STEMWARE or EIDOLIC or EOBIONT, when it seemed I had her pinned to the mat.

I am told that her last club game, three Saturdays ago in Aliso Viejo, was a come-from-behind nail-biter against Sophia Woldemariam. Sue went 3-1 that day, which brought her club winning percentage for the year to .734 and her bingo per game average to 2.3.

You went out on top, Sue Kararuk. I hope one day to play LACRIMAL, EARLOBE, or SOWBELLY in your honor.

In other club business, our 9-year-old phenom Potter Oh is selling chocolate bars in order to raise money to fly to Orlando this summer for the National Youth Scrabble Tournament. Please consider buying a few.

Also, a week from Tuesday, I'll be in New York, visiting family. Thanks to Steve Pasternak, who's volunteered to fill in for me as director that week.

And thanks as always to the indefatigable Mary Loupe, who picks up the ruglach, chips and salsa, and juice every week, so that we all have refreshments to enjoy.

See you all again Tuesday night!

Jerry Gottlieb
Director, Scrabble Club #1781

A CONFESSION IN THE SPIRIT OF OPENNESS
RIGHT FROM THE BEGINNING

Mina,

Thanks for the great date. I've been on more than twelve of these things since I went on this site, and tonight's was the best one by far. I would love to see you again. Is the feeling mutual? I just wanted to clarify one thing.

At the end of our date, when we were walking back along Garvey Avenue toward the lot where we had both parked, I asked you if your ex had proposed to you or if you had proposed to him, and you said of course he had proposed to you, and I said, Not of course, and you said, Why, and I said, Sometimes women ask men to marry them, a woman once asked me to marry her, and you said a woman once asked you to marry her too, and I said, Really, and you said, Yes, she was serious, and I said, But you were already married, and you said, That's right, and I said, Well, how serious could it have been, and you said, Serious, and I said, You wouldn't have actually married her if you were single, would you have, and you said, I might have.

At that moment, as I glanced back across the street at the Shanghai-style dumpling place where we had just had dinner, I wondered if you were serious when you said you might have married this woman. Here you were this lovely—this tremendously lovely—woman I had just been out on a date with, this woman, you, whom I couldn't keep my eyes off, whom I could imagine greeting every morning for the rest of my life over café au laits in a breakfast nook, telling me, in your own perhaps inadvertent way, that you were leading a false life as a straight person. That you weren't actually interested in men (me?) at all. Or maybe you were positioning yourself at some middle register on the homosexual-to-heterosexual continuum and saying you were comfortable with men or women. Once I had considered the possibility that even though your dating profile says "Straight," as does mine, that you might prefer men or women, you'll recall that I met your honest disclosure (that you might someday marry a woman) with an honest disclosure of my own.

And this is the part I want to clarify, so that you don't go around thinking I'm something that I'm not.

When I said I was a 6.5, I meant that I find some men to be handsome and even physically compelling but that, so far as I'm aware, I do not want to have sex with them. (I would call that a 5.) Occasionally I have feelings for a man that keep me up at night out of curiosity about what it would be like to spend more time with him, but I would not call this sexual arousal. I would call it emotional connection, intellectual attraction, sympathy, combined with the feeling of liking to look at and listen to this person so much that I must sometimes avert my attention from him in person so that I don't seem too interested. If that makes sense. And while it's true that I don't want to have sex with another man, I also don't identify as the kind of man who says he would never have sex with another man.* I guess I would say that I am very happy being intimate with women and when I lack physical intimacy with a woman in my life, I miss it greatly.

You'll recall that at the end of our date, as we stood in the half-empty (or half-full, I'd prefer to think) parking lot, there in Monterey Park, you not wanting to show me where your car was because it was our first date and that's totally understandable—there *is* such a thing as privacy—I became embarrassed about admitting that I am a 6.5. I worried that you would not understand what I meant by 6.5, that you would find me less appealing. Believe me when I tell you: If I wanted to have sex with men, I would. I have opportunities. (In fact, during the last six years, when I've had only one short-lived girlfriend, and only sporadic dates, it has often seemed that I've had more opportunities to have sex with men than with women.) And to be completely honest, I sometimes find gay men to be more interesting, sensitive, and insightful than heterosexual men. For one thing, gays are an embattled and historically despised minority, and I find myself drawn to members of such groups. Gay men are often more eloquent than their heterosexual counterparts. They are often darkly funny. I have a friend here in Los Angeles, an indie filmmaker, who is gay, who is among

---

* Clearly, I think about it.

the most brilliant and compelling people I know. I love spending time with him (though our friendship is perhaps complicated by the fact that he resents me for being, in his view, a closeted homosexual, the proof of which is that I have never married, talk about homosexuality as if it is not a foreign land, and like musicals, Plato, Virginia Woolf, Barbara Stanwyck, ballet, Morrissey, and John Cheever). (For the record, I also like Bruce Springsteen, eating contests, the Sports Illustrated swimsuit edition, and so on.) My three closest friends are heterosexual men; all wonderful—brilliant, sensitive, creative—and married with children. I have heterosexuality in common with them, although they are probably 7.5's, 8's, or 9's.

I remember right after I said I was a 6.5, you gasped and said, I'm a 9, and my heart sank, first because I couldn't understand how someone who identified as a 9 could want to marry a woman (can we discuss this on a future date?) and second, out of fear that you would not want to get close to a 6.5. I said, Do you mind that I'm a 6.5? And you—shockingly, since this never happens, since no woman, I sometimes feel, is ever going to accept me as I am—you said, I like it, it makes you unique, most people are 9's. And I said, How do I know you mean that and are not just saying it to be polite, people often don't express their true feelings, particularly to complete strangers that they just met online. And you said, Well, you'll have to find out. And then you added, I actually wish I were a 6.5, it seems a lot more interesting. I've always wanted to be a 9, I said. I've craved it, probably out of insecurity, and you said, Don't be insecure, and I said, But wouldn't you prefer to date a 9 since you yourself are a 9? And then you said—and this was so sweet of you—a 6.5 might be all right.

Okay.

So.

There's one other thing I'd like to bring up. In the spirit of openness. My mom has warned me a hundred times against doing this. Don't talk about this on dates, she'll say. Don't bring it up, you'll scare them away, give it some time, give it five dates, give it ten. But I feel strongly about this. There's a stigma attached to talking about mental illness that's not so with alcoholism any more. Maybe there was stigma attached to talking about alcohol abuse in our grandparents' era. But now people tell people they meet at parties they're alcoholics within ten minutes of meeting them, and it's all right. It's on the table. These alcoholics might even be admired for openly doing battle with their addiction. But with mental illness it's not that way. People are ashamed to talk about it. People don't have the vocabulary to talk about it. They have countless misconceptions. And the larger society reinforces the ignorance and the prejudice. So if I come across as being a little more forward in this area than some other people, now you'll see why.

I suffer from severe depression. Severe depression with two major episodes, both of which required hospitalization in excess of three months. I'm not going to go into the details here. Oversharing: bad idea. Except to say that with the second episode, six years ago—and remembering that episode still makes my bones hum—I experienced depression that was so grave, nothing the doctors did, including electroconvulsive therapy, could bring me out of it. I am told that I sat next to a pay phone with my head in my hands for seven weeks. It just had to run its course.

Then again, I worry that I may not make it through the next episode.

Do you have mental illness in your family? I hope not, for your sake. It seems to run in families. I was reading not long ago that scientists are on their way to piecing together the genetic components of schizophrenia. That's cool. So many suicides in previous generations could have been prevented if the sufferers had had the range of psychiatric medication that we have now. Of course, nobody can make a person take a pill.

And then, lo, there is the example of my uncle Fred, which offers no grounds for optimism of any kind. My uncle Fred experiences a low-grade depression twenty-four hours a day, three hundred and sixty-five days a year. He can't escape it, no matter what medication he takes, no matter how much he exercises and does yoga and follows all the conventional advice. His depression is like a news ticker, constantly broadcasting the particulars of a middling madness. The buzzing in his ears, the never-ending omens, the insulting slips of the tongue, make him try to avoid people, so that he doesn't subject them to his pull-downs, from which they might not be able to protect themselves.

You say you're close with your family. You say your parents had hard lives in China—Cultural Revolution, ration tickets for everything, mass suicides of intellectuals. You say that your mother, a singer, didn't feel loved by her parents. You say that your father's parents, a theater director and an actress, died young. Once, you say, toward the end of their lives, for the entertainment of friends, your father's parents wrote and staged a play about two boys and a giant moth. In Chinese tradition, you say, it is often believed that the souls of departed loved ones return as moths. Some Red Guards heard about the play. Only five plays, approved by Mao, were allowed to be performed in China at the time. Your grandparents' play was deemed counterrevolutionary; they were severely beaten and forbidden from ever performing again. That's tough. I would love to talk more about all this on our second, third, or fourth date.

Have I told you enough times yet that you are fascinating?

You say that both sets of your grandparents had arranged marriages and that your parents were the first ones in your family to choose their own spouses but that you aren't always sure if they have been any better off because of it. Interesting contrarian position! You say that your father, a physical anthropologist studying pre-human and human craniums, and your mother, emigrated to the U.S. as soon as they were able to, in 1978. You were born the following year. You say neither of them ever pressured you to marry anyone, much less a Chinese guy, though you knew they wouldn't mind it if you did. For my part, I've always faced a certain pressure to marry a Jewish woman. It's not direct pressure. My parents live on the other side of the country and I'm my own person and have been for a long time. However, something in me really, really wants to tell you, right from the get-go, that I think you're super attractive, super smart, and super funny, and I don't *need* to marry a Jewish person. I don't segregate the world, like many people I grew up around, into Jewish and non-Jewish. Or maybe a little, but I'm uncomfortable with the part of me that does that.

Which brings me to the Jewish guy-Asian woman thing. Many years ago, when I was living up in the Bay Area, I waited tables at a restaurant in Berkeley. It was a high-end pan-Asian place, twenty-five tables. All the watercolors on the walls, I remember, were of parrots. The chef was Jewish—he had traveled all around Asia collecting recipes and learning everything he could about the different cuisines, and he had a wife from Shandong province in China and two kids from that relationship. And one night, he was sitting out on the floor with her, in a booth—I remember it was a Friday night, date night—and the entire restaurant filled up, and I'm not kidding you when I tell you that twenty-one out of the twenty-five tables, including their table, had a white guy and an Asian woman seated at them. No exaggeration. And I don't know why exactly, but it made me sick. I wanted to put some kind of pill in all the guys' ginger martinis. Not that there's anything intrinsically wrong with a white guy dating—or marrying or whatever—an Asian woman. I would be most pleased to marry one myself. But that night it felt like it had just, I don't know, gotten out of control.

So what is it with all the Jewish guys and Asian women? I mean, this has been going on since the '90s at least. I've been to three of these weddings myself. You hear different theories: that Jewish guys prefer Asian/Asian-American women because these women tend to be educated, loyal, thin, youthful-looking, low-key, adept in the kitchen, yielding, financially self-reliant, family-oriented, exotic. Of course, in your case, you've made it clear that you like Jewish people, in general, and Jewish men, in particular. That's great. That's really great. I think on that score alone, we're off to a nice start.

But, you added warily, as that steaming-hot plate of rice cake with minced pork and cabbage (yum) arrived at the table, Please don't tell me you have a thing for Asian women. And I said, I like all women. Which is true. I like Jewish women, I like non-Jewish women, I like Asian women. And, as I have mentioned, I like some men. I have never been in love. No woman has ever been in love with me. (The woman I told you wanted to marry me just wanted a green card and was willing to pay me $17,000 for that purpose.) Do you think that's strange? I guess for some people love takes longer to hatch than for others. Let's leave some things to fate.

I do very much want to thank you again for going to the dumpling place with me. From what I've heard, Asian-American women don't usually want to go out on a first date to a restaurant, they want to just have coffee, then go from there. And if they agree to go to a restaurant, as you did, they don't usually want to go to one that serves food from the country, e.g., China, where their family is from. So I was happily surprised when I proposed the dumpling place and you agreed. Did I possibly charm you when I said you'd have to beat me down with a club to keep me from wanting to eat Chinese food in the San Gabriel Valley as often as possible? I hope so!

I once met a 96-year-old woman at the Y. She was actually lifting weights and doing jazzercise, and we just started to talk. And I asked her if she could boil down everything she had learned in her life to one sentence, and she said, "It's all luck." I thought you could relate to that. You say you feel lucky you have had a good life. (You play the cello professionally, for God's sake!) I feel lucky we went on a date. If I'm coming on too strong here, I apologize in advance. Chalk it up to being inspired by you.

Let's perform a thought experiment. Say you would like to go out with me again. What would we do? What adventure might we go on? I was thinking that we might try something a little romantic but not too romantic. We want to pace things, not turn up the flame too quickly. I know the assistant curator of the photography collection at the Huntington Library. Really nice guy. He helps oversee a million photographs. With emphasis on the history of Los Angeles, of California, of the West. With him as our guide, we could look through any batch of photographs you might be interested in—their collection is unbelievably great: Carleton Watkinses, Alfred A. Harts—then take a walk and check out the Rose Garden and the Desert Garden. You can't beat the Desert Garden. Over five thousand species of desert plants, with the wildest shapes and flowers. You'll be amazed. Then maybe we could go eat the hell out of some under-the-radar place in Little Tokyo or Koreatown. What do you think? :)

Thanks again for your loveliness.

See you real soon, I hope.

Sincerely,

Glenn

P.S. You have the same first name as my great-aunt from Vienna, who made it out in time!

DIGNITY SHORES

I've got my hands full at the moment. My best client, Charlie Sorroff, founder and former president of Peabody Containers, the third largest manufacturer of plastic medicine bottles in the United States, is in the hospital. The other night I had to take him to the emergency room. End of life stuff. Depression. Threatening suicide. The aide called me at ten p.m. He was having a hard time breathing and, she said, was crying uncontrollably.

I visit him every day on the psychiatric floor of King of Plantation Hospital. I bring him a smoothie and the *Wall Street Journal* in the morning, a tri-tip salad or blackened grouper for dinner. He's started to get demented so there are days when he'll just stare at the front page of the paper as if trying to remember what to do with it; then after a while I'll say, "Hey Charlie, you want to check your stocks?" or "Hey Charlie, the Dow gained 1 percent." The night after he was admitted, he managed to sneak up onto the roof of the hospital and climb halfway up a chain-link fence topped with razor wire, then just stayed there in a gown, trembling and clinging to the fence until a nurse found him. Every day I update his sister Dottie in Boston, who has power of attorney, about his condition. It troubles her the ways he's losing his mind—she clearly loves him—but she's also, not very subtly, exhausted of his battles and hoping for him to die.

Then there's Margaret Abendroth, from Ohio, who I see on Wednesdays and Sundays. She's eighty-seven and frail. I met her a couple years ago in the waiting room of a probate lawyer we were both using. She had no one. Her husband had just died, her brother had just died, she had never had kids. She was falling to pieces. She and her husband, though only middle-class breadwinners, had been obsessive savers and now she had a bigger nest egg than she would ever need. That first time I talked with her, widow to widow, in the lawyer's waiting room, she told me, proudly, that she hadn't purchased a single new item of clothing in thirty years. She was living in a second-floor condo with no elevator (a broken hip waiting to happen) and could still drive but was nervous being alone—with no husband or brother to take care of. She was losing weight, wasn't cooking for herself, wasn't eating out. I gave her my card and said if I can help you I'm here for you.

It took her a while—as it takes all of my clients, or my clients' families—to decide that they need me. Even my title, geriatric care manager, is off-putting to many. To need me means that a person can no longer take care of herself entirely and will never be able to again. In Margaret's case, she needed help getting things done that she hadn't needed help with a year before. Grocery shopping, for example. I started taking her to doctors' appointments and the pharmacy and church. I took her to lunch on Sunday afternoons at a beachfront café in Fort

Lauderdale. Then, after a few months, when she had regained some of her strength and peace of mind, I started the process of convincing her to move into the Polk Houses in Tamarac, one of the best South Florida retirement communities. There she would live among people of similar backgrounds, Lutherans particularly. There would be church services on campus, a full-time nursing staff available, and Saturday night movies and popcorn at the clubhouse.

So that's where she is now. I still take her out to shop and do errands, help her pay bills, brainstorm how to rewrite her will so that she leaves all of her savings to low-income Lutheran pastors in Ohio and Florida. And, unlike Charlie Sorroff, who has been in the midst of one crisis after another for the last several months and cannot stop raising his fists to heaven, Margaret doesn't make a peep of disgruntlement about anything.

The crisis, however, that really has me shaken up, even more so than Charlie Sorroff's psychotic depression—which a whole medical staff is committed to treating—began two weeks ago at a bank. Rosa D'Avila, a manager there, who, for a time, worked as a financial advisor to one of my now-deceased clients, called to say that she had recently had her eye on a very, very old and small lady, who had been coming into the bank for eleven years. About three years ago, she started coming in with a large male attendant. Now she never comes in without him.

"I have a bad feeling about this relationship," Rosa told me. "Would you call her and make a date to just drop by and see how she's doing?"

I called the lady the next day.

As it turns out, she—Elaine Zilbergleit—lives right here

in Coral Springs, in a third-floor apartment in the largest retirement community in Broward County, Millennium Vista. Millennium Vista is made up mostly of professional-class Jews from the Northeast who started wintering in South Florida in their fifties and sixties and then eventually retired here. I took the elevator.

As I was walking down the sunny stretch of open-air hallway toward Ms. Zilbergleit's apartment, I was suddenly overpowered by the stench of urine and feces. The smell was shocking. I've spent countless hours in low-budget nursing homes and understaffed retirement facilities, and this was beyond anything I had encountered. I knocked at the door.

Nobody answered.

I knocked again.

When there was no answer a second time, I tried the door knob.

This time the door opened into a small, dark, fetid living room. The curtains were closed, the air conditioner was not on. Curled up on the two-seat sofa was a tiny lady, on oxygen, whose back was so hunched over that her forehead was practically touching her knees. She couldn't have weighed more than seventy pounds. On the seat next to her, a jumbled stack of papers came up as high as her shoulders.

"May I come in?" I said.

"Please do," said the lady. Her voice was barely a squeak. She tried to raise her head in order to make eye contact with me but she could barely do it.

"Marcia Newman?" she said.

"That's me," I said, cheerfully.

The room was filthy beyond description. Every sitting

surface was stained yellow and stank of urine. Next to the front door were two unlined plastic garbage cans that reeked of excrement. The same reeking odor was also coming from the direction of the kitchen and the back of the apartment. I could hear a television going in the front-most room, a den.

I walked over and shook the tiny lady's hand.

"My husband's in the bedroom," she said.

Neither she nor Rosa D'Avila had mentioned a husband.

I followed the path of the lady's oxygen cord, through the kitchen and dining room area (where it would be all too easy for her to trip over it and break her back), past the smells of rotting fish and fruit, and into the bedroom.

There, in a room crowded with a king-size bed, a triple dresser, a highboy, and an oxygen tank, I found Mr. Zilbergleit sitting in a wheelchair, feet dangling, in only a diaper. He was squirming in discomfort, facing dark curtains.

He had a small orange bottle of pureed baby food stuck between his bare legs. "Is your husband aspirating?" I called out to Mrs. Zilbergleit.

"Yes, he is," she peeped.

In the couple's bathroom was another unlined trash can, stuffed with diapers full of fecal matter. The bed, the carpet, the bathroom floor rug, it was all soaked in urine.

Finally, I went back into the front of the apartment and peeked inside the den. There, I found myself standing over a large young man, no doubt the aide, easily 250 pounds. He was sprawled out barefoot across a striped chenille couch, belly hanging limp, watching a television infomercial about how to reverse hair loss.

When I came into sight, he paddled the couch until he was

sitting up straight.

"Who are *you*?" he barked.

"A friend of the Zilbergleits," I said.

"Nobody told me you were coming," he said. "She's going to hear it from me."

"I just stopped by to say hello," I said, unthreateningly, and went back into the living room. There I removed the piles of newspapers, tissues, bills, and other mail from the seat next to Elaine Zilbergleit and sat down next to her. The young man stayed in the den.

I asked her to tell me her story.

She again struggled to lift her head to make eye contact with me. But when she did, she said in her tiny squeak that she and her husband Howard had both grown up in Trenton, New Jersey, children of uneducated Jewish immigrants. They learned early on to make do with what they had. Howard became an accountant and she, Elaine, helped him during tax season. They raised two sons in Hopewell Junction; both died in their late forties of cystic fibrosis. It was the hardest thing she had ever had to do, outlive them. By this time, she and Howard had retired to Coral Springs. The first ten years in Florida had been okay. Then Howard began suffering from dementia. Eventually, he needed twenty-four-hour care. That was three years ago. So she, Elaine, hired this male aide to work seven a.m. to seven p.m. and his female cousin from seven p.m. to seven a.m.

I glanced around at the rank chaos of her apartment. "When you were growing up with your immigrant parents, and learning how to make do, you never lived like this."

"Oh, it's not so bad," the old lady replied, almost in a whisper.

She was looking again at her knees.

"How much do you have in savings?" I asked her.

"Four-hundred thousand," she peeped.

It was lower than I had been guessing but not frightful. Four-hundred-thousand will get you three-and-a-half years of round-the-clock aides. This couple didn't have three-and-a-half years. The lady's back was so bent, her lungs would soon fail to expand when she breathed; and the aspirating husband could contract pneumonia any day.

"It's nice of you to come over," Elaine sighed. "But we can get by."

"Listen to me, Elaine," I said. "I can reduce my fee for you. We can make it work. Give me a chance to help you."

"Let me talk it over with my husband," she said.

The following week, I paid another visit, no charge, to the Zilbergleits. This time when I arrived, I found the aide in the kitchen, standing over Howard, who was naked again except for urine-stained pull-ups. Howard's wheelchair was crammed up against the kitchen table. His head was lobbing forward. A plastic bowl of green pureed baby food sat in front of him.

"Sit up, Howard," the aide was snapping. "Sit up."

The aide grabbed Howard by the shoulders and tried to sit him up but Howard kept slumping forward.

When the aide saw me staring at him, I said, "As a physical therapist, I have to tell you that you should not let his feet dangle from the wheelchair. Use the footrests so that he'll be more comfortable."

"I don't work for you," he snapped and banged down a metal spoon.

Elaine looked away.

"You want to feed him?" he said to me. "You want to feed him?"

He picked the spoon up, smashed it down again, and charged off to the den.

Howard grasped the spoon. He stabbed at the bowl of green puree in front of him, then slurped up what he didn't drip onto the floor. No wonder Elaine Zilbergleit weighed seventy pounds. Who could have an appetite watching this day after day?

I wanted to tell Elaine that I could clean up her and Howard's lives. But more often than not, when you try to help people, you don't get the chance to help them. You'd be surprised what gets in the way. The person might not be able to afford you. Or she might think she can't afford you. Or she might not be able to admit to herself that she needs help. Maybe a niece or daughter who's controlling the money isn't really interested in prolonging her life. Or else maybe the party controlling the money will pay you but won't listen to you or get out of your way because they have been visiting medical websites lately and so they know more about geriatric care than you do. Also, elderly people often feel stuck with the unsatisfactory home health aides that they have hired. It is as if they can no longer imagine a better life than the one they have now.

I said to Elaine, "I can give you a new life. But you're going to have to fire this aide."

Her face took on a cast of horror.

"You and I could make a contract to work together for three months," I told her. "After three months, you could decide if you still want me on."

Her downcast eyes were seized with worry.

"Think about it," I said. "A new life."

Another week passes and Charlie Sorroff is still in the hospital. He has been having psychotic outbursts followed by bouts of screaming tears and the staff doesn't always let me see him. One evening when I bring him dinner, he is sitting alone at the table where we usually eat, but this time his face is plunged into his hands and his elbows are riveted to the table. His doctors keep trying out different antipsychotics, different antidementia agents, different antidepressants, heavier dosages. One thing's for sure: the new medications have dimmed Charlie. He has gone from being an outsized leading man, a man who directed boardroom meetings for decades and burned with competitiveness and the joy of the hunt, to a tremulous old man with a waning light. After dinners, I often give Charlie a roll of quarters. Since personal phones are not allowed on the psych floor of King of Plantation, Charlie has to be walked down the hall by a nurse's assistant to a wooden chair by the pay phone, where he can talk to Dottie for the third time that day.

Dottie is the only family member Charlie talks to. More than once Dottie has sworn to me that she will never move to Florida, that hellhole. But she does fly down from Boston for one long weekend every six weeks to visit Charlie. She stays at the Plantation Hilton. Otherwise, Charlie has no family around. Fifteen years ago he and his wife Maddie moved down from Boston into the Hear O Israel luxury retirement condos in Plantation. After Maddie passed, Charlie still had friends in Hear O Israel and enjoyed taking walks and playing cards with them. But then dementia came along and Charlie reached end-stage cardiac disease and he needed twenty-four-hour help. His friends visited him less and less. He passed most of his time with home health aides in a large white condo ringed with enormous black-and-white photographs of Peabody Containers' plastic bottle factories in Puerto Rico, Mexico, and the Dominican Republic.

This week I actually have news for Charlie, but I don't give it to him until a few evenings later when he looks less despondent.

His estranged daughter Lisa called me from Los Angeles. She wants to come to South Florida for a visit.

"Would you like that?" I ask him.

"I don't care," he says.

"Of course you care," I say.

In my only other conversation with Lisa, seven months ago, I had heard through the ice of her voice a hint of warm feelings for Charlie. This time when we talked, the one thing Lisa told me that she didn't want was for Dottie, whom she called evil, to know that we had spoken, but I couldn't help telling Charlie and Charlie told Dottie and now Dottie is irate.

"That ungrateful bitch deserves nothing," Dottie says to me the next time we talk. "What did she tell you? She wants peace? She wants money. It's the only thing she's ever wanted from him."

But Charlie is visibly affected when I speak the name of his younger daughter. He does want to see her; he also can't forget that Lisa, who dropped out of college to run off to Los Angeles with a charismatic musician, didn't attend the funeral of his and Dottie's only brother twenty-five years ago. Neither did Charlie's older daughter, Michaelina, now a community organizer in San Francisco, who appears to live in a state of immovable anger. Seven months ago Michaelina told me that she would never talk to her father. Under any circumstances. Nor would she attend his funeral—so don't bother asking.

When I call Lisa back, I tell her that Charlie would like to see her. I say I don't know how long he has—a day, a month, maybe a few months. With the cardiac disease, probably not more than four.

"Then again," I say, "he still has these cloudbursts of energy. You'll still recognize him, I think."

While I am waiting for Elaine Zilbergleit to decide what to do, I call the Florida Department of Children and Family Services, who agree that the care the Zilbergleits are getting is abusive. The aides must be removed.

Next I call the Coral Springs police, who agree that the aide and his cousin—who, on top of everything else, owe the Zilbergleits $11,000 from a personal loan never repaid—need to be fired, and that if Mrs. Zilbergleit is too afraid to do it herself, then the police will send out someone to help her.

After that, I talk to my friend Jacqueline Dupuy in Delray Beach, a certified home health aide and single mother of three A students, who hasn't had work for so long that her electricity was just turned off. The supply of qualified home health aides in South Florida far outstrips the demand, which makes it all the more outrageous that the Zilbergleits are living the way they are. Jacqueline has big, strong shoulders and loving-kindness in her heart; she doesn't see patients as agglomerations of needs but as whole human beings. I tell her I may have work for her.

Finally, Elaine calls. She tells me she is trembling like a leaf and I can picture her hunched over on the couch, her forehead nearly touching her knees, the large young man with his scant bristly hair and monstrous belly, barking commands to her from in front of the TV set.

"Can't you just train them to do the job properly?" she cries out to me. "Can't you just teach them? They're not so bad!"

I never imagined that I would go into business for myself. I am a woman of a certain generation, whose parents did not go to college, who took a practical degree, in physical therapy, specializing in the elderly, and worked my way up from low-paying nursing home jobs through the ranks of my profession. I helped establish the Broward County Alzheimer's Association, learning the business of Medicare reimbursement, until, in my late fifties, I was hired by VitaTher, the company I had been working for, to be vice-president of operations for the Southeast region. I was nervous and honored and thrilled. VitaTher is a national rehab company that provides occupational therapy, physical therapy, and speech therapy clinics within assisted living communities in North Carolina, South Carolina, Georgia, and Florida.

From the start, the pressure to grow the business and be profitable was greater than I had imagined and I spent a lot of time on the road, trying to win or renew contracts. But mainly—and this was why I liked my work so much—I trained younger people to be good therapists for an elderly population, to understand what it means to be elderly and experience decline in most areas of your life every day. Countless days I pinched myself; I had grown up with nothing expected of me professionally, just to become a wife and mother, and now I had a well-paying, respected, and useful job.

Then, after seven years of total commitment to VitaTher,

I was told that the company was cutting costs and that I was being let go—no thank you for my service, no severance pay.

Not knowing what else to do, I started madly printing brochures and calling cards and telling everyone I knew that I was going into business.

Who knows what finally convinces Elaine Zilbergleit to get rid of the aides? But as soon as I have her go-ahead, I arrange to have a policeman come up to Millennium Vista the following Friday at 6:45 a.m. This way, he'll catch the young man starting his shift and the cousin ending hers.

All week Elaine is in a panic. She is sure that if the two aides find out what she's planning to do that they will kill her and Howard, put a bullet in each of their heads, then just vanish into thin air. They hate her and Howard enough to do it, they really do. I stop by the apartment twice that week to try and calm her.

Then, when Friday morning comes, I meet a Coral Springs police officer at the Millennium Vista guard gate. He looks too young to shave. We shake hands.

When I hear his voice, I say, "You're not from around here."

"How can you tell?" he says. "I'm from Valdosta, Georgia."

Few people have visited more Southeast regional elder care facilities than I have. When I name one in Valdosta that I have spent time at, the young policeman, whose name is Crowder, says, "I'm impressed." Then, "Let's go take care of this."

When we arrive at the Zilbergleits' reeking apartment at seven prompt and no one answers the door, we let ourselves in. Elaine is not in her usual place on the couch. There is no sound coming from the den. I tiptoe toward the bedroom. There I find

Elaine in bed, eyes wide open in the dark, huddled in next to Howard, oxygen tubes in her nose.

I tap her lightly on the shoulder—she is shaking—and ask her where the female aide is.

"She usually leaves early," Elaine peeps. "And the young man usually gets here late."

"Wait right here," I say.

In the living room, I give Officer Crowder the male aide's cell phone number.

Fifteen seconds later I hear him saying, "You're supposed to be here at seven o'clock. A couple in this condition should never be left alone. Do you understand that?"

There is some silence; the aide is no doubt plying the officer with excuses.

"Don't bother showing up. Okay? You're fired. And your cousin is too. Just turn your car around and go home."

There is more silence; then Officer Crowder warns the aide never to come to this residence again.

I turn on the living room lights and go back in to check on Elaine. She has lifted herself up in bed and whispers to me that she wants to say something to the aide.

I help walk her into the living room; the stench in the house ripples through my nostrils.

"Forget it," the police officer is telling the aide. "You already owe these people $11,000. Tell your story to the judge."

By now, Elaine has reached the officer. She taps his arm and he hands the phone over to her.

"I just want you to know," she says brittly to the aide, the phone shaking in her hand. "I just want you to know. That the way you treated us. Was abominable. And you know it."

And at that she practically faints and falls back onto the couch.

On Sunday, I bring Margaret Abendroth an African violet, its ten delicate blooms held aloft by yellow threads of stems. I screw a hook into the ceiling and hang it out on her balcony, which, by now, has quite a dense assemblage of hanging plants. The three native-Florida air plants I have brought fascinate her; her favorite is an epiphyte, which has attached roots to a piece of driftwood that it uses for support. She has tiger fern and blue star fern. Moss rose and verbena. In the first two years after I lost my husband, nothing helped me more than clearing out my front yard, replanting the row along the house with gold-, copper-, and red-leafed bromeliads, and watching them grow.

On this day, as we are driving to our usual beachfront café in Fort Lauderdale, it starts to beat down rain and Margaret asks me about my daughters. I have three, the first an emergency room attending in Miami, the third a Jewish day school teacher in Atlanta, and then the middle child, Hannah, a poet, who supports herself—and she has only just revealed this to me— by conducting writing classes at prisons, women's shelters, and halfway houses.

"Doing well," I say.

Six months ago, I made the mistake of mentioning something personal to Margaret—that Hannah had just published a book of poems. In fact, I had been carrying the book in my purse and I showed it to her at lunch.

She riffled through the pages.

"Please show me your favorite," she said.

I got a lump in my throat. The truth was, I didn't understand any of Hannah's poems. As a child, Hannah had been creative and there was a time, when she was nine or ten or eleven, when she wrote poems I could understand. But starting in college, as her difficulties maintaining mental stability set in, she stopped showing me her poems, even the ones that were—I now know—getting published in good literary magazines.

I showed Margaret the title poem of the book, "The Firebird." I have read this poem many times and I don't know what it means but if it is about anything, then I would say it is about a magical glowing bird that can confer marvelous powers to its owner. Many ambitious young men, in particular, go out hunting for this bird, hoping to acquire its might, but in Hannah's poem, it is a young woman who ends up with the bird, not because she has gone out searching for it—on the contrary, the firebird has attached itself to her. And now this wild flaming potent creature, which she can neither release nor tame, and which sets her mind on fire, becomes more a curse to her than a blessing.

"Hmm," Margaret said after she had read the poem.

Now, driving through the rain, I gently change the subject away from Hannah—who lives all the way in Portland, Oregon, and will not let me help her with money or advice or anything—so that by the time we arrive at the café, Margaret and I are talking about subjects I am more comfortable with, which are to say, ones pertaining directly to her.

The following Friday, Lisa Sorroff comes in for a long weekend to see Charlie, who is still in the hospital. I have suggested the Plantation Hilton but Lisa can't afford such a place. So I reserve her a room in a clean bleached-white flat-roofed 1950s-era motel off A1A in Deerfield Beach that is more in her price range.

At the start of visiting hours, I meet Lisa at the hospital. I don't know what I'm expecting—maybe someone youthful and exciting—but middle age has hit her hard. Her face is melancholy and worried, and she keeps a physical distance from me.

"The doctors have got the psychosis under control," I explain to her after we get out of the elevator on the psych floor. "But the dementia's unpredictable."

To see Charlie, we have to be let in through an eight-foot-high steel door with a wheel-shaped handle, almost like a vault. This puts us in the visiting room, which has rows of tables bolted to the floor, where we can have a meal with Charlie and pass along approved items to him.

While Charlie is being brought to us, I tell Lisa a story. For the past couple weeks, I say, Charlie has been sharing a room with a bulky younger man named Lalo. Lalo seems to feel some kind of connection with Charlie because when Charlie is not in the room, Lalo repeatedly goes into Charlie's closet and puts on Charlie's clothes—his blue oxford, his khaki pants, his navy socks—then walks about the floor in Charlie's tight-fitting clothes, saying that he is King Charlie and making everyone call him by that name. When Lalo inevitably runs into the real Charlie on the floor, he accuses Charlie of being an impostor. This confuses Charlie, who starts to cry. At this, another patient comes up to Lalo and shouts, "You're not King Charlie, you're not King Charlie," which enrages Lalo so much that he picks up the wooden chair from next to the pay phone and brings it down on the patient's head so that within thirty seconds Lalo is being swept off to a back room and strapped down in restraints, not for the first time. But the next day, loaded with even more tranquilizers, Lalo is back to wearing Charlie's clothes and calling himself King Charlie again.

"It's been an adventure with your father, I guess I'm trying to say," is what I say to Lisa.

The two of us are sitting across from each other against the far wall. At a nearby table, three obese children are clutching plastic bottles of brightly colored soda; at another table, a disheveled elderly couple seems to be visiting their blank-eyed adult child.

When Charlie shuffles into the room, arm in elbow with a nurse I have gotten to know, he appears to be sleepwalking.

"Here he is," the nurse sings. "Mr. America."

Charlie doesn't look good. His eyes are wet, his confusion profound. The nurse has combed back his hair neatly and dabbed bay rum on his neck. He looks like a man who has seen something terrible.

I spring to my feet and take hold of Charlie's elbows.

"Do you know who this is?" I say to Charlie, rotating him toward Lisa.

Lisa appears to shrink in her seat.

I slide Charlie into my former seat, across the table from Lisa. Then I put takeout containers of pepper-encrusted salmon, Israeli couscous, sautéed kale, and bread rolls in front of the two of them, as though they're on a dinner date.

"It's Lisa," I say in Charlie's ear. "Lisa Sorroff."

"Lisa Sorroff," Charlie says, and nods.

"Hi Pop," Lisa says.

Then, as if lightning has struck, he says, "My Lisa Sorroff?"

Lisa laughs sadly.

"I came to see you, Pop," she says.

But then the curtains draw again around Charlie's mind.

I head over to a table on the other side of the room.

From there, I mostly don't watch Lisa and Charlie, who have forty-five minutes together, so that I don't jinx them. I answer emails on my phone. I call my youngest, the Jewish day school teacher, in Atlanta, and catch her while she is bathing her toddler.

Finally, after it seems that a long time has passed, I glance across the room and see that Charlie and Lisa are leaning across the table and have put hands around each other's heads, like blind people. They are touching each other's hair, almost as if trying to read it. Their lips are not moving.

I have the feeling that Charlie's confusion has been battling Lisa's conciliation and that Charlie has been winning.

When their forty-five minutes are up, the nurse re-enters the visiting room and I follow her over to Charlie and Lisa's table.

"Time to say goodnight and take our meds," the nurse says to Charlie and reaches for his elbow.

"Your daughter Lisa's going to come back and see you tomorrow," I say to Charlie.

Once Charlie has shuffled off with the nurse, I see that Lisa has been crying.

"I thought," she says, but then doesn't finish.

"Listen. Tomorrow's another day," I say.

I can see that she is trying to say something like "I should have come sooner" or "What have I done?"

"You did your best," I say. "As long as he's alive, you've got another chance."

But still she doesn't say anything and by now all the other

visitors are exiting, and as Lisa gets up and arranges herself next to me—we are about the same size—I am hoping that sometime this weekend Charlie will come back from the other side for long enough that this woman will have the chance to say whatever it is she came here to say.

Cleaning an excrement-filled apartment from top to bottom is not fun, but on this day there is a certain joy to it. Jacqueline Dupuy is with me. We are going room to room with 44-gallon black contractor bags and filling them with the flotsam of this place. Twenty-nine bags and two weeks later, we have thrown out most of what the Zilbergleits owned, torn out their rugs, and Cloroxed all the floors. Elaine Zilbergleit now gives me the go-ahead to put in new rugs, a new bed, a new sofa, two new recliners, a new 42-inch TV, new patio furniture, and new paint. Jacqueline starts caring for the couple twelve hours a day and I hire another certified aide for the other twelve hours. Elaine Zilbergleit gains ten pounds. We keep the curtains open. The apartment seems almost brand new.

Howard Zilbergleit can still follow some one-step directions but his mind is getting worse. He can barely self-feed, and more and more of what he eats is ending up in his lungs. He's become incontinent of bowel and bladder. He needs to be turned in bed. And Elaine is having her own problems—heart, kidney, breathing. It is in the nature of my job that my clients deteriorate and die; the only uncertainty is how quickly. This is why I'm always looking to bring on new people. If all of my clients died at once, I'd be in quite a state.

Today is the fourth anniversary of my husband's death, and I take off a couple hours to go visit his grave. What can I say? Staring at a flat stone with your husband's birth and death dates is an awful, extremely final way to spend part of a day. Since I paid for everything, I am aware that his remains are shut up in an unfinished pine box with a carved Star of David above the head, just like the boxes his parents were buried in. The rest of him, though, is somewhere else.

I came over and bought the two plots right after he was diagnosed. It was a horrible thing to do alone but I did it. I know many people who have been buried here, so that was a help. The cemetery's out in western Palm Beach county, in what's still farm country. The funeral director asked me where I wanted us to be buried. Near a lake? Under an oak tree? I didn't want our graves to be in the middle of a long, green field, so that people who visited us would have to broil in the Florida sun. So I picked a shaded location near the western edge of the cemetery that has a bench nearby, so that people don't have to stand. Across the road from our plots is a place we've gone many times with our kids and grandkids to pick strawberries. The strawberry place is also at an entrance to the Everglades, which gives visitors the option of going for a family bike ride along the nearby highway.

The official name of the cemetery is Mount Sinai Memorial, but everyone I know calls it Dignity Shores. That may have been its previous name. I don't know. The cemetery lawn stretches out for fifty-five acres; there's an immense American flag outside the front gates and numerous yellow earth-moving machines parked along the sides of the roads.

My husband Louis was a judge on the Seventeenth Judicial Circuit in Fort Lauderdale for twenty-seven years. When I stand over his stone, I would like to remember the good times but often I don't. It was a long marriage. There were years, when the girls were still at home, that we slept in different rooms, when I would sometimes squeeze into bed with my oldest or curl up on the pullout sofa in the back room. Louis had bushy eyebrows that, in those years, registered his predominant states of mind: sternness and indifference. He started out in his forties as a judge who wanted to repair the world and soon became one who found his work—found *life*—monotonous and embittering. Would our lives have been different if he had ever been named to the Fourth District Court of Appeals? Such a judgeship would have been more secluded and intellectual, requiring lots of research and writing; it would have suited his temperament far better than the zoo of the circuit bench did.

But then Louis retired and we started to travel a little, for the first time in our lives. The girls were all grown up and it was as if we had a chance at a second marriage. Louis stopped obsessing about what he lacked. He began to see me as a partner with needs and wishes that he could fulfill. Not long after, though, the doctors found the huge tumor in his pancreas, along with a bunch of other smaller tumors, and they told him that the only way he could survive would be to undergo a nine-hour operation that had a success rate of only ten percent and would increase his physical suffering afterward. Naturally, he wanted to keep living. But he was not one of the ten percent and, after a quick period of uncontrollable explosions of diarrhea and endless vomiting, he was dead.

My cell phone rings and I have never been so happy to hear it. I can see that it's Dottie, no doubt reporting on a new crisis that has engulfed Charlie, who was discharged from the hospital last week. Sometimes when I'm talking to Dottie it'll dawn on me that in the back of my mind, I am calculating the number of billable hours it is going to take me to put this latest fire out. I have a knack for estimates. I guess it's that I have a lot of expenses and no other way to know what my month-to-month income will be. I help my youngest daughter with her mortgage, I have an aging house that requires lots of repairs, I have car payments and self-employment taxes and a retirement account to fund, and, four years to the day, I am still paying off these two shaded plots, which, when I told my husband we'd have so we'd always be together, gave him comfort during the last few weeks of his life.

ACKNOWLEDGMENTS

Grateful acknowledgment is made to the following publications in which these stories first appeared: "The White Spot" in *Kenyon Review*, "The Kind of Luxuries We Felt We Deserved" in *Playboy* and reprinted in *Playboy's College Fiction* (Playboy Press), "Roger's Square Dance Bar Mitzvah" in *Gulf Coast*, "Apples and Oranges" in *Green Mountains Review*, "I Should Have, Believe Me, All This, The Way I'm Doing It Now" in *Zaum*, "New Pocahontas" in *Northwest Review*, "Panels" in *Angels Flight • literary west*, "Boca" in *New York Stories* and reprinted in a Mandarin translation by Mia Guo in *Shanxi Literature*, "Weekly Status Report" in *Sonora Review*, and "Dignity Shores" in *Carolina Quarterly*.

"A Confession in the Spirit of Openness Right from the Beginning" was written with the assistance of a Hawthornden Fellowship.

*

I'd like to thank everyone who read one or more of these stories in draft form. Particularly valuable have been the insights of Holiday Reinhorn, Andrew Porter, Harriet Collier, Matthew Goldstein, Amber Dermont, Marilynne Robinson, Greg Downs, and Julie Simon. Also, thanks to the editors of the magazines in which these stories first appeared: Sergei Lobanov-Rostovsky, David Lynn, Alice K. Turner, Leslie Daniels, Christopher Puppione, Janice MacRae, John Witte, Shilpa Agarwal, Daniel Caplice Lynch, Janet Towle, and Rae X. Yan. I am grateful for the abiding friendship of Michelle Remy, Kristy Guevara-Flanagan, Amy Margolis, Hazel Walker, Michael Silverblatt, and William Deverell. Thanks and love to my family, who have given me so much. Thanks to Sevy Perez for the cover. Finally, this book owes its existence to the wonderful Caryl Pagel and Daniel Khalastchi of Rescue Press. There's nothing like being believed in.

Jonathan Blum grew up in Miami and graduated from UCLA and the Iowa Writers' Workshop. He is the author of a novella, *Last Word*, which was named one of the best books of the year by Iowa Public Radio and was featured on KCRW's Bookworm. He has received a Michener-Copernicus Society of America Award and a Hawthornden Fellowship in Scotland for his short fiction. He was a guest writer at the Tianjin Binhai New Area International Writing Program in China. He lives in Los Angeles.

RESCUE PRESS